Snap Chance

For
Dualena
Spooks Ms Hollywood
Doc Baritz
All Right Starlight
&
Buster

SNAP CHANCE

A MODERN WESTERN MYSTERY

NOVEL BY DON WELLER

Published in the United States by the
Weller Institute, PO Box 518, Oakley, UT
84055

Ian Tyson's lyrics are used with
permission. He retains the copyright.

ISBN: Hardcover   978-1-7328832-3-9
        Softcover   978-1-7328832-2-2
        eBook   978-1-7328832-4-6

*Ah, but there is magic
in the horses' feet in
the way they jump
and the way they sweep ...*

——Ian Tyson, Non Pro Song

Prologue: Wind Rivers

A cold steel sky hung low over the Wind River Range in western Wyoming. On a high and craggy mountain, where the forest surrendered to stone, a lone man picked his way carefully across a dangerous field of scree.

Finally, out of the sea of rocks, he paused for a moment, welcoming the improved footing and stability. Suddenly the stillness was broken by the crack of a big game rifle. The muzzle velocity was such that the bullet arrived before the sound that continued to echo against the steep rocky walls. The body slid down the steep mountain several feet, and then launched off a sheer rock face, falling into a boulder field ninety feet below.

Across the chasm, an old gray Big Horn ram stepped out from behind the twisted remains of a lightning-struck conifer. He raised his nose to the crisp thin air and surveyed his domain. Then he silently crossed a smooth granite face on footholds only he could see.

The Party

Salt Lake City lies crunched against the Wasatch Mountains. They are spectacular and right in your face if you happen to look east. This feeling of being next to such majesty is seldom more dramatic than in the area south of Parley's Canyon and north of Little Cottonwood. There is a section of the city in the shadow of the Wasatch where large lots and huge trees make it seem almost rural. This neighborhood is sometimes referred to as 'Holladay'. Big homes with tennis courts in the back yard separated by thick hedges or wooden fences, signal new money.

The old money mansions of brick or stone are northeast of the Temple and the Capitol, in what they call The Avenues.

But it was in Holladay that Peter Ernst built his huge home, set back from the street, hidden. The streets are winding, confusing, dark, and empty. And that's the way they planned it. Dense, heavy foliage set the scene, and the absence of sidewalks adds the exclamation point. Quiet, and private. The area suggests prestige, elegance, and success. Any traffic conducting the city's business stuck to the grid designed by Brigham Young: Straight streets, north and south, east and west.

Peter was feeling on top of the world.

It had been his best year ever. The new house was finally finished and his enterprises, at least the important ones, were profitable beyond his most optimistic projections. The 1995 Utah cutting horse season was over and he'd won his share of awards, including a championship belt buckle and a trophy saddle. And he had a hunting guide who had found a huge Big Horn ram in the Wind River Range and was keeping an eye on it from the air. When it became a little more accessible, the guide would let Peter know, and he could come up and shoot it. Furthermore, a brand new 1996 Sebring Silver Corvette with the LT4 special edition 330 horsepower engine had just been delivered. It sat gleaming in his driveway.

Life was good.

To celebrate his good fortune Peter decided to throw a party for his cowboy and hunting friends.

Marvin Thompson and Jake Oar were in their mid-twenties and involved with cutting horses. That was the subject of gossip in the front seat, as they headed west down Interstate 80 through Parley's Canyon. Marvin was a horse trainer, and rode a mare called Golden Peppy San that he hauled to competitions all over the West. Jake was a friend and student of his, a rancher and talented horseman. In the back their wives, Mae and Kay, were enjoying an excuse to dress up.

"Now, we don't have to stay all night," came a voice from the rear, and they all agreed. It was code for the universal question: are we going to have fun this evening?

In the city they got lost a few times before they found Peter's home. Slightly late, they had to park in the bushes along the street, but they weren't alone. The long curving driveway had already been stuffed with cars.

"Welcome. Come on in," said Peter at the door. He had on a dark blue, slightly fancy sweater over a pale blue dress shirt, slacks and loafers. Dress wise, he was neutral, neither hunter nor cowboy. You couldn't always say that about his guests.

Peter was an average man with a large presence. He looked very much like the successful entrepreneur he was. Jake couldn't remember ever seeing him without a hat. Peter's forehead started higher than expected and the eyebrows looked like caterpillars in confrontation.

The coat closet, like the driveway, was overflowing, so Peter said, "Just toss your wraps on that table."

There was no surface visible, just a mound of clothing precariously balancing above wooden legs.

"Drinks are over there by the giraffe, and there's tons of food in the kitchen. Make yourselves comfortable," he said, and gave the wives a warm smile.

Giraffe? Jake thought. Out loud, his mouth mumbled "Giraffe?"

"I was hunting lion in Kenya," Peter explained, "and we were staying in a tiny village. This old giraffe had been terrorizing the natives and they asked me to shoot it. They ate the meat, and I brought home the skin, head, and hooves."

Jake didn't know what to say, so he said, "Amazing."

Marvin said, "lucky there's a high ceiling. That thing is tall."

"When we built," Peter said, "we kinda planned around the giraffe. We call him George."

Like a very quiet pet you don't have to feed, Jake thought.

As they moved further into the house, they realized it was a museum of trophy animals and birds. There was a wall of dead ducks, each one a different kind, and they all appeared to be going south, right wings reached for the ceiling, left wings stretched toward the floor.

There was a stuffed lion here, and a fierce tiger there. The lion's expression suggested he was surprised to be here. A mountain goat stood with his front feet elevated on a plaster rock, and he glanced at Jake, eye to eye, with a glassy stare that revealed the depth of his cold dead soul. His snow-white coat had been combed and bleached, looking like he just came from a Beverly Hills shop.

One room was full of the heads of creatures with antlers or horns. There were several kinds of deer, of course, a huge elk, antelope and buffalo from both Wyoming and Africa. It was a zoo of the dead.

And that wasn't all.

A small but important looking display case stood in a place of honor, protected by a black panther on a log. Smaller trophies were on shelves behind glass. What looked at first glance like a little golden forest was actually a group of marksmen, all different sizes, standing in close formation. Each little gunman had a plaque explaining the honor, when it was bestowed, and what it was for.

"A little army ready to shoot birds," Marvin observed as he tried to read the tiny lettering.

Finally, he said, "Prizes for shooting skeet."

Another shelf held several silver belt buckles with lettering spelling out the glory won. There were a few framed photographs of Peter competing on his cutting horses. They were all pictured in the midst of some dramatic athletic turns, nose to nose with a heifer, the rider looking grim. The front view of horse and rider meant the rear view of the cow they faced.

Lower down behind the glass was a strangely artistic knife resting on a dark green velvet pillow. Crafted of silver, steel, and brass, it looked more like a weapon than a trophy, but there was a plaque near it announcing something in Latin: 'Una sumus potentes.'

Jake and Marvin moved over to share the case with one of the hunting crowd. He had come to see the amazing knife his friends had talked about.

"That's an amazing knife," he said, "lion charges, do you hit it or stab it? It's for a man that can think fast."

The tendency for the wives to gather comfortably near the food preparation was on full display. Luckily, the house had been planned for parties, and the large kitchen was behind a food-laden island, centered in the stream of guests. The pungent smell of curry followed folks with loaded plates as they floated into other rooms.

Peter's guests were an odd collection of sights and sounds. The hunters hung in clusters, talking about trips and guns, wearing jackets that tended to have too many pockets. The cow cutters wore starched, pressed Wranglers, and talked to each other about bloodlines and horse prices.

At least once there was a strange collision of cultures when Jake and another horseman, Wally Archer, found themselves trapped in a corner, between a fierce wild boar, and a hunter named Steve. He was a large man dressed from an upscale outfitters catalogue, nothing too extreme, but you could tell.

Steve was anticipating an upcoming trip.

"I'll soon be heading for Afghanistan, and I'm dealing with the paperwork right now, and it's driving me nuts," he said.

Jake tried to imagine Afghanistan. There are gophers right here in Utah, if you want to shoot something, he thought. He found this hunter very interesting.

Wally, who sometimes imagined himself an outdoorsman, wondered out loud about the permits required for that kind of travel. As Steve explained it, things sounded rather exotic. Nothing like a cruise ship vacation in the Caribbean, or deer hunting in the Uintas. These specialized trips were like assembling a small army.

"Not too complicated really," Steve explained. "I am working with an outfitter and guide service over there, and they can put the whole thing together. They take care of most stuff, but the focused nature of this trip is adding some complicated twists and turns."

"I always thought of Afghanistan as dry hills and rocks," said Wally.

"Oh, they have some real mountains, and National Geo called it the roof of the world. Some very tough people live up there, twelve thousand feet or more in the thin air. They have tiny herds of long haired, horned beasts they herd around, and use for wool and meat."

Noticing he was talking to a couple of horsemen, he continued, "They have a strange sport called buzkashi, played on horseback, that is basically a wild struggle for possession of a decapitated goat. I think they fight for it until there's nothing left but grease and hair."

< 6 >

Wally said that it sounded like fun, although his expression suggested sarcasm.

Steve explained he'd been doing some research on the culture, and the geography. He described an account of scientists putting radio collars on two snow leopards, and how the next day one of them had traveled seventy-five miles.

"Picture a cat like that, going that far, with nothing to eat but rocks."

His enthusiasm for the trip had been infectious.

"When are you going?" Jake asked. "I bet it's cold at the top of the world."

"Boys, I'm hunting for a special kind of leopard that lives up there, and it's going to be put on the endangered species list. So I've got to get there first. Just as soon as the paperwork is approved, I'm gone."

Jake almost said 'Good Luck' reflexively but thought better of it. He really didn't know what to say. He looked at Steve.

"Hmmm," he said.

Wally said he thought it was gonna be chilly.

As the evening progressed, Jake consumed a plate of broccoli, rice and curry while seated on a rock at the foot of the mountain goat, listening to Peter describing his up-coming hunting trip to an intrigued Wally. He was getting deep into the details, and since they were on the other side of the goat, Jake felt free to look for a place to discard his plate and find a different conversation. Maybe something equine.

An excellent evening finally began to wind down. Kay and Mae emerged with Marvin, and lured Jake from a discussion involving Steeldust bloodlines and the influence of a little stud named Doc Bar. In the car they realized it would be well after midnight before they got up the mountain, and home.

"We didn't have to stay all night, but we did, so it must have been a good party," came a voice from the back seat.

Twenty-five years later a freeway separated the Holladay mansions from the Wasatch Mountain Range, the 1996 silver Corvette became a classic, and Peter Ernst's Wind Rivers hunting death was all but forgotten.

America's longest war put Afghanistan on everyone's map.

< 8 >

Sandhill Cranes

The sandhill cranes had been marching around the hay fields on stilts, their beaks finding bugs no one knew were there. Twisting heads rose higher than the fence posts when they looked south. Then they started to fly. Flocks of them circling the valley, calling to the stragglers, scolding, commenting, and giving each other weather reports. And then in a few days they were all gone. The valley seemed quiet and a little lonely without them.

Fall was coming, that period when all the summer projects that must be done have been done, and the summer projects that should have been done, may have to be postponed. Time is running out. Winter may be just over the hill. Snow powdered the top of Hoyt's Peak, and it had begun turning peach color in the late afternoon light. The valley floor was already in shade.

Jake stared at the mountain. It seemed to him that if he could concentrate with enough focus, he would be able to watch the shadow line crawl up the side, rock by rock, tree by tree. He wondered about the deer up there. Deer season seemed to coincide with the first really serious weather. Wet and cold. A breeze blowing from the north suggested it could happen early again this year. But you never knew for sure. Sometimes a beautiful autumn could last into December.

His own urge to hunt had waned over time. He had inherited the tradition from his father. Enthusiastic in his early teens, he loved the little rituals, shopping for shells, cleaning weapons, getting the deer tags, scouting the mountains, and selecting companions. Gradually hunting buddies had grown up, moved on, drifted away, or wanted to bring noisy sons along. It began to seem more like work and less of an adventure.

Jake hadn't hunted at all since Mae died. She had been taken in an accident, a car vs. her bike. But in fact, he thought, he hadn't done a lot of the things he used to do before. There was the long loneliness of course, but animals must be fed, hay needed to be cut, and life, this new life, had to be lived alone.

He had been taking it one step at a time.

He was in a large round pen full of sand. It had solid walls that kept the attention of a horse or cow focused within, although a six-foot man could easily see out. Jake took another long look at the mountain, and then turned his attention to the horse. A sorrel, with a white snip and strip down her elegant face, she had been born in the pasture just across the irrigation ditch.

He pulled the latigo up carefully and put a toe in the stirrup like a man who hoped no one would notice. Then he stepped onto the little filly, in a smooth motion, and sat very still. Not exactly like sitting on a powder keg, he thought, but at this age a bucking horse is not the fun it once was.

She'd been saddled several times, but this was only the fourth time she'd borne his full weight. She was ready for the next step. Their first step together. Jake moved his legs around and began bumping her a little with his heels. She tipped her nose around and looked back at him. He relaxed and sat still a minute, then bumped his legs some more. He slapped her rump ever so gently with the reins. He squeezed his legs. She took a step, and instantly his body completely relaxed. So far, so good.

He rode her like that, a step at a time, for about ten minutes. Then he got off and on, about five times. She acted calm about it all.

He looked at the peak again. The shadow seemed to have moved about a third of the way up, and the peach color was giving way to pink.

He stood beside the filly, looking south across his saddle, toward some aspen trees lining the irrigation canal. The leaves were mostly gone; those remaining were blinking in a raising breeze, flickering as though they wanted to fly south with the cranes.

Something moved on the other side of the ditch. At first he

< 10 >

thought it was a cow, but it moved again, and he wasn't so sure. Jake stood still watching. The little filly had her head raised, ears up, watching too. She trembled and quivered.

There was a commotion as the black object got to its feet and stirred panic in the horse. She swung around at the end of the hackamore reins, head high, eyes large, and she snorted loudly.

The moose was a two-year-old female, larger than a riding horse, and coal black. She stood looking at them, concerned but unafraid. Then she nibbled at some willows beside the water, turned clear around, looked at Jake again, and trotted off. Sixty yards away she came to a wire fence. She stopped, then trotted this way and that, stopped again and stood still. As he watched she jumped the barrier, her rear legs sliding over on the wire. It was not graceful, but efficient. She headed south in the gathering dusk.

Jake wondered about her. She was headed for the hills, he knew. Probably lost and lonely. Taking her life one step at a time. She might make it to motherhood, or she could get hit by a car.

His horse relaxed and bobbed her head. She sniffed Jake's elbow. He turned and put a toe into the oxbow stirrup. At his urging the filly moved off. No bumping this time, just his legs squeezing. They walked and trotted a little. The temperature dropped a few degrees, and the shadow was near the top of the mountain. He dismounted and led her to the barn.

< 11 >

The Cutting Lesson

After the Civil War the cattle business bloomed in the 50-million-acre unfenced pasture called West Texas. It was an arid grassland, where a man's cattle could mix with his neighbors. Ranching this big country required new methods and practices.

One of the tools that grew out of necessity was the cutting horse. A special horse with quickness and ability to separate a specific cow from a herd, prevent her return, and drive her somewhere. Cattle come with a strong separation anxiety that makes this difficult. She may dodge and dart. On a normal horse the rider can only struggle with reins and spurs trying to keep up. But a horse that could read a cow, watch her eyes, ears and body language, anticipate her action, well, that was something.

These special horses were called 'cutting horses'. They were prized by their owners and treated with respect. The working men all took pride in their companies' cutting horses.

Bragging is one thing, but in 1898 a three-day Cowboy Reunion was held in Haskell, Texas, and it included the first cutting contest for prize money. The best all came, and the winner was an animal named Old Hub who won in a work-off, performing without a bridle.

Nowadays the open range is gone, but not these unique equines. No longer a tool, they are still respected and admired, competing in arenas and colosseums.

A sport or art form? It depends on your point of view.

Another winter was in the history books; a fresh calendar from the feed store was on the wall.

Jake had been on horseback for over two hours and was walking slowly around a black cow in his large round pen. He rode a chestnut three-year-old Quarter Horse. Her neck showed a light sweat; she was not tired but relaxed. As they approached one of

< 12 >

the three gates, Jake rounded his back and pushed his heels down, and the filly glided to a soft stop. His hand on the reins didn't even move. With his legs he adjusted her position, so he could unlatch and swing the gate open while he remained horseback. Then he resumed walking the big circle, reins swinging. His movements were calm and seamless, his communication with the horse almost invisible. Without being asked, a black and white dog scooted across the sand and sent the lone cow out the gate.

There was a mature gray gelding saddled and tied, just outside another gate. And a red Mercedes-Benz approached on the driveway. Jake checked his watch.

"Right on time," he said to the dog.

Soon there was a woman in a cowboy hat with a stampede string and a colorful neckerchief at the gate. She waited as Jake continued his circle and drifted up, the gate between them.

"Hi." She gave him a nice smile.

"Howdy Missus Jones," Jake said as he touched his hat brim. He was a middle-aged guy with some old-fashioned habits.

"Am I dressed, OK?" she asked, a little self-conscious.

"You're fine, ma'am."

"Please call me Stef."

"I'm Jake, and that's Buster." He pointed at the dog.

"And who's this little cutie?" she smiles at the horse.

"Cats Countin' Checks, but I call her Sis, Jake replied.

"I understand you've ridden a lot."

"Hunters and jumpers as a kid in Pennsylvania, but since college it's only been trail rides on rental horses," Stef said, "I've always loved horses."

That's what girls usually say, thought Jake, but what he said was: "I bet these cow horses seem smaller than you're used to."

"I don't care. I've always wanted to ride a cutting horse. They're so quick, jumping this way and that. How do you stay on?"

"We'll get to that," Jake said, "but I have to warn you, you could get hooked, addicted, and it could ruin your life."

< 13 >

"I'm ready," Stef announced.

The gray gelding was introduced, and stirrups adjusted. Then came a short conversation about the reins: that they are not used to maintain the rider's balance or make steady contact with the horse's mouth as they might in English-style riding. When the reins are picked up, the animal collects himself, alert to the rider. But when working, they are loose, and the horse does his own thinking. He and the rider will be focused on the cow.

"He can feel a fly on his ear or the weight of the leather against his neck. If the rider's hand moves, he knows," Jake said. "We try to build on that sensitivity in our horsemanship."

"A horse's natural reaction to pressure is to escape or push back. But we train them to give to pressure, move away from it. I want to use the least pressure needed to get the response, trying to keep everything as light as possible.

"As you are walking, move a leg away from his side and he'll drift that direction. If you relax and push your heels down, he'll stop, move one leg away, push with the other, he'll draw back and roll over his hocks. You can steer with legs only. Of course, all this only comes after you learn to trust each other."

When Jake was reasonably sure she understood, Stef rode around the pen a while, as horse and rider were getting the feel of each other. Jake watched closely from his saddle.

When he thought they were ready, he called a meeting.

"OK let's start, Jake said. "Are you comfy?"

"Yep. I like this little guy," she claimed, and put her fingers in the mane of the muscular little creature.

Jake explained how she should ride when working a cow. To slouch her back when stopping. Push on the saddle horn to keep her butt from rising up, and to maintain her bearings when the action got hot. To imagine her center of gravity changing from her chest down into the horse, just below his withers.

"A hand on the horn guides you when things go fast. You cannot use your eyes because they must always be watching the cow.

< 14 >

She tells you what is going to happen next, and if you are watching the cow, you can keep up. If you glance at the horse, or anything else, you will be left behind."

And they discussed Stef's legs. When to touch the horse with your calf, and when to get those legs out of the way.

Jake knew the instructions were theoretical and would become quickly forgotten in the heat of battle. There was a lot to think about in the beginning. Later it would become easier as the student developed reflexes and muscle memory.

"I don't mind repeating myself, and we'll start slow with just one old cow."

In an hour she had worked a single cow on the fence, learning to step into its comfort zone, referred to as its 'bubble', to cause it to move. How to stay in position, or to curve away to be defensive, to hold a straight line to be correct, and when to step forward to stop the cow.

After the slow cow, she squealed as she worked a faster one, clinging to stay on, and forgetting all she'd been told. They reviewed things and she settled down and improved.

"Not too hard to explain," Jake said, "but difficult to do, especially at speed."

"Wow!" she said, her heart beating fast, gasping for breath.

When it was over Stef wanted more. They rode side by side, talking, and letting the grey gelding cool down.

"A horse that can move like that and think so quick is amazing. How much is a horse like that?"

"The horse is only the first financial problem. Remember hay, stall, vet bills entry fees, a trainer ..."

"But start with the horse ... how much do they cost?"

"Somewhere between ten grand and a million," Jake said, "and I don't think ten'll get you very much."

Stef smiled but she didn't look like she understood the answer. Jake thought a story might help.

"So, there's this guy, and he calls a trainer. He says 'I wanna

< 15 >

get a solid cutting horse. One I can ride and learn and compete on and not embarrass myself too badly, and I wonder if you know of anything like that for sale?"

"And the trainer says 'Hmmmm ... I think I happen to have a horse like that right here in my barn. Fifteen-thousand bucks."

"Oh," the first guy says. "I was hoping for a little more horse than that."

The trainer says, "Ok, I'll look around and find one for you."

"A couple weeks later the trainer calls the man back. "I think I've found just the horse you're looking for. Twenty-five thousand."

Jake paused, allowing Stef to fill in the blanks and get the point.

"It was the same horse," Jake said, just in case.

They squirted the horses off with a hose and had a beer.

Stef, looking invigorated, told Jake she thought there were a lot of old habits to unlearn if she wanted to ride cutting horses, and that he had been a good teacher. She had to go to California but would call as soon as she got back.

"It's unique among any horse sports I know," she said. "The rider and the horse trade off the decision making, and when he's deciding, you just have to keep up ... and when it gets fast it's really fast."

"I know a professional bull rider that, when he retired, went to training and showing cutting horses. He said the adrenalin rush was similar, but in cutting it lasted longer," Jake said.

"I can understand," Stef said, "and, in cutting, your dance partner isn't trying to kill you."

Cutting Hay

Jake had been on the John Deere since 5:45 am. Now, well past ten, he'd cut the grass in his small meadow, and was working on one of the larger alfalfa fields. The wet spring had created a nice first cutting, and if the television weather girls were right, this would be a dry week. It should be a fine start toward filling the hay barn. Jake had his fingers crossed.

Two hours had passed since he'd noticed Tina Valentine's silver Toyota headed toward Park City. You must pay attention to your work cutting hay, but there was plenty of time to notice things. Cats and rabbits jumping from hiding places, running into the uncut legume, disappearing. A fox following the fence row sneaking up to pounce on a gopher. And it was hard not to notice the plume of dust a car made on the usually deserted Monroe Springs Lane.

Much later, as Jake turned from west to south, he spotted Tina's car again. This time it was parked at the southwest corner of his field. As he got closer, he saw her get out and lean on the hood, watching him. It was her Toyota, surely it was her, but something was different.

He realized that although he'd seen her many times, she always appeared rather bland, even mousy. She had usually been in jeans and a work shirt. Her hair was rabbit brown, and she seldom wore makeup.

But here she was, in a skin-tight exercise outfit. The sort of getup Jake had only seen on the covers of women's health magazines in the barber shop. Amazing. She wore a black leotard with a yellow sports bra, partly covered by a red thing that sort of covered the bra, but didn't, and was cut very high in the hips. The effect made her legs look very long, and when he glimpsed her rear as she moved around the car, it seemed almost spectacular: Two black cheeks separated by a thin red line. For some reason she reminded Jake of the red-winged blackbird that nested by the irrigation ditches.

Well, well, he thought, there's more to Tina Valentine than baking pies, and weeding the garden. What he said was, "Howdy."

He was talking to himself, so he could hardly hear the words over the chuckling and banging of the machinery. The big green and yellow equipment rattled to a halt, and he waved, opened the little cockpit door, and climbed down to the ground, to escape the noise.

"Hi," she said. "Please excuse the outfit, I've been to yoga." She smiled, a little self-consciously. She had been sweating and her face was a little flushed. There were freckles on her nose he hadn't noticed before. Her hair was damp, darker than usual, and looked interesting.

"Howdy," Jake said again. He hoped he didn't appear to be staring.

"I'm sorry to interrupt your work," she said, "but I was pretty sure it was you in there driving."

Jake waited a second for her to continue, then said, "Yep, it's me ... realizing then that she had started to speak again. A second or two of silence, each waiting for the other. Then both grinned.

"Anyway, I saw Karen Kelly in class this morning," Tina said, "and she reported her cows have attracted a visiting bull, and she wondered where it belongs. It's been messing up her fences."

"Ummm."

"Any ideas?"

"What kind is it?" Jake asked.

"Well, I don't know. But she said it was black."

That'll be Angus," Jake guessed. "I suppose she should call Ken Hargraves; it could be his. Or maybe Jim Clementis. Most of the others have their cattle on the mountain by now."

"I'll tell her," Tina promised.

"Tell her to start with Ken first. He has cows with a bull in a pasture that backs up to hers at the southern corner. Most likely

< 18 >

it's his."

"I will."

She seemed a little out of place on a country road colored like a bird. Ready to fly, he thought. She moved around as though she might have had the same idea.

Jake shifted a little, too. He didn't like to shout over the tractor, but he also felt a little uncomfortable. He had been easy with Henry Valentine and his wife, but Tina, alone like this? He put it out of his mind. Same Tina. Just different.

"I hope this weather holds," he said, making conversation.

"Me, too."

What a lame cliché I have found, he thought. Out loud he said, "My alfalfa will all be down by tomorrow night, God willing; maybe Henry would like me to do his too, if it's ... if the weather is still dry."

Oops, Jake thought. Her costume has me flustered.

"Henry's gone to California again this week," Tina said, "but he'll call home and I'll ask him. I'm sure he'd like you to cut it whenever you think is best."

"California?" Jake looked slightly quizzical.

"He's doing a little research in the library at USC, and getting some new computer stuff," Tina smiled. "Henry loves new stuff."

"Stuff?"

"He's a stuff magnate."

"I don't envy him those freeways," Jake said. "There's a lot of cement there, and most of it's at seventy-five miles an hour."

"There's something about Henry that loves long drives," she said. "I'd rather stay right here, but he's different. Sometimes he'll take a notebook and his laptop, and just go for a day or a week, just 'cause he likes to be alone, and drive. He loves the desert."

"Plenty of desert between here and there."

"Well," she said. "I better scat. I must look a mess."

"Hmmmm," Jake announced. "You look very healthy."

When she turned and got back in the Toyota, Jake got another fine look at the thin red line. That image remained number one in his memory the rest of the morning.

After about forty minutes, Jake began to toy with the idea of a woman. Since Mae died, he had no close women friends. No, that wasn't right. He did have several but none that were close, and most were married. He reviewed the single women he knew, but there weren't many. No one seemed to strike a chord. Is romance even possible after so many years of neglect?

He wondered if Mae would forgive him. For what? ... moving on? He would always love her, he knew. But for the survivors ... there is the old saying: 'Life goes on'

Then his mind suddenly stopped wandering. His eyes focused on the silver auto that appeared again, leading a dust cloud. It stopped at the field gate and waited.

Jake stopped the slow cumbersome machine and killed the engine. He was about sixty yards from the road, and he knew he'd get there quicker on foot. He left the John Deere in its tracks, jumped down and walked toward the car, smiling. When he crossed the rows of cut legume, he giant-stepped over them dramatically, like a schoolboy showing off.

Tina greeted him at the gate, dressed in the more familiar denim jeans and baggy work shirt. She looked showered and smelled fresh, lemony.

"Do you like tuna?" she asked, "I made us lunch."

"Sure," he laughed.

She withdrew a bag from the passenger seat that held two sandwiches and a thermos of lemonade. From the hatch-back she pulled out collapsible director's chairs.

They sat by the fence, ate and chatted comfortably for about fifty minutes. Jake felt more relaxed with this woman than any he could remember. The sun was hot, and it would be easy to neglect his hay. He was a 'job to do, get it done' kind of guy, but found he was truly enjoying this diversion.

< 20 >

He had known Henry and Tina as a couple, but he knew Henry best. They had talked of topics that needed discussing, irrigation water, burning ditches, snow removal and haying. But never personal things. This conversation was a first. He found her smart, chatty, and pleasant. She had ideas that made him think. She loved the valley.

Finally, reluctantly, weather creeped into his mind. A rancher with hay down was always a nervous rancher.

"Would you like to take a tractor ride?" He realized a stupid question as soon as it popped out. He must focus on work, not talk. And the cab was small. Probably impossible with two people.

They had collected the remains of their lunch and Tina seemed to think about the invitation a minute.

"Sure," she decided. "Sure."

The plexiglass cab of the tractor was tiny, and in the center was a seat big enough for only one large farmer's bottom. Any extra space was filled with levers, buttons and gauges. The floor was home for some equipment and tools. Hammer. Wrench. Shovel. A toolbox, a rolled slicker, a lost horseshoe, and a coiled lariat.

As he opened the little door, Jake realized the hopelessness of the situation. But forging ahead, he climbed in and tried to squeeze to the other side.

With the tractor turned off, sitting quiet, the normally air-conditioned cab was getting warm.

"Come on in," he said, wondering what she'd do.

Up she climbed and stuck her torso through the opening. Then she stepped in, trying to arrange her feet around the tools and levers. She couldn't stand, and she couldn't squeeze beside him.

"I guess you'll have to get seated first," she said, "and I'll slip behind you."

Jake didn't have a better idea, so he took the familiar seat.

"OK," he said, but he knew it wasn't going to work. He had levers at his knees and the steering wheel above them. He adjusted the seat forward, but it still didn't allow enough room.

A fly buzzed during a moment of awkward silence. Then he felt her struggling behind him. It was impossible, but Tina was in a playful good humor, trying her best.

"I'll have to ride on your lap," she joked.

Jake slid the seat back as far as it would go, and she squeezed in. It was apparent this wouldn't work either, but he held her hips as they experimented with positions.

"I guess they didn't build this cab for two," she announced laughing.

Then she stood, hunched over by the low roof, and turned, passed a leg over his lap, and sat down astride him. His hat was getting crushed. He pulled it off, then tossed it out the door. Her upper body was twisted because a sleeve had caught on a lever, so she unbuttoned her shirt with her free hand, and struggled out of it. She sent it out the door after the hat. Then, sitting straight, her lips met Jakes's forehead. His nose pressed in her neck. She had to arch toward him because the steering wheel was in the small of her back.

They were smiling at the ridiculousness of the situation. Slowly they became aware their arms were around each other. There was really nowhere else to put them. The mood changed, and they held each other quietly for a long time. His fingers found her bra, and he unhooked it, without really thinking. Naked arms, shoulders and tummy changed the atmosphere.

Four grasshoppers were trapped with them, taking turns jumping at the window. The door was wide open, and one hopped out. The tiny space was warm and getting hot.

"Jake," Tina whispered "I ..."

His face was buried in her neck, her hair all over him.

Jake felt Tina's rush of emotion.

She seemed to float in the moment. Right here, right now,

< 22 >

in the heat and dust, with the grasshoppers. Her feet moved among the tools. There was comfort in the touching arms and bodies.

They remained like this for a while. Finally, fingers fumbled to unbuckle belts and searched for zippers. She tried to stand, wiggled out of her pants and panties. Her bra, hanging loose on her shoulders, went out the door.

She bent to help Jake, and soon his pants and shorts joined hers on the floor with the tools. She was astride his lap. Jake didn't know who did what, but he could smell perspiration everywhere. Her back was wet and slippery.

A primal urge surfaced in the River of No Return and took control. It narrowed, shutting out the world in its rush headlong toward the inevitable sequence: coupling, climax and release.

Afterwards they remained locked together. Everything moist and glistening.

Gradually as their focus widened, the wild river calmed and became a lake of reflection.

After years of waiting, they felt no urge to move. Jake's legs went to sleep, and sticky moisture trickled on to the tractor seat. They listened to their breathing, their hearts beating, and the sounds of insects. And they smelled the odors of alfalfa, dust, diesel fuel, and sex.

But the situation gradually changed, from uncomfortable to unbearable.

Only then did they untangle, crawl out of the cab and climb down, where they lay in the uncut alfalfa, shaded by the tractor. That's where they remained nearly two hours.

At last, Tina began to wonder out loud if her bare bottom could be seen from the road.

Jake realized lying there wasn't getting the hay cut.

There were about sixty yards of cut alfalfa resting flat and three feet of alfalfa standing, between where they lay and the road. They had been performing in a tiny plexiglass theater, about six feet in the air, and there was no telling if somebody might have witnessed their passion play. It was a troublesome thought as Jake climbed up and in with the grasshoppers to retrieve some of their clothes.

< 24 >

Mirror

After the struggle in the tractor, Tina had been on Jake's mind most of Wednesday, Thursday, and Friday. Simon Banuelos, neighbor, friend and employee was his main helper with the ranch. They were trading time in the tractor cutting hay and turning it over later to dry. The plan was to bale it early the following week.

Jake's mind seemed to move in two directions. Opportunity and guilt. He needed a distraction that might help cool the emotion Tina's memory raised. He realized a new door had opened, and horizons had expanded. How she fit in, or if she did at all, he did not know. One step at a time. But nothing was as simple as it had been.

Simon took over the chores on Friday, and Jake gathered a couple of horses and left town.

Saturday morning he awoke in the Best Western Motel in Delta, Utah. When he looked out of the window, the night was beginning to brighten. The land here was flat as a table. He could see the mountains many, many miles to the east, so small they were just a wrinkle at the edge of the sky.

Jake punched the television to life, but without Trump or pandemic, there was nothing interesting. Cartoons, click, cartoons, click, cartoons, click, talking heads. He turned it off.

His head. That's my head, he realized. He looked again in the mirror.

At home he had a small mirror in the bathroom to shave with, but here it covered the entire wall, sink counter to ceiling, wall to wall. It was well lit, with a long row of lights across the top. It was suitable for a Prom Queen or a Vegas showgirl. Lighting to put on eyelashes or find a stray pimple. He'd stayed in motels with big mirrors before, but never noticed, or paid any attention. He'd

< 25 >

taken his face for granted, hadn't really seen it in years. This huge reflection seemed to say, "Take a look, Jake, is that really you?"

Jake did look. The strange face appeared older, with more wrinkles than he remembered. From the eyebrows up it was pale white, the lower half was worn leather. He wondered what Tina thought of that face.

He shaved, then put the face out of his mind. Thank goodness he didn't have to look at it.

He dressed then and drove about a mile to the Millard County Fairgrounds to feed his horses.

In half an hour he parked at the motel again and crossed the street to the cafe. Inside there were some cowboy hats, and he spoke to most of the people under them. An old friend, Mark, and his wife Deb had not ordered yet, and they made room for him in their booth by the window.

With coffee and eggs under their noses, they discussed the price of cattle, the chance of rain, and some details about a future contest in Farmington. They gossiped about a trainer who was moving from Utah to Idaho, and they worried about the cattle they would cut next month in Vernal.

"It'll probably be those wild cattle off the reservation," Deb said.

"They were the toughest cattle we faced last year," Jake remembered.

"Fast as bullets."

"Came in all jacked up and wouldn't settle."

They discussed a rich developer, who, with his family of four, had been competing on cutting horses for three years. They had used a private trainer and were just now getting out. With at least four show horses and other horses for practice, equipment and so on, they must have spent millions. At two and a half minutes each 'run', how much had each minute of pure fun cost? A question of money spent required accounting, and nobody at the table liked math well enough to answer.

< 26 >

"One thing for certain, there'll be horses and stuff for sale," said Deb.

When the eggs were gone, and after the third coffee refills poured, they were joined by a twenty-year-old named either Lena or Lela. She was one of twins, and at this table only the elderly horseman could tell them apart. Jake and Deb addressed her as "Lenaorlela." She was Lela but had long ago stopped worrying about her name. She had worked for a trainer in St. George, and they discussed his exploits a while, then they helped her analyze her goals, and plans for the future: horse trainer, or dental technician. They were unanimous that she would have to clean her fingernails more often in dentistry.

"Hmmmmm," said Mark, looking at his watch.

"Maybe we should go," Jake suggested, and picked up the check.

His friend reached for his wallet, but Jake sprang up, and headed to the cash register.

"I'll get the tip," Mark said, and he did.

"Thanks, Jake," said Deb.

"Thanks for the coffee, and the advice," said Lela.

There were covered stalls at the Millard County fairgrounds, ample parking, trucks, trailers and people. Horses were tied, waiting for something or someone, others gone somewhere, to do something. People were doing chores. Familiar sounds featured nickering and hellos. There was all the focused confusion before and during most large horse events across the West.

Jake breathed in the bright, cold, high-desert air as he looked in on his horses, then walked to the large steel structure that contained the arena. He stepped inside, where the cool florescent atmosphere was thick with humidity and the pungent smells of ammonia and sweating horses.

The large space was divided through the middle with panels, and a parked pickup truck with a chair in its bed for the judge.

< 27 >

A tractor was dragging the ground to provide good footing. The cattle would enter dead-center on the north side where the cutters would compete.

The other end, south of the panels and truck, was open for warming up horses. Saddled horses were tied along the sides, and riders were walking, trotting, and loping circles, virtually filling the remaining space with motion. Bumper cars on horseback. Each rider was lost in his own cocoon, psyching up or calming down, perhaps focused on finding a private game face. Distracted drivers, most of them.

Crossing this area was like jaywalking at noon, not Jake's favorite memory from New York City. No wonder the professionals were safely elsewhere; their assistants, friends or others did the dangerous warming up or cooling down.

Jake picked his way through this confusion, with a series of smiles and "Hellos." Most riders were friends or acquaintances; many were also his direct competitors.

An elevated box in the northwest corner was his destination. It served as the office for Hope, the show secretary. Entering, he noticed the chill was gone and it was warm. She had a tiny propane heater at her feet.

"Jake, how are you?"

"Good," he said. "You?"

"You missed some excitement yesterday when a cow escaped into the bleachers, but I'm glad you made it today."

Hope was everyone's pal, and advisor. She had a little news for Jake; twelve entries in the open, and there should be fresh cattle through the Three Thousand. The youth will have re-runs. The judge was from Texas.

Jake entered his horses, Little Pete in two classes and Starlight, a four-year-old, into the Three Thousand Novice. He visited with Hope until another contestant came in to enter.

About two hours later he was circling the warm-up area beside a fellow named Loren, and they talked and gossiped a little, as their horses walked.

"There was this golfer," Loren said.

"Yeah?"

"There was this golfer, who was lining up his shot, you know." Loren looped his reins around the saddle horn, so he could demonstrate with his hands as they rode.

"So, he's at the tee, looking out, then looking down, getting his feet set, lining up his club, and a voice says, 'Hey' and he looks down and sees it's a frog in the grass, and he ignores it, and lines up his club, and the frog says 'Hey you',' and he tries to concentrate, and the frog says, 'Hey you. Hey, if you kiss me, I'll turn into a beautiful princess, and you can do anything you want.' And the guy ignores the frog and hits his shot.

"So he's walking toward his ball, and the frog is hopping along beside him, and the frog is goin', 'Hey, stupid, pay attention here, just kiss me, and I'll turn into a beautiful princess, and we can have great sex all night.' So the guy just keeps walking, and the frog keeps following, and they get to the ball, and the guy is lining up to hit it, and frog says, 'I mean it, are you listening to me? Just one kiss ...'"

"The guy reaches down and picks up the frog and puts it in his pocket. He's getting his putter out and lining it up, and the frog sticks his head out and says 'Hey stupid, have you been listening to me? Just one kiss, I'll be a beautiful princess. Great sex.'

"The guy says, 'Well, at my age, I think I'd rather have a talking frog.'"

Jake chuckled and they kicked their horses into a lope.

After the Twenty Amateur, they had another cattle change and lunch break with pizza for everyone. Some people remained on horseback, settling the new herd or keeping a horse warmed up for the next class. But almost everyone else clustered under the raised office talking or relaxing on the bleachers. The judge sat apart, because the rules forbid anyone but the secretary to speak to him.

Someone asked Loren how come his luck had been so bad in the draw. He'd been next to last in the non-Pro, and very last in the Fifty Amateur. It is the secretary that supervises the draw, although the judge usually does it.

"Well," said Loren, "this morning it was pretty cool around here, and when I went to sign up, Hope said her ass was cold, and asked me if I had a heater she could borrow."

He held his pizza in his teeth, glanced at Hope's bottom as if judging the width, and spread his hands about three and a half feet apart, then took the pizza into his right hand again.

"I said, I don't think I have one big enough," he said, and Hope squealed.

"I think she's been a little miffed at me ever since."

"You will draw up last, for the rest of your life," she announced loudly, but she had a big grin. Everybody within ear shot cheered.

Jake ate supper at Steak Ranch with a collection of his friends. They were tired, and pretty dusty, especially from the knees down, and wore their boots, spurs and hats, with some of the esprit de corps a gang of black-leather-wearing bikers might exhibit in a small desert town in Nevada.

They talked of horses and cattle, kidded each other and the waitresses, and generally had a nice time. At a cutting nobody cares who won or lost, but Jake won enough checks to cover his entry fees, motel and gas, and still be a few dollars richer. That's not easy, and Jake was feeling good. Tomorrow he'd be home. By nine fifteen Jake was in his motel room, showered, and ready for bed. But as he passed the large mirror, he saw his reflection again. It was like confronting a stranger.

"Who?" he said to this image, "Who the hell are you?"

< 30 >

Sunday

Sunday morning, when Jake arrived home, Tina was still on his mind. He was unsure what to do about it. He unhooked the trailer and put the horses away. He and Buster checked the waterers, and the horses in the pasture. And he glanced at the cows. He put the saddles in the tack room, bridles on their pegs, and hung up his chaps.

Buster's tail was still wagging. A lot had gone on in Jake's absence but the only way the dog had to explain it was through his tail, and it was on auto pilot.

Jake entered the house from the back door, put his hat on the kitchen table upside down. The room was like he'd left it, except the clock now said 11:06. He picked up some loose magazines and put them in a neat stack by the television. He moved a jacket and a vest to the closet. He put his good hat away; the usin' hat was by the door. He realized he was seeing his house as a stranger—a woman perhaps, might see it. He caught himself and stopped that unfamiliar behavior.

Then he spied a note peeking out from under the front door. He picked it up carefully and sat down. It said:

Saturday
Jake
You've been on my mind.
I am trying to think things out.
Henry will come home Monday sometime.
Maybe we could talk today or tomorrow, if you get back in time.
Do you go to church?
If you get home before Monday, please call me.
I don't know how I feel. I want to sound you out
about your feelings.
Tina

< 31 >

Well, there you are, Jake thought. This conversation is inevitable, he knew. Jake opened the curtains, and things seemed to brighten up. Then he picked up the phone.

By 1:30 pm Tina and Jake were in his old farm truck, on a two-track excuse for a road, and had climbed up into the hills high above the valley. This country was high, wide and handsome, with grass and sage dominating the south-facing slopes, and evergreen forests residing on the north sides.

Jake and several other ranchers ran cattle here through the summers, sharing access and Forest Service permits with a lumber company that harvests trees. Outdoorsmen in search of sport or exercise, trout or deer, also explored this edge of the wilderness. It was the western end of the High Uintas, a mountain range that starts at the Kamas Valley and crosses much of northern Colorado, just below the Wyoming border. After the first few miles, roads disappeared into paths, and finally were gone. The chance of meeting another person was remote.

When Jake stopped the view was endless. The last evidence of civilization, tire tracks through slender wheatgrass, had ended thirty yards back. It was a scruffy hilltop, plunging northward into a dense forest of pine. Southward, sage stumbled into patches of evergreens and aspen and expanses of grass. To the west a youthful cluster of white bark and flickering leaves protected a beaver dam, and a large pond.

"This might be my favorite view," Jake said. "I used to come here on my horse, when I was a kid."

He turned off the key, and they climbed out. Perched on a rock, side by side, facing the panorama, they sat quietly at first.

"I understand why you keep this old truck. It's amazing it could get up here, with no road," said Tina, making conversation.

"Mostly it's used to repair fences, or for odd jobs where it'll probably get scratched up, and to take hay to cows in the snow. That's why it's full of hay string and old tools. It's a truck and a

< 32 >

toolbox. It gets no respect at home, but here, it's in its element."

"Looks old but works good," Tina said.

Just like me, Jake thought.

"The battery is brand new," he mentioned.

And from that careful beginning, the real discussion evolved.

Tina explained how her marriage had gradually gotten stale and loveless, like the cottonwood behind their house. As time passed it got older, the marriage longer, the tree taller. But branches died and memories faded. What was the attraction in the first place? A tall gray dying thing with a few pathetic leaves at the very top.

She and Henry had not been intimate for many months. Probably years. He had become too controlling. She was feeling trapped.

There was a lot she needed to say out loud, examine in daylight, and Jake was supplying a sympathetic ear. Relaxed and realizing it was going to be a long conversation, they stood and meandered down toward the beaver dam. They settled themselves on the grass, lying side by side, watching the clouds. She talked to the sky. Her words, soft as cotton.

Carefully Tina unwrapped her childhood, her family and school. Raised on the western edge of an exploding Phoenix, an only child to a quiet couple. Her father had been a dentist, and in the long hot pink evenings, a poolside alcoholic. There was the high school swimming team, and her pets. She had many, including a chinchilla and a snake, as well as the usual dogs and cats.

Not an unusual childhood, Jake supposed.

She told of a high school romance that lasted almost three years until it burst like a long festering pimple.

But if she spent an hour on her youth, she spent four more on Henry and his family. She unloaded a trunkful of his family's dirty laundry.

In his youth Henry Valentine had been a rock and roller. His band played country rock in Kansas and Missouri, usually near

Fort Riley, where the soldiers had come and gone from Vietnam.

His formal education at KSU had been in art, the department with the reputation for the best drugs. After the band broke down, he spent three years in New York City planning to make a big splash in modern art.

Sharing a loft in the West Village, he took some all-night chemical tours of life's deepest meanings, and its highest awakenings. With a deKooning print for inspiration melting on the wall and a Jackson Pollock squirming like the inside of a car crash, Henry realized he had found the center of a freaked-out universe.

Wallowing in personal growth and stumbling through a lake of self-pity, his system seemed to cleanse itself, and he retreated to the universe of his youth.

Back home he tried working in the family business. With a monster Toyota dealership at four locations around Kansas City, and a large car stereo store, the family was rich and getting richer.

Henry had four brothers. Two became executives in the auto business, leaving the others free to share the profits and travel the world. Henry's new "work" was journalism, and his business card said, 'freelance writer'. That, Tina explained, was debatable.

She described a greedy brother, another worthless one, and sisters-in-law who drove her crazy. One of them actually considered herself K.C. aristocracy, which was her excuse for becoming a Royal Bitch. There were annual get-togethers that were the worst sort of punishment. On a tiny lake where the family mansion stood, the 'Blood members' got to see the books behind closed doors. Tina and her sisters-in-law sat around, comparing status, who was more important than who.

Tina met Henry after college in Phoenix when he wrote some corporate literature for her boss. He lived with an independent income that varied year by year, depending on the automobile sales, and she met him in a good year. Her first impression as they began dating was: Big Spender.

Gradually she brought her story up to date.

< 34 >

Henry always had a horse, as long as she'd known him. It was always an Arabian, never ridden nor trained, boarded and admired at a stable somewhere. Whenever it died, he'd just get another one. He would say "It's an A Rab." The current horse was a mini, and sometimes he'd let it in the house. A "Mini-A-Rab." Her marriage had gotten to the point where expressions she once thought were cute, now just sounded stupid.

Marriage to the car family, and life in Phoenix, had started out just fine. They even considered starting a branch dealership there.

But gradually Henry changed. Controlling, and tighter with her allowance. He didn't enjoy what she cooked and didn't like the way she kept the house. And she was tired of picking up after the goofy mini horse.

And Phoenix changed too. It got bigger. More cement, more traffic, and more heat. Every year was hotter than the last.

Finally, Henry had an affair with Tina's best friend. It had been brewing for months under the covers but arrived like a thunderstorm at a church picnic. Tina blamed Henry, but she blamed Phoenix even more.

Four months later they moved to Utah.

Jake and Tina got up and went downhill a ways. The grass covered ground had gotten harder and positions needed to be changed. They sat again, this time about thirty feet from the pond.

"You'd be amazed at the wildlife here," Jake said. "This is an active dam. Bet there's a beaver or two somewhere."

Jake felt more relaxed than he'd expected. Her one-sided conversation had dissolved into a very long story. He had no advice to give, just an ear to lend. He knew any decisions were hers to make, but sex, he had decided, was not an option. Her life was already much too complicated.

"Are you hungry?" Jake asked suddenly.

"Not very," she smiled, and looked at her watch. "Maybe I could eat something."

"Let's see what I can find," Jake said. He realized he hadn't eaten more than a snack since his breakfast in Delta.

"Are you a hunter or gatherer?" she asked. The mood had suddenly gotten lighter.

"I'll hunt in the truck and see what I can gather."

Tina sat, feet together, her arms hugging her knees, staring at the crystal-clear water with the dark bottom, and Jake hiked up the hill.

Rummaging around, he found five energy bars, a plastic bottle of water about two thirds full, and three cans of Bud Lite, warm but unopened. Further digging revealed a small bag of unopened peanuts. He gathered it all and started back down with supper.

After they dined, the sun headed west. The aspens started to develop shadows on their eastern sides.

"I'm gonna swim with the beavers," Tina said.

She got to her feet. It was not the springing up of a teenager, but it looked to Jake like a very spry adult. She unbuttoned her shirt and pulled it off. The movements suggested efficiency rather than sexuality, but it definitely had Jake's attention. She turned her back to him modestly, facing the pond, and took off the bra. Then she wiggled out of her jeans and shoes and stepped gingerly past the boneyard of old bleached sticks and twigs, then into the mud, hard and dry at first, sculpted with the tracks of deer, elk, and moose. Then her footing turned gooey, and slowly she moved into the water.

She looked very white. Her tender feet stirred up plenty of the dark bottom, but where the pond was undisturbed it remained clear. Within a few feet, it was deep enough to swim, and she did.

Tina's strokes were slow, deliberate, and strong. Sometimes she would jackknife at the surface, and go straight down, toes to the sky, last to leave. A tiny splash and a bull's eye of ripples. Jake enjoyed the show.

Finally, she climbed out on the far side, onto the dam. Careful of her footing, she maneuvered to the top, stood facing him, and

< 36 >

called out, "I think they live in there." She pointed.

Her skin was silver and shining, and her wet hair was slicked back on her head. The panties had been white, but wet they were transparent, almost invisible. They concealed nothing. She seemed very naked, surrounded by all that nature. A porcelain doll on a bird's nest, was how Jake would remember her.

He was enjoying full frontal nudity, when Tina raised her arms and made a graceful dive, back into the water straight toward him.

Oh oh, he thought. But he didn't move as she dried herself, wiped mud off her feet, and dressed. Her life was complicated enough. Jake remained stoic and the mood remained light.

Very gradually the air cooled off. The sky was spectacular, and clouds turned rose with silver edges. They were sitting very quietly, had been since Tina's swim, lost in their own thoughts. A mule deer appeared, dreamlike, from the forest at the furthest edge of the pond. It looked at them for several long minutes, and then stepped carefully to the water's edge for a drink.

A little later the sun finished its descent behind the Wasatch Mountains, and the beavers came out to play in the dusk. They swam to and fro, much as Tina had done, then floated on their backs, disappeared, and then reappeared.

Finally, Tina clapped her hands, and they instantly produced a loud tail slap, and were gone. But in about two minutes they'd be back.

It was hard to tell how many creatures performed that evening, but there were probably three or four. Five if you counted Tina.

"I'm going to ask him for a divorce tomorrow," Tina said, as they got up to leave.

< 37 >

Tuesday

Tina called Jake late Tuesday morning. Her demeanor was subdued as a puff of vanilla smoke. She reported that she had told Henry everything. His controlling nature, the blood brother wives, and their pretensions, what she wanted and didn't want. How she felt.

They had talked for hours, sometimes in anger and others, actually communicating. They revisited their history in Phoenix. Periods of accusation led to times of remorse. In the end they agreed to work on their marriage. She said this had been the first time the word divorce had been used out loud, and the millionth time professional counseling had been suggested. Finally, Henry agreed to see a therapist, and she would be able to get a dog. The mini-arab would stay outside.

"So, we're going to try to make it work." It was a strange little voice followed by a pause.

"You and I have a friendship I would like to keep," she said.

"That is if you want to."

"I'd like that," Jake replied.

"And I loved Sunday. I'll remember it forever," she paused ...

"I love you and need you, Jake," she said earnestly.

"I'll always be here, just call."

After another quiet moment he asked, "Tina?"

"Yes."

"You told Henry everything?" Jake asked softly.

"Yes."

"About the alfalfa field?"

"No, Jake. That's off limits. That was our private day."

After they hung up, Jake sat still a long time. His sense of guilt was in check, and he had a strong feeling of relief. He acknowledged some loneliness. He also thought it might be time to clean up his house.

< 38 >

News

In the sheriff's office at the Summit County Courthouse in Coalville, Marvin Thompson relaxed. Training horses had been a dawn to dark profession with no way to slow down. Even the weekends had been filled with travel and contests, showing clients' animals, or helping everyone else. But, as a sheriff, he had time to unwind now and then.

It had been a serious career change with no regrets. Well, maybe some, but at last he finally had a steady income and time to read the paper.

Examining the *Salt Lake Tribune,* he learned about a car chase that ended as a stolen maroon Mazda hit the concrete support of a freeway overpass at about 68 miles per hour. It sent the driver, a notorious gangster, spinning across the street to finally rest, inert, in the gutter with some old newspapers, beer cans, and a banana peel. There were sirens and a rotating red and blue lights, and the torn metal remains of what had been a car. A bloody broken mess that smelled of grease and spilled gasoline.

Of course, the smells, colorful lights, and loud crash were not in the paper. But that kind of a scene was quite familiar to Marvin the sheriff.

He could remember the familiar odor and read between the lines.

What Marvin didn't read, the part not covered by the news, was that a unique switchblade knife-brass knuckles combination was in the wreck, and had flown, spinning out with the body through space, and then bounced and disappeared into a sewer drain.

It was a strange implement, beautifully crafted and would have reminded Marvin of the one just like it he'd seen in Peter Ernst's trophy case many years ago.

But he didn't see it.

Lost forever.

< 39 >

First Date

John Farnsworth wore a brand-new beige shirt and under his hat, his hair had been combed. His truck had been through the car wash at the Chevron on Interstate 80 about an hour earlier.

He parked beside the old fire station where he could see the Kamas Kafe, but probably not be noticed. He was blocking a right turn lane if there had been one, but east-bound cars could pass him easily and most traffic was on State Road 32, the crossing street. When a blue car came up behind him signaling for a right turn, John glided forward when the red light turned green, rolling south and circled the block to resume his former position. For a full three minutes he stared at the Kamas Kafe like a Doberman watching for the mailman.

A plumber's van pulled up behind him, so he put the truck in gear, repeated circling the block, and waited again.

Finally, his persistence was rewarded. He saw a young woman in a white waitress uniform walk down the street and enter the cafe's door.

A minute or two later a car pulled up and a girl jumped out at the curb, circled the vehicle and pecked the driver's cheek. John could see her, probably only a year or two out of high school, with pink cheeks and long blond hair. She was talking to the motorist. They seemed to be sharing a joke. She too, wore a waitress uniform.

Then she sprang away, as the cafe door opened and out came a mature woman with big hair, Mildred, followed immediately by a full-figured lady. Her name was Trixie. All three wore white outfits. They chatted a moment as the car pulled away. The young blond flitted to the door, and ducked in. Mildred headed south, down the sidewalk, and the other woman, Trixie, headed north. She walked like a person who had spent many hours on her feet. She stopped at the corner, and then crossed on the green light

< 40 >

going north.

John signaled for a left turn, but lost his nerve when Mildred changed course. He turned right instead, tipping his head reflexively, hoping the hat brim might hide his face.

He looped around the block, this time turning left at the light. Trixie had passed the tiny theater, the pharmacy, and a couple of stores before turning west at the next street. John smiled to himself when he saw the white uniform strolling on the north side. He pulled slowly up beside her, lowering the passenger window with the press of a button. When she glanced at him, he stopped.

"Hi kid," he said with his best smile and a tip of the hat. "Need a ride?"

He paused, then continued, "Expect you been exercising since about five thirty this mornin' ... Hop in."

She looked at him a long time, as if he were a notorious something or other. Maybe a woman snatcher.

"How come you're not on a horse or under a tractor in a pan of oil or something? I haven't heard you retired yet."

"Not yet," he said. "Hop in."

She slowly moved toward the truck, and John jumped out, ran around the front. His sudden action startled her, and she froze. He jerked the door open for her.

"First gentleman I've seen in twenty years," she said squinting at him.

John exaggerated his spryness as he headed for the driver's side.

"Is that a clean shirt I see? I've seldom seen you so sparky."

"Yep. I'm comin' courtin.'"

"Well, my hell," she snorted.

"Yep."

"Who's the lucky prom date gonna be?"

"Ain't goin' to no promenade," John said. "I'm a courtin' you."

"No you ain't."

Trixie leaped out of the door as though the seat was hot as a griddle.

"Git back in here, you silly girl! I'm a lot handsomer than I look."

Trixie's legs were tired and try as she might, she didn't figure John was anything but harmless. They'd flirted at the cafe for years. He'd often suggested that she run off to Oklahoma with him. So, she just looked at him and he grinned back. Then she got back in.

"You got two blocks to do your courtin', cause I'm tired," she said.

The truck crawled slowly down the street, like an armadillo crossing a highway on a hot day. An Oklahoma speed bump.

"You're single and I'm single and I wanna buy you a milk shake," he said.

She didn't say anything but smiled at him like a Hallmark card. He stepped down on the gas, made a mid-block U turn, and headed for Dick's Drive In on the Mirror Lake Highway. It was a six-block ride, and Trixie said nothing and neither did John. At the window Trixie corrected his order of two milk shakes.

"One shake and I want a big lemonade," she said.

Dick's was quiet. It was shortly before school let out, releasing hordes of teens with their pent-up energy, hormones, and appetites.

"Thanks for the lemonade," she said.

John suddenly had a strong urge to light a cigarette, but he thought a moment and postponed it.
"This is my first date in about twenty years, I bet," he said. "So far I'm having a great time."

"Well cowboy, I guess we've found your thrill threshold. You probably better take me home before we stress out your heart."

"Oh no, we're just getting started. I figure we go to supper, catch a movie and park somewhere and watch the city lights, and neck."

< 42 >

"What city?"

"Hmmmmm ... Guess you're right. No city close enough for this old truck to make it without an oil change. But we can have supper at least."

"My heck, we're just having a big drink, we won't be hungry for hours. It's only three o'clock in the afternoon, for Pete's sake." She paused. "I'm tired, by the way."

There was a moment of quiet and Trixie relaxed her tingling legs. She was off her feet and the truck seat was comfortable enough. It felt good to just sit.

"Help me here kid." John smiled his toothy grin at her. It was a kind smile. "It's my first date in years. Bear with me. I'm planning it as I go."

"Hmmm."

"I really thought you'd be too particular to get in this old truck in the first place. Now that you're here, I sure don't know what in the world to do."

"You can take me home and forget it. Tomorrow I'll give you some coffee and a smile, and you can invite me to Oklahoma some more, and then leave a big tip."

"No, serious."

"I am serious, and tired."

"OK now, I got a plan." Thinking fast, there was a slight desperation in his voice. "It's a spur of the moment plan, but basically it's a good'un."

"I can't wait." Sarcastically.

"OK kid, here goes. So it's three now, or really, three thirty, so we go for a little drive in the hills, toward Mirror Lake, let's say, then maybe we come back and go to the Snake Creek Grill in Heber, and then we go bowling, then dancing if we can find a dance." His eyes twinkled like a little kid on the fourth of July.

"Hey, this is Thursday, and there are no dances."

They sat a moment; Trixie felt the soft seat supporting her tired thighs. Her calves tingled in relief.

"Let's start with the drive," she suggested.

"Yee Haw!" John said and tossed the half-consumed milk shake into the trash barrel as they pulled onto the highway, headed east.

Trixie was feeling a little younger and sensed that she wasn't quite as tired as she thought.

At fifty miles per hour up the familiar road, she studied John. He was a pretty wrinkled-up old guy, but not really bad looking, in the same way a worn out farmhouse might appear quaint to a real estate salesman in a slump. John could certainly use a fresh coat of paint. She tightened her grip on the little handbag that held her makeup.

They stumbled into and out of some conversations. After a while they were chatting like actual friends.

About forty-five minutes passed when John turned off into a little parking area. The feisty waitress might have asked if he'd run out of gas, but the mood was now kinder, gentler, more sincere. She let the thought pass.

Nearby, the Provo River slid across a sheet of rock, then fell fifty or sixty feet into a rage below. Although they had both seen it before, more than once, they strolled down a path to the water's edge. They sat on a flat rock listening to the roar and watched the green water rush past and plunge into space.

The sound eliminated conversation, but they sat with their feet on the pine needles, smelling the conifers for quite a while.

By the time they arrived at the Snake Creek Grill the sun was setting. And later, over dessert, John confided that he had very much enjoyed their first date.

"First?" Trixie repeated. "That implies there may be more. Let's just call it our date. I think we have both enjoyed our date."

"I'm glad we enjoyed it ... are enjoying it," he corrected himself. "It ain't over yet."

When at last the truck pulled up at Trixie's house, John turned the key and killed the engine.

< 44 >

"Thanks for a wonderful time," Trixie said honestly.

"You, too, kid."

They looked awkwardly at each other for a moment, and Trixie smiled.

"Past my bedtime," she said, and slipped out into the warm evening.

"Thanks, and good night."

John sat watching as she went up the steps one at a time. Strong straight legs he noticed. One of the things a horseman always looks for.

She opened the door and switched on the front room light. Now a full figure silhouette, she turned and waved, trotted back down toward him. He sat still as she sprang up to the open passenger window like a teenager.

She leaned in and stayed like that, looking at him. She was rim lit, the illumination coming from behind. Her edges seemed to glow, especially the hair. He could barely make out her features, couldn't see the blue eyes at all, but he was aware she was smiling. Her's were very white teeth.

"It did sort of seem like a first date, didn't it?" she asked, and then was gone, back up the stairs.

In the bright room he caught a glimpse of her pretty face, and the halo of golden hair, as she glanced at him. She waved and quickly shut the door.

John decided he would never again think of her as the fat one.

He sat quietly for a couple of minutes, staring at the darkness where the door had been, gathering his thoughts. Suddenly he realized he hadn't had a cigarette for many hours. He reached over and patted his heart. The pack's familiar shape was still there, so he pulled it out and automatically shook one up. He pinched it with his lips. Without thinking he lit it and drew in the smoke. Then he looked at the glowing end for a long time and stubbed it out.

Fundraiser

An Oakley City Councilman and his wife hosted a table at the annual fundraiser for The Summit County Land Conservancy. His guests included Bill Jones and Stefanie, Jake, and a divorcee from California who had just built a combo barn slash house on twenty acres. Two more couples filled the table. The Councilman cleverly maneuvered the seating, so Jake ended up between the hostess, always great and perk, and the single lady from Pasadena. Her name was Flicka. Jake gave a couple seconds of thought to the notion that someone might be playing cupid.

This grand affair was held at the Full Moon Ranch. It was a development with a huge auditorium, stage, restaurant, and more. The crowd that evening gave legs to the expression, 'All hat and no cattle.' Since it was a fundraiser, the attendees were rather upscale, and dressed up. Jake wore his newest hat, and his navy-blue sports jacket.

Everything from a small bronze sculpture of a winged buffalo to a Mexican cruise, was displayed for a silent auction. A guitarist in the corner played gentle country music, and a no-host bar kept busy filling glasses. The crowd was milling about like lost zombies, talking and moving. But on closer inspection Jake could imagine folks making connections and exchanging business cards. That's what people often did wearing suits and ties.

The councilman's wife had disappeared when he introduced Stef and Bill to Jake. Stef gave a little squeal, and smilingly said, "We're old pals."

Bill smiled at Jake, "She doesn't stop talking about your cutting horse."

"Well," said Jake, "he's a very interesting individual."

"Marvin Thompson certainly sent us to the right guy," Bill said with enthusiasm. "We really appreciate it. Now we have to figure out where we go from here. Can Stef get a schedule and

< 46 >

take lessons? How do we find a horse? She surely loved that horse she rode at your place."

"I wanted to come back the next day," she said. "I had to go to California to help my sister, and it took a lot longer than I expected. But I'm back now."

"I'm just a pusher, an enabler," said Jake, "an addict myself. But, of course, I know the suppliers."

The councilman disappeared and the three of them stood at the table.

"We could get together for lunch sometime and talk," said Jake. "There are several ways to approach it, if you're serious. A little advice at the beginning could be useful." Then he said "Kinda hard to talk here."

He saw John Farnsworth and Trixie the waitress headed their way.

"I could bring sandwiches to your house tomorrow," Stef said. "I want Bill to see the little gray gelding."

"Works for me," said Bill with a smile.

"Me too," said Jake.

A few people were searching for their tables and there was a thirsty line at the bar.

"Can I get you guys a drink?" Stef asked as she drifted in that direction. A serious fellow drifted by, grabbed Bill's arm, attention, and his ear.

John Farnsworth cruised up and Jake noticed Trixie looked rather fetching. She seemed slimmer than he remembered. She gave Jake a pretty friendly hug, and admired his clean shirt.

Jake knew many of the men and several of the women, so there were many greetings and some short exchanges, before he bumped into a good friend from long ago. Marvin Thompson.

"Out of uniform," he observed.

"Yep," Marvin said, and they shook hands warmly.

"That Bill Jones seemed to be a nice guy," Jake offered. "His wife, too."

< 47 >

"Yep, I think he's a straight shooter."

"She rides very well. A lot of habits to unlearn, I'm afraid."

"Yep," Marvin said. "Usually the case when they ride as kids. They come with confidence and a good seat, but heavy hands."

"Marv, do you ever miss training cutting horses?"

"Every damn day," Marvin said, and paused. "I don't miss showing. Hauling Gold Peppy San for the world just wore me out. It was a great year, and I wouldn't trade it for anything. Memories, good and bad, friends, enemies, and the phone calls in the middle of the night from an owner who couldn't get his head out of his ass."

Marvin smiled at Jake. "You're doing it right. Enjoy the horses and forget the politics."

Marvin seemed a little older. It had been ten years at least.

"In the old days, we sure had fun though, huh?"

Jake gave a thoughtful, "Yep."

"Maybe cutting's changed a little. Too much money involved. People too serious. They forgot how to have fun."

"Or," Marvin continued, "maybe it's just me, that year just wore me out."

They both pondered a moment.

"Speaking about the old days, do you remember Peter Ernst? Used to show a gelding named Lenas Goin Peppy. Died in a hunting accident in Wyoming?" Marvin asked.

"Sure. I remember him. We were at a big party at his house once. Cutters and hunters."

"Well Jake, I have a friend who guides hunters up there, and we talk every year or two, and last time he said there was news on our dead friend. Might not of been an accident. Might have been murder."

"Really?"

"That musta been nearly thirty years ago."

Marvin glanced around. "My friend said a guide there got in some trouble with the authorities, helping some poachers bending

< 48 >

the rules or something. They're gonna make an example of him, throw the book at him. He's old and grumpy, can't stand change, hates rules, nobody can tell him anything. Anyway ... that kind of guy.

"So now he's in real hot water and looking to make a deal, get 'em to lighten up a little. Trade some information ...

"Information about this old hunting accident, which nobody really thought was an accident. His claim is he knows a guy who knows the man who guided the fellow that shot Peter. Of course, the real rumor is that the guy dealing information was the actual guide for the murder. Probably got paid a lot, too."

Marvin paused as an acquaintance passed, saying hello, smiling.

"Interesting," Jake said to Marvin.

"Yeah, it is interesting.

"Guess the guy realized he could be making things worse for himself and is trying to be careful. Could be, he knows everything, if he could remember it. Or could be, he's making it all up. One lie on top of the next. Digging himself in deeper. Accessory to murder or colorful liar, take your choice.

"Maybe there will be more to it later. I suppose the law is looking for proof."

Marvin paused. "Anyway, I do miss the horses. Surely I do."

Finally, the crowd was asked to find their seats. Supper was served, followed by announcements, and speeches. The Land Conservancy had some success stories to tell. Three large pieces of land that would be preserved as open space forever. Or so they said. Developers had been dividing up the valley, and the hills, and the rural character was in retreat. Jake was well aware that his retirement was in the value of his land, not in the price of hay or beef.

Another speaker reviewed some deals and trades in the works they were optimistic about. Possibly this time next year there

< 49 >

would be more good news.

Jake wondered how long this was going to go on. He had been up since five am., and had enjoyed a rather stiff vodka tonic, and two or three beers, and had consumed a delicious supper of roast beef piled high. It had been a long day, and it was well past his bedtime.

But slowly Jake realized there was something familiar about the diminutive lady speaking on the stage. He knew her. At least he had known her, somewhere in his past.

That was Darcy, he thought. She had been married to an acquaintance of his, who passed away a few years ago. Jake tried to remember when he had last seen Darcy. Perhaps ten years ago, maybe more. Gosh, she must be forty or fifty. Maybe forty. She certainly looked younger. Is forty the new twenty? he wondered. Or maybe he had that backwards. He was feeling too mellow to worry about it. The point was, she looked very nice and sounded plenty smart.

Watching more carefully now, she seemed confident up there, moving and talking, in front of maybe seven hundred people. Well, maybe five hundred, but Jake was sure if he tried it, he'd be a nervous, shaking puddle. He knew most of this audience was with her in spirit, but the whole conservation thing was controversial, especially here in the rural West.

When Darcy finished, she thanked everyone, and answered several questions. She was followed on stage by a loud auctioneer who got everyone all jacked up and sold several big-ticket items to the noisy crowd that cheered each sale.

Jake felt more awake now and took inventory of his current environment. Hoppy had melted away, leaving an empty chair on his left. The tall California girl was on his right. She was wearing a black sweater with long sleeves, leading to graceful hands and long fingers with silver nails. A very complicated piece of Navajo squash blossom jewelry was climbing down from her throat and between her breasts. She appeared feline, elegant, glamorous, and

< 50 >

expensive. Memorable. He struggled to remember her name. She was pretty, and in his younger days, he would not have forgotten. Zoie, Zoomie, something like that. She and another couple were discussing the ins and outs of outsiders trying to settle in Mormon Country.

With only mild interest, Jake listened to observations about how most important local political decisions were made in the parking lot, after church. This led the tall husband, Ed, into a story:

"We had a piece of property in Peoa, and we finally decided to build our house. The location was at the north end of town on the west side of the highway."

Jake knew Ed, a retired high school coach, as a pretty good storyteller, so he listened closely.

"About sixty yards north of our property is that little square white house under a huge tree. It's directly opposite the cemetery. It's sort of a landmark on State Road 32 if you're coming from the north."

He leaned forward looking at the California girl, and she indicated she knew right where it was. His wife rolled her eyes. She'd heard the story before.

"Well, before we built, I thought it would be neighborly to introduce myself around and kind of apologize in advance, for any inconvenience my construction might cause.

"So, one fine day, I walked to that little white house, and knocked on the door. I listened, and heard a 'Who's there?' I said who I was, and the house said, 'Whatcha want?' I said I was going to be your new neighbor and wanted to talk. The voice said I could come on in.

"Inside was an older guy. He didn't get up. He was sittin' in a well-worn overstuffed chair, and his missus was at the other side of the room, at the sink.

"'You can build a house if you want, but you'll never be one of us,' he said.

< 51 >

"Well, he had been born and raised right here. He'd gone to college back east somewhere, Michigan or Ohio State, and had a degree in geology. He scouted the west looking for uranium, hoping to strike it rich, and now he had gotten old, and retired back home in Peoa. This was about thirty years ago."

Ed was into his story by now. Having fun.

"His name was Moroni, the same name as the gold statue blowing the trumpet on the tip top of the LDS Temple in Salt Lake City.

"Anyway, as he's talking, still sittin' in the chair, he reaches behind him, and lifts a 22-rifle leaning against the wall. He shoulders it, and calmly shoots a mouse that had paused next to the baseboard. You can't imagine the noise that little rifle can make in that tiny enclosed space. I jumped out of my skin, but the wife didn't even move, just kept doin' something in the sink."

Ed paused for breath. Jake, and the California girl, were eating this up.

"We built the house, and moved in, and I'd look out the kitchen window, and sometimes see old Moroni, sitting in our driveway in his truck. I'd go out to see what's up, and he'd roll down the window.

"'Moroni, are you all right?' Then he'd tell me the local gossip, for about as long as I'd listen. His family, extended family that is, was all over this area. Uncles and nephews, and they were always feuding. Lawyers may be still getting rich on their lawsuits, even to this day.

"Anyway, after several years of these driveway meetings, one day he seemed particularly perturbed."

"'Moroni, what's wrong?' I asked.

"'You gotta take over,' he said. I tried to get him to explain what he meant.

"He said that there's going to be that dang bike race again this year, and his cows were up on the mountain already. He has no cows in town.

< 52 >

"The bike race starts, and ends, in Park City, goes up and down and all around, through Kamas, north through the valley, into Oakley and up on to the bench. Then it turns directly west, goes down into Peoa, where it makes that sharp right hand turn to the north, past the cemetery and back to Park City.

"Moroni said when he hears about the scheduled race, he moves his cattle the day before, slowly, from his land, south through town, and when they come to that 90 degree turn, he goes straight south onto Wooden Shoe Lane aways. Then, he takes them home on the same route. He said he likes the sharp turn freshly greased for the bikers."

There was a pause in the story in case the California girl might not understand what cows do, how they might create a slippery road. It was unnecessary, and all the listeners were enthralled. In fact, Ed's audience had grown to five.

"So," Ed continued, "I asked Moroni, 'What can I do about it? I have no cows.'

"'See your spreader sittin' out there?' he said. 'Just hook up your tractor Friday night, and pull it through town; and, see that rope attached to that lever? Just pull that now and then and leave a nice thin coat on the street.'"

The band was playing now, and Ed's audience dispersed. Jake could have asked the California girl to dance, but he really was tired, and not a very good dancer anyway.

He did remember her name finally, and was proud of that. It was Flicka.

The Day After

The next morning the first light caused a glow on the profile of Hoyt's Peak, and gradually turned the sky a series of spectacular colors. The clouds, a minimalist's fantasy, were just thick enough to provide a series of dramatic reflectors. For twenty minutes a sunrise, as good as it gets, performed a series of slow-motion circus acts above the Kamas Valley.

Jake had opened one eye for just a blink, but all he saw was darkness. By the time the hungry feline stood on his head, the sky's colorful presentation had ended. He got up then to feed the cat, but was moving a little slowly, getting the coffee going. Buster was hungry too and let Jake know, and when the back porch door squeaked open, the horses welcomed him with some over-blown nickering, snorting, and head tossing.

A couple of hours later, when the red Mercedes pulled up, Jake realized he'd wasted the entire morning.

"Nice night, last night," Bill Jones said with enthusiasm, as he reached to shake Jake's hand.

"Howdy folks," Jake replied.

"Hi Jake," said Stef, full of optimism, and carrying a bag of food and drinks.

"Can we show Bill around first?"

Jake said something that sounded like "Sure," and thought his visitors seemed unusually wide awake.

With Buster as their guide, they saw the small pasture with three brood mares, a retired gelding, and two foals that Stef thought were just the cutest.

At the larger pasture a small herd of heifers lay chewing their cud. These were used for training his cutting horses, Jake explained. His older cows and calves were on the mountain this time of year.

Next, they visited the big round pen full of sand, and the other pens and alleys needed for handling livestock.

< 54 >

Bill commented on the efficient layout of a one-man ranch.

"It is organized and works well," Jake acknowledged, "but there are plenty of times it's not just one man. I have an almost full-time employee named Simon Banuelos. He lives pretty close, and we have two freelance helpers, when we need 'em."

"Arf." Buster wagged his tail.

"And of course, Buster is full time."

They toured the barn, where five horses lived in stalls with outside runs. One was the gray gelding Stef had ridden, and she made a little fuss over him. The hay, Jake explained, was in a loft above.

"I drop it through a hole above each manger. The horses think hay comes from Heaven."

The tack room was neat, with a wall of bridles hung on pegs. Two director chairs and a black and red rug occupied the middle. Pictures of cutting horses performing were on one wall.

"Wow," Bill said.

"So many bridles and bits?" Stef asked. "How do you decide what to use?"

"They all have different functions," Jake said, "but there are two or three I use most of the time." That was the short answer he knew. The complete answer would take all afternoon. Actually, it could take a lifetime.

Bill asked why there were five saddles. "You can only ride one at a time, right?"

"The one with the big flat horn is for roping, the others are cutting saddles, one for starting colts, one for practicing, two for showing."

Jake gave a big grin and said, "Let's eat, and I'll tell you about cutting horses.

They enjoyed Stef's sandwiches at the kitchen table, and then moved to Jake's office, the only large room in the house. It was a comfortable place with a view toward the barn and pens, with

< 55 >

trees in the background. Jake's big desk, and a huge old coffee table shared the center of the room, holding down a well-worn rug of Navajo descent. Shelves, waist high, filled the wall behind the desk, stuffed with books, some for reading or looking, others for accounting. The top shelf supported a few magazines and some trophy sculptures of cowboys cutting cows. A bleached cow skull with dangerous horns and a bullet hole, hung centered high above the shelves.

There was a computer on the desk, looking embarrassed and out of place. The knotty pine walls had aged to an agreeable shade of burnt umber.

"Definitely a man's room," Stef observed, as she studied a watercolor cowboy in an important frame, some smaller photographs of a young woman, smiling, one in a truck, and several on horseback. In a corner was a basket full of trophy buckles, and a saddle stand with two saddles, one on top of the other, lettering tooled on the fenders.

After exploring the interesting room, Stef and Bill sat in the dark leather couch that tried to swallow them.

As a couple, Jake thought they fit together very well. Bill seemed to lend stability, while Stef furnished a likable enthusiasm. A comfortable looking pair. Her affection for horses was the hook, but Bill seemed much more involved than just a supportive husband.

Jake had promised to tell them about cutting, and so he did. He had bored listeners before; this time he'd be more careful. For a sport that was so generous with its action and thrills, yet so hard to really master, where do you start?

"Well, I'll just start at the beginning," Jake said.

"Way back, Marv used to be a trainer, and he got me interested. I've seen many people get into it since, and lots of people get out. Their stories hold a collection of life lessons."

Jake explained that cutting could be approached many ways, depending on what had been the attraction in the first place.

< 56 >

For some it's admiration for these special horses. At the other extreme, an urge to gamble on a dream.

He gave some examples and entertained them with some stories.

"I really think the attraction is different for everyone. The common denominator is the adrenalin rush "The Ride," Jake said. "But if you can examine your reasons, that will help you determine the next step."

Jake paused, unsure where to go next. Buster, who had heard this all before, got up and went to check on the cats.

"Is it going to be expensive?" asked Bill.

"Uh huh," said Jake. "Of course, expensive for me may not be expensive for you. I have friends who do it in a limited way, on a budget. And I know several who jumped in with both feet, checkbook wide open. Everyone finds their own path, but however you do it, it'll be great fun."

With encouragement from his audience, Jake rolled on, describing a friend "who practices at a trainer's arena, where his horses were boarded. He meets his equine partner at the contest, warmed up and ready to show. He'd ride it into the cows when his name was called. Cut his cows for two and a half minutes. At the whistle, he'd ride out, hand the reins to an assistant, and listen for the score. He writes a check every step of the way, never gets his boots dirty, and has been doing it that way for many years.

"For others, the trainer rides and shows the horse with the owner cheering from the sidelines. Trainer is the jockey. Excitement and pride of ownership, I guess is the thrill.

"Those are two expensive ways to do it, but most people step in the shallow end first. A solid older horse, lessons, and work up from there. Takes more of your time and less of your money."

"After a few years, some of us try to train our own. Any problems, we go to a professional for help. That's the time-consuming way to go, and you get to know the horses intimately, but not a good way to start.

"My best advice is find a trainer you like, who will give you

< 57 >

lessons and help you get a horse that fits you. Some people who are anxious to win, buy an expensive, fancy horse, way above their ability. As they begin to learn, the horse loses his shine, and value, and comes down to the new owner's level. For a beginner an older, steady, solid horse is usually the best."

They talked, becoming more a conversation than a lecture. Jake was hoping they weren't getting discouraged.

"They win money though, not ribbons?" Bill asked at one point.

"Yes, they do. No ribbons."

"So there's a chance for profit?"

"That's pretty hard to do, and the IRS looks at the horse business as a magnet for an audit. But yes, winning helps cover expenses. Personally, I'm better off thinking of it as a hobby most years. If I win enough or sell a horse or two, I could come out on top, once in a while."

Jake thought a moment. "My friend writing all those checks has winnings close to a hundred thousand, but I bet he's spent twice that much to do it. Expenses represent money gone, but the horses can be investments."

A cat had entered the room unnoticed until it jumped on Stef's lap. It looked into her eyes. A feline psychiatrist with unusually long white whiskers. They stared at each other until Stef spoke.

"Well?" she said, as the cat sat down and looked away.

"Probably the first thing to do is find a trainer," Jake said, back on subject. "I can't be it, because I hold a NCHA non-pro card, and I can't afford to lose it. I must own the horses I compete on, and can't train other people or horses, for money. The good news is, I know most of the trainers around here, and several in Texas. I can help and you can come over and cut for fun, but you need a real trainer."

This news was unexpected, and there was a quiet moment.

Stef was still trying to get her head around a stranger giving

< 58 >

her lessons. So Jake talked about local horsemen she might consider. Abilities, personalities, and locations.

Since they knew Marv, he would be a good source also. While his connections were decades old and he was definitely out of the current loop, his knowledge was solid and deep.

"We know Marvin pretty well, but I didn't realize he'd been a trainer," Bill said.

"It was about thirty years ago. When Marv arrived, everyone would smile, he was that kind of guy. I think the sport misses him. I know I sure do."

"What if you just want to ride them?" Stef wondered out loud. "Just working a cow was plenty thrilling."

"That would certainly simplify it," Jake answered, "but to keep themselves employed, trainers— actually the whole system— is set up to make you hungry to get better; to keep moving up to a tougher class and always needing a flashier horse.

"Competition keeps us from getting sloppy, and it keeps us from getting too full of ourselves."

Jake thought a moment and continued.

"But the truth is that at a show you get what every cutter dreams about. A whole pen full of fresh cows, the best helpers, good ground, all your pals, all things you seldom get at home.

"That is why we are addicted to a sport that most people have never heard of."

Stef's earlier question had been in Jake's mind for thirty years. Why do it? For Jake, the answer was the horses.

The conversation had lasted all afternoon. When Jake finally suggested it was time to feed, they wanted to go along and help. He guessed this was a good sign.

"I'm looking forward to a grand adventure," said Stef.

< 59 >

Folk Art

About two years after the maroon Mazda crashed, Marvin and his wife Kay enjoyed a supper of homemade chicken pies. The sheriff was washing dishes and Kay was doing something in the sewing room. The television was on in the background because they had watched the *PBS News Hour* as they coaxed poultry onto their forks, then gradually moved to spoons for the delicious gravy.

Marvin paid attention for a few moments as the Antique Road Show came on. It happened to be an episode from Salt Lake City and about ten minutes into the segment an unusual knife was featured.

It was part switchblade, part brass knuckles.

"This is a beautiful example of folk art," said the chubby expert in the gray suit and bright tie. "Tell us about it, please."

The camera panned across the knife to a cute little old lady who smiled and wiggled her nose.

"Well, I saw it at a garage sale in Sandy City, and I just found it very curious. It was marked $8.00, and I thought that was a good price."

"So you paid eight dollars ..."

"Oh heavens no. We negotiated. I paid six seventy-five."

"Well," the gray suit said, "well what you have here is one of the finest examples of metal craft I have ever seen. Truly magnificent craftsmanship. There are no markings identifying the maker, so finding a comparable price is impossible. It is unique, one of a kind. Folk art, utilitarian and beautiful."

There was a closeup of the elderly face carrying a concerned expression and a tension-building pause.

"My best guess, is ..." the expert, smiling ... "Two hundred and fifty to five hundred."

"Dollars?" she asked.

"And at auction, I think if two or more knife lovers wanted it

< 60 >

and were bidding, I think the price could go into the thousands. Really, there is nothing like it. Totally unique."

The woman squealed, and Marvin glanced at the television, but the knife was gone; he caught only her animated face. If he had looked a few seconds sooner, he'd have recognized the knife he'd seen years ago, on a green pillow, at Peter's party.

< 61 >

Supper with the Joneses

Bill looked at Stef, who was doing some project in their kitchen. Pot and pan sounds suggested a meal was in the works. Just noise, the smells would come later.

"Honey, why don't we invite Sam Skidster to dinner and get to know him a little better. Especially if we're going to spend money with him. Seemed like a nice guy," Bill said.

Stef was quiet a moment, thinking.

"Good idea," she decided.

Then, after a while she said, "Let's invite Marv, Jake, and Clint, too."

Bill, thoughtful; "OK. It'll let Skid know we're kinda keeping our options open. Also, we want nice horses and don't care where they come from."

"Wives, of course?"

"Of course."

"A week from Friday, maybe?"

"It's good for me Honey, if it works for them."

"Bill, Jake's not married. Suppose we invite that lady from California we met at the fund raiser. She was nice and a new-comer, plus she was a horse lover, I think."

"If you want. I hope it doesn't look like we're setting them up."

"OK. What was her name?"

"Flicka something as I recall. I'll find it."

The Joneses' house was southwest of Kamas in a ritzy develop-ment called Victory Ranch. It was large and warm and new. It had a great view, temporarily obliterated by a semi-serious storm. A mixture of snow and sleet. A preview of winter.

That weather was forgotten when Flicka took her coat off, unveiling a graceful arm with an intricate sleeve tattoo that blossomed with flowers growing down to envelope her wrist.

< 62 >

No anchors away here; it was a work of art in at least three colors, maybe more.

Body marking had just exploded across Jake's radar, unexpected and startling. He knew this image would stick in his mind a long while. Marvin mentioned that he liked it, and Clint's wife caught him staring a time or two.

The arm full of artwork started an evening that moved seamlessly through introductions, cocktails, small talk, and into the rich scent of a beef stew cooked in red wine. Then, more drinks and on into the soft seating in the great room. There, Stef and Bill steered the conversation to cutting horse, specifically from the beginner's perspective.

"I suppose you all had to start somewhere," Stef prompted.

"Well," said Skid, the ex-Prince Charming, ex-ski racer for OSU, ex-ski instructor at Deer Valley. "Learning to cut was the hardest thing I ever tried to do."

There were nods of understanding and some rolled eyes, depending on whether they'd seen the sport from between the horse's ears or from the stands.

With everyone feeling relaxed, many stories followed.

Skid told of a birthday present from his wife that got him hooked. It was a three-day cutting lesson in Texas.

His first time to compete was at a contest for beginners, optimistically named The Novice Spectacular. Skid was bridling his horse, when a slightly familiar guy, Morty, came by. He had been learning for a few weeks and knew everything. Always helpful, he said "Here let me show you how."

He grabbed the bridle and jammed the bit in the horse's mouth, banging the teeth. The horse jerked free and split. Morty disappeared. Skid had to retrieve the animal, who had run into the lunchroom where all Skid's heroes were eating. It was many years before he tried again.

"Speaking of Morty," Skid said, "he jumped into cutting with a splash. Got an expensive animal and a six-horse trailer, then

< 63 >

contacted a trainer in Warren, a tiny town in a grid of narrow streets through pastures and hay fields. When Morty turned into the driveway for his first lesson his trailer hooked the corner and took thirty feet of wire fence in with him ... Hello."

Flicka told of her only ride on a cutting horse. At a big event in Paso Robles, she watched her friend cut, and then rode the horse quietly around, cooling it out for about forty minutes, while her pal had a nut bar, a juice, and socialized with other competitors and family.

"Now you know the horse, maybe you'd like to cut a cow in the practice pen. See how it feels," the owner offered.

Flicka said OK, and the friend sat on the fence guiding her step by step. Sure enough, she was able to separate a cow. Then the cow went this way and that and the horse jumped out from under Flicka.

She was invited to get back on and try again, but sanity prevailed. She was smiling as she told the story, so apparently there were no hard feelings.

A brave, sensitive girl with an amazing tattoo.

Marvin told about the days he was training cutting horses and had three beginners as students. One of them was Jake.

About once a month he'd take them, their horses, and his young equine prospects, to southern Utah to cut fresh cows.

"You will find that the search for fresh cows dominates your life if you pursue this addiction," Marvin warned, interrupting his own story. He was looking at Bill and Stef.

Continuing, he told how they'd go to Antimony, a village far from anywhere, located on a road to nowhere.

"We'd leave the asphalt there and go straight south on a county road the next pavement forty miles of gravel and dust away."

Jake's memory stirred to life, and he took over.

"The road was straight and wide, but most of it was washboard that could tear up a Mac truck. The ranch was halfway to Bryce

< 64 >

Canyon's western entrance, but those twenty miles could take forever. You could never find a comfortable speed for travel. We tested everything from 5 miles an hour to twenty, but nothing fit. You could feel your teeth rattling loose, and the horses in the trailer thinking their shoes were coming off. The bumps were that bad. Then we'd come to a smooth patch and get it up to thirty, but look out, more's coming, and you're back down to five."

The destination, Marvin explained, was his friend's little arena, and a lot of cattle. That was dry lonely country where the road had four strands of barbed wire on each side collecting tumbleweeds and a dead deer.

"We watched that deer for several years," said Jake, "it was a landmark that meant six more miles to the ranch. First year it was dead, developing a brisk odor. We learned that over fifteen miles an hour the smell wasn't quite as bad, but the bumps far worse."

"Second year, dead and dry, third year hide and bones. After that the bones started falling off."

Jake nodded at Marvin. "Just adding color," he said.

Marvin grinned and picked up his story again.

They would gather the cattle and stay all weekend.

The rancher and his three sons had built a tiny cabin in the bottom land near a little river. Since the well was about ten feet deep, the outhouse about ten feet from the well, and with a flashlight the bottom of the hole appeared about ten feet down, no one but the owner would drink the water. So, besides horses and his students, Marvin brought three days' worth of Pepsi and Coors.

"Those evenings on the cabin porch were just the best," Marvin said.

"After supper we'd sit and watch the moon rise over Bryce Canyon and talk.

"At about nine, our host would go to bed.

"'I'm going to bed,' he'd say. 'You folks stay up as long as you like, and sleep in late. We've got the cattle gathered, so there's no hurry in the morning. Sleep in, I insist on it. Early morning

< 65 >

is my quiet time.'

"His wife would stay with us, and the topics would move from horses and cattle to the meaning of life. We could get pretty deep. We were usually on the porch way past midnight. Lifelong friendships forming.

"He was a large intimidating guy, and at 5am he'd be up crashing around in the dark kitchen, banging pots and pans, while we lay cowering in our bags, wondering who would be first to get up and invade his quiet time."

Marvin paused, everyone calm.

"But those evenings, quietly discussing life's mysteries, our futures and pasts, dreams and plans, were soft and deep. Pockets of time that refresh a hectic life," Marvin said.

There was a moment ... Marvin and Jake remembering, the others imagining.

"Reminds me," Bill said, "of a scene in *Missouri Breaks* where Marlon Brando is singing 'Life is Like a Mountain Railroad' and plucking a mandolin. He looks at Dennis Quaid and asks, 'Do you think life is like a mountain railroad?' Quaid says, 'I don't know but it's not like anything I ever seen before.'"

They thought about that a second or two.

"Hon, think I remember Brando drowned Dennis in the next scene," Stef said smiling.

Marvin nodded. "Movie written by a Montana cuttin' pal of ours."

"Guy writes about the meaning of life from the back of a cuttin horse?" Bill asked.

"Tom McGuane," Jake said. "The meaning of life is certainly important, but I also remember the jeep jumping contests."

Jake paused to let his audience catch up, then explained how, some evenings, especially if the beer supply had run out, they would drive the gravel road twenty more miles south, to the highway that brings tourists into the Bryce Canyon National Park. Since their pickups were hooked to horse trailers, they would

< 66 >

all go in the ranch jeep. It was old but had a new-ish Corvette engine.

"When the gravel ended at the highway there was a bar named 'The Dog House' that had a sloping parking lot," said Jake. "If you backed the Jeep into the pansy bed next to the building, pointed straight north, you could go down and across a flat area then up an incline to the highway. There was enough room that if you really gunned it, you could get airborne, as you went up onto the asphalt. And if you were quick enough with your foot, and hit the brakes in midair, you could make your landing with a skid mark of rubber. All the elements for a good contest."

"I think it may have annoyed the bartender squishing the daisies and spraying gravel with our drag race starts," Jake said, as he finished his story.

There were stories about cuttings so windy, that even the professionals couldn't keep their hats on, and weather stories remained popular for a little while.

Once at Meadow View, it rained so badly the arena was a slippery puddle, and although they cancelled the cutting, no one could leave, because all the trucks and trailers were up to their axles in mud.

After many tales were told, and exaggerations made, the wine bottles were mostly empty, guests started to look for coats and hat, Bill made an announcement.

"Try as you might, your stories have not discouraged me," he said.

"My news is, we are looking for two solid cutting horses, one for Stef, and one for me. We'll stay in touch, but please give us a call, if you discover anything."

Then, in an ocean of thank yous, smiles, and hugs, Flicka put her flower tattoo in a coat sleeve, and people began to depart. As he told Bill thanks and goodbye, Marvin mentioned that the cutting Futurity could be seen live on a computer starting next week.

"The finals will be as exciting as it gets," Marvin said. "Unless

< 67 >

you go in person, packed in the Will Rogers Colosseum with the cheering aficionados."

"Or in the saddle," said Jake. "Old Buster Welch used to say the saddle was the best seat in the house."

Outside the warm house, the night was chilly. The storm was moving on and there were patches of sky full of stars.

< 68 >

Aloha

When Jake looked at his mail the next morning, the storm that left the night before was being replaced by another, newer, fresher, and dark.

A postcard sparkled out from under the *Cutting Horse Chatter*, a newsletter that grew into a monthly magazine. 250 gray pages of tiny type listing results, and standings after the hundreds of recent contests across the country. There were also ads, mostly for horses standing at stud.

Jake tossed it away and picked up the colorful picture postcard.

A period painting of a hula girl wiggling in full color looked at him, a pink flower behind her ear. Dimensional lettering said "Wish You Were Here." He examined it several long seconds, then turned it over.

A hand-written message resided on the left.

Hi, Jake.
Having fun in the sun. Henry says "Hi."
It was signed: *Tina.*

Interesting, Jake thought. Talk about mixed messages.
He looked at Buster and said "Bow Wow."

< 69 >

Trophy Wives

Americans from the coast look down from windows thirty-seven thousand feet up, to see what is sometimes known as flyover country. What could possibly be going on down there?

For the curious, however, there are ways to get a little closer look. In a slower century there was Route 66.

A modern traveler might choose Interstate 80, a long cement snake that stretches full length to reach from sea to sea. As speed limits increased and more lanes were added, the snake lost many of her curves. There are still some, the Rockies, Wasatch, and Sierra Nevada mountains saw to that. It's mostly horizontal on every map, but west of Wyoming it curls within a few miles of the old silver mining town, Park City.

Fifty years ago, a small road sign and the ski runs were about all you'd notice at sixty miles per hour. The remains of the actual town were hidden behind a big hill. Now growth and urban sprawl have brought the town out to greet the Interstate. Swaner Park Nature Preserve protects about 150 acres of lake and wetlands, delivering enough open space to allow a speeding traveler forty seconds to see that hill that hides the original town.

In its shadow lies what the real estate brokers call horse property, and Sam Skidster bought his from a team roper. It included a log home, arena, barn, and pasture. Skid remodeled, adjusted, and added, as he evolved from ski instructor into horseman.

Carol DeClaire's history with horses had been hot and cold over many years, and she found that flirting with western riding was pretty interesting. She was not particularly excited about cows being involved, but she liked Skid's other students and his gentle way of teaching horse and rider together. He could explain the human body's relationship to horses or skis, where the most subtle shifts elicit results. That he looked like a Disneyland Prince

< 70 >

Charming, all grown up, didn't hurt either.

She was sitting in his tack room, which had been redesigned into a wine cellar, complete with comfy chairs, coffee table, sound system and curtains. The change started when Skid's first two students, Suzanne and Barbara Sue, began boarding their horses full-time. That made Skid a professional horseman, if only slightly.

But quickly two more women with horses joined the party. Collectively they were known as the trophy wives, since they lived large, and had lots of free time. Skid's actual wife worked at home and could check on him if things got too loud in the wine cellar. When Leslie, a reined cow horse owner, Carol, Stef, and Bill were added, Skid had found his new career.

When two trucks with trailers pulled in, Carol was starting her second glass of the Sauvignon Blanc she found open in the fridge. Selecting a fresh bottle was reserved for the ring leaders, Suzanne or Barbara Sue.

Carol listened to the slam and squeaking of aluminum, stomping of hooves, and voices chirping. She smiled, and sure enough, four of the cow horse enthusiasts started filtering in. Pat, first to enter, had come to Skid afraid of her horse, and became his most dramatic success story. She grabbed a Bud Lite and flopped next to Carol and grinned.

"Missed ya gals, where'd ja all go?" Carol asked, although she could tell by the smell, it had been with cows.

"Jake's."

"You all get yer fun?"

"Sure did," said Pat, catching her breath and settling in.

"Always fun. Made some turns on the fence with a black cow, while Skid yells 'left leg,' or 'sit' or 'ride.' Jake, always on horseback, might show us somethin'. This gang of girls takes some getting used to, videoing each other with their cell phones at the drop of a hat, and constantly chattering like magpies. Document-

< 71 >

ing smiles is as important to some as the horsemanship. Jake takes it a lot more seriously. But I suspect he enjoys the company."

"What's his deal anyway? Lonely bachelor, goin' to waste in the Kamas Valley?" Carol asked.

"He was married, long ago, but now he's not. He does seem a little lonely, maybe, but seems busy and content. Skid has known him for a long time, probably knows the details."

"Well it's a shame to see one wasted. Bet if he came to Park City, he'd get discovered ..."

Their conversation was eclipsed as a commotion burst through the door and consumed the empty space, filling it with dusty, invigorated ladies. Beers were acquired, wine was selected, poured, and chairs arranged.

"Well, what does Skid think?" asked Leslie who had entered with Suzanne.

"I think he agrees with Jake, but he's more diplomatic," Suzanne replied. "Jake wanted to talk about conflicting goals, but I don't need that shit. Heard it all before." It was apparent she had a position staked out and only wanted confirmation.

"Bring us up to date, girlfriend," Carol requested. "You gotta concerned brain trust here, ready to help."

Leslie explained, "So Carol, you know Suzanne is buying ... oops, actually it's bought. A gelding with super blood lines, whose early trainer was a Texas hot shot. It sold at the Western Blood-stock Auction as a two-year-old, for sixty thousand. Couple or three years passed, and now it came for sale for twenty thousand, and we all saw it here for a week. Skid rode it, Suzanne rode on the trail, and both worked it on a flag. It checked all Suzanne's boxes, and we all approved. Today, Skid, Jake, and Suzanne, all rode it on cows. It had cow sense, and, with Skid's help, we think it could become a finished cutting horse. Maybe great."

"We all practiced our ponies on cows," Pat said, "but Suzanne's horse was the star, and the main subject of conversation. Skid wants to keep it in training for cutting, but Suzanne has been

< 72 >

thinking success will come fast and easy in team penning. She was picturing herself going that way."

Skid finally joined them, but stood near the door with a Coors, listening.

So, Leslie picked up the story and continued.

"Jake liked the horse and agreed Skid could probably make a dang good cutting horse out of it. The only reason we can think of for the price drop, it's missed its Futurities and Derbys where the big prize money is. Now it's two years behind its age event competition. Suzanne, however, could compete in 'money won' classes, you know, ten-amateur, that kind of stuff. She'd be hot there, we expect."

"Did it get a vet check?" Carol asked.

"First thing we did," said Suzanne, calmer now.

"Anyway," Leslie said, "there was a lot of talk, everyone giving Suzanne ideas. What to do with her new purchase, and Jake listens but doesn't say too much. So she asks him, point blank, if he thinks it's a good idea to have Skid finish its cutting training, while she takes it to team pennings some weekends.

"She thinks she'd end up with a fabulous horse in two sports, her ultimate dream. Just so you know, Carol, a lot of cutting horses that have fallen through the cracks, turn out good for penning or sorting.

"Well, you know Jake. Cutting is his passion, and I don't think he's any good at fibbing. So she asks him straight out, can she do both at once on the same horse, this particular young horse in training.

"Jake rides closer to her, his way to make a point. Basically, what he says is: You need to write down your goals, look at that list, and make sure you don't have any conflicting goals." Leslie paused a beat and said, "I think that was his way of saying no."

"Jake comes at it from the horse's point of view," Skid said from the doorway.

"He thinks you'd end up with a horse confused, because the horse

< 73 >

handling and training are so different. In cutting you're asking him to think for himself as he works the cow, but in penning you're going to punish him if he does."

Skid glanced around then and said, "Horses are trained by consistency."

He was looking professorial. He had their attention.

"Let's compare cutting to baseball. This may be a little tricky, I'm making it up as I go along. But imagine a horse is a baseball bat. Suppose our bat is made of special hard wood, hickory, or whatever they use. Carefully turned on the finest lathe, and polished by elegant over-paid polishers, the grip is precisely wrapped by a professional grip master. It then goes into the hands of a skilled athlete who trains and tests it against hard balls coming at it at various speeds, up to a hundred miles per hour. And, at a prearranged time and place, let's imagine Dodger Stadium, since some of you are from California. Anyway, there's the big crowd. Here stands our batter with his excellent bat. Game on the line, the goal is to hit the winning run."

Skid, proud of his story, relaxed and scratched his nose with the edge of his beer can.

"That's Jake's version of a cutting contest, but I'm sure he wouldn't put it quite like that."

He took a sip. "Now let's imagine our same bat, this time resting somewhere in an Arizona beer joint. The parking lot is dirt, full of motorcycles. Imagine a fight breaks out, chairs flying, and glass breaking. The bartender yells 'stop' or 'get out' and grabs our bat and starts swingin' ...

"I think a lot of cutters might look at team penning kinda like a bar fight."

Skid looked at Suzanne. "You wouldn't take a bloody, dented bat to Dodger Stadium, although you might hide a nice new bat behind the bar."

"Uh huh," said Suzanne.

When she was sure the story was over, Carol glanced at

< 74 >

Suzanne.

"Well, girlfriend," she said, "looks to me like you want yer cake, and eat it too."

The sisterhood was supportive, and when Carol was feeling feisty and spreading unwanted wisdom, it was delivered equally among them all, without malice. It was just Carol being Carol.

While inside the wine cellar, things were getting noisier, looser and spirited, the red Mercedes pulled up outside and nosed into the limited space between trucks and trailers like a brand new yacht seeking sanctuary at a slip in Belize.

As Stef entered the room, she attracted lots of smiles and little cheers.

"Sorry to be late to the party. Did I miss much?" she asked.

Barbara Sue scooched over, making space in her large chair. Stef smiled her thanks but sat on the arm only.

"Is that cow I smell? You guys been playin' without me?"

"Yep."

"Where'd ya go?"

"Jake's."

"Dang, I hate to miss that. How's Jake?"

"He's good," Leslie said. "He's always good. We sometimes get fresher cows at Clint's but have more fun at Jake's."

"Clint's is fun too," said Suzanne.

"He's a stick in the mud," said Pat.

"Jake likes our spirit, gotta nice pen, good views, and he doesn't charge us," said Barbara Sue, "and he can sure sit a horse."

"Well, I love cattle, and I'm sure sorry I missed it. Won't miss the next one, that's for sure."

It was a workday for Skid, and he led Stef out for her lesson.

"See you," and Stef was gone.

"That's a nice horse Stef has," said Pat.

"Real nice and it's just gonna be her practice horse," said Leslie. "Nice lady too."

< 75 >

"Fits the sisterhood good," said Barbara Sue, "and Bill, when he comes, kinda balances out Skid a little."

"Helps get the 'teacher' edge off him some," said Pat.

"Bill's always busy. Men, always too busy to have fun."

"Too busy gettin' rich."

"Sometimes I feel sorry for 'em. I think we make them twitch when we spend it faster than it comes in," Barbara Sue said.

"Don't y'all worry, girlfriends, they're doin' jess fine." Carol, back in the conversation again.

"Wanna pursue a little exploration about the attraction you all have so much fun with, the cow," she said, adjusting her posture. "I suppose you get used to the smell?"

"Yup," Leslie answered.

"My question, what I wanna get my head around, is why do cows attract cowgirls. They attract flies, that I get. But girls? Why?"

Carol seemed to be poking around for a cage to rattle.

"You call what you ride 'cow horses'. Does a cow horse attract more flies than any regular horse?"

"Flies are everywhere, you know," Suzanne said, pointing at the table.

Pat started for the flyswatter, but Barbara Sue was closer. She grabbed it and took careful aim.

Crack.

It was a good try but missed.

"I know exactly what you did wrong. Want me to show you?" Suzanne said, as she took the weapon and did a slow-motion demonstration.

"You missed," she said. "Cuz you looked at your target, therefore your arm slows up just enough before the strike, and your quicker fly will escape every time. When it's hot, the flies will get quick."

She sounded serious, and her pals thought it over.

"Know how I know?" she continued. "Learned from Skid,

< 76 >

father of a high school baseball legend. Cuttin' hay bales open, feedin' our horses. I asked him why not use a knife. He uses a hatchet. Says hay strings dull his knife quick 'cause they're so tough, you have to saw away, but the hatchet stays sharp much longer and is harder to misplace. But you can still bang away before it cuts unless you think about 'follow through.' See the string, then focus below the string a few inches, and aim there. This way the string will cut, because it's in the path of your swing.

"Aim below the fly. The fly is in the way of your attempt to swat through the table's surface. Try it next time."

Suzanne put the swatter down dramatically and folded her arms. Then she smiled.

The women looked impressed, and the sisterhood had forgiven her grumpiness about written down goals.

"Before I was interrupted by a fly, I had hoped to learn the attraction of cows," Carol reminded everyone.

"I have learned a lot here, from the many happy days I spent studying western horsemanship, and cowgirl-ography, with all you all.

"But cows. Why? Let me review what I've picked up, mostly from osmosis."

She smiled, "Just curious, we're not mean-spirited here."

There was a pregnant pause, as though she were gathering her thoughts.

"So, let me get this right. These cow horses are extra special cause they're so smart they can see a cow?"

"Yep."

It had been a rhetorical question, so Carol continued.

"Actually watch it? Tell which way a cow is facing?"

"Yep," again, from someone.

"That does sound intelligent."

"Yep."

"But it sounds more like an eye issue," said Carol. "These horses are so special they can see which way a cow is pointed.

< 77 >

Cow pointed west; we suppose it might go west. Pretty smart, I grant you, but I think you could probably pick up a horse with two eyes for fifty bucks if you looked around. He could probably tell you which way the cow was pointed too. If he could talk."

"The only way to explain it, is to take you with us, when we go work real cows again," said Leslie, offering the last chance for a serious debate.

But Carol was on a roll, and the women were rolling with her.

"Before the West was all chopped up with barbed wire, your cowboys scampered about on these two-eyed cow ponies, playin' their guitars and watchin' which way the cows gonna go."

"Yip."

"Of course, now a days the cows are in pens, and ride on the truck."

"Yup."

"So, to recap, these horses usta' do what real cowboys need done, before fences. But no longer having economical application to agriculture horses just stand and eat. They are now a problem, no longer a solution.

"Can't race 'em ... too slow. Can't eat 'em cause France is too far away. They're too small to jump fences. They have no use, therefore no value.

"Somebody decides the solution is to invent a sport they can do. That way the good ones will have a use and be desired. Their worth would be based on how good they look watching a cow. That was the only thing special about 'em in the first place, and I'm using the word special loosely."

Then Carol asked, "They call this a sport?"

"Yep."

"Surprises me they found a judge who could stay awake long enough to decide which 'cow pony' came out best."

Her audience was still playing along.

"So, girlfriends, let's analyze this. Let's compare these things you're calling 'cow horses' to real cows that give us meat and

< 78 >

leather and milk. That have actual value, independent of whether or not they're able to play sports with a horse.

"Now forget that cow, back to the horse.

"Well, my new girlfriends, you have your little system to find the best at watching a cow, then that one is more valuable than the others. So now you are in constant search for new buyers who want cow watchers. The more newcomers you get, the more the prices go up. With a little greed and a lotta inbreeding, we're building something special here. A pile of two eyed horses. Best one on top. Newbies coming in at the bottom."

She paused.

"Looks from here, like we're building a dang pyramid scheme, girlfriends."

She stood up and said goodbye.

Her husband, a Delta pilot, three days gone, then three days back, was due home soon. Long hours trapped thirty-seven thousand feet up in a cockpit watching gauges, dials, and clouds, would soon fade in his memory. He was coming home to a sweet woman and the clean quiet mountain air.

"The husband's gonna wanna play," Carol said. "I'll see you 'all in about three days."

Out the door she went.

"Pretty good," said Leslie. "But she'll change that tune if we ever get her on one, workin' a real cow."

< 79 >

Island Park

On the eastern Idaho plateau, the twisting Snake River attracts trout fishermen worldwide. Approaching from the south, signs spaced along the highway announce the year various sections of trees were planted. It serves as a visual history of the area's forest fires, logging, and replanting. It is an education in how fast conifers grow.

Island Park is where the evergreens make room for cabins and lodges, some old, others new. There are a couple of gas stations and markets. It's a very small town spread out intermittently along fifteen miles of highway, with no real beginning or end. In the winter it hunkers down and disappears under sixteen feet of snow. It lies just north of the Averell Harriman Estate, managed by the Park Service, and is about an hour south of West Yellowstone.

The J Bar M, a working cattle ranch with extra cabins and occasional entertainment, also functioned as a guest ranch in the short summer season. It had an Island Park address but lay many dusty miles west of the highway. In August it hosted a popular three days of cutting, with excellent cattle, and spectacular scenery. It attracted some of the best horses from all the neighboring states, and others from far away hauling for world championships.

It was 10:15 am, with the sun getting high, as Jake rode Little Pete out of the sandy pen, past the refreshment area and through the trailers. His mind was reliving the final seconds of his performance. He had worked two very good cows, and been error free, with extra credit for challenge and time worked and was looking forward to a good score. He had about twenty seconds left of his two and a half minutes, so there was a split-second decision: to go into the herd slowly and try to have one cow out just at the buzzer.

Or, chip one off the edge of the herd, and be working it for several seconds before time ran out. It's a choice: safety up, and

< 80 >

get your score, or invite danger, and maybe win the class. Jake had gambled. No guts, no glory, is how the saying goes.

He'd chipped a cow. But three others had come with her, and he'd rushed to get her set up. It was not the smooth cut he had hoped for. She broke hard to her left and took him to the back fence. It was the fence that turned her, just as the buzzer sounded. A three-point penalty took him out of the money, just like that. It was a good draw wasted. A hundred and sixty bucks, shot to hell.

He passed someone he didn't recognize, saddling a horse tied to a trailer with Texas license plates.

"Morning," Jake said.

"Cool morning," said the cowboy. "Nice day."

Jake turned left and rode between trailers, crossed an open area and rows of temporary pens of green twelve-foot panels set in a grid. There were more trailers on the other side.

The three-point mistake was still on his mind. Thankfully, one trait of horses is to forgive most human error.

Suddenly there was a noise that caught his attention. It was a loud pop, or bang, he wasn't sure. A halter rope stressed and breaking, a horse kicking aluminum? The sharp sound seemed to bounce around among the trailers, distorted. The pop was followed by a human exclamation. Jake's gelding had jumped at the sound.

Although a couple of trailers were in the way, Jake caught a glimpse of a swinging door and a man in motion. Thinking maybe he'd been kicked by a horse, Jake rode through a maze of parked outfits hoping it was nothing serious. In a few seconds he saw Buck Francis lying at the rear of his open trailer. Jake jumped off and crouched by the man.

"Are you OK?" he asked.

It had probably been less than fifteen seconds since the sharp noise. Already Wally Archer and Buck's Mexican helper, Arturo, had arrived. Another cutter appeared quickly, and other voices were on the way.

< 81 >

Buck Francis lay still. He was in a dark blue shirt, lying on his side. His hat lay nearby upside down.

"Buck." Jake was kneeling, bending close.

Buck mumbled something, his mouth in the grass. Jake thought he said "wannship" or "one ship" or something like that. It could have been "Oh shit."

Buck moved slightly, then lay quietly with not another word. But he groaned.

Jake reached to hold his head, wondering what had happened. Then he touched Buck's torso, thinking he might help him get more comfortable, perhaps on his back. Something felt sticky. Looking down, a pool of blood was forming on Buck's blue shirt.

He looked around, guessing Buck had been kicked. Built to carry six horses, the trailer was deep and long. It was dark shade in there and looked black from Jake's sunlit position on the grass. The trailer moved slightly with the motion and sound of a nervous horse. That, and the rich odor of horse manure and a faint smell of cedar shavings, were what Jake noticed.

Looking down again at the head on his knee, and the blood stain spreading on the dark shirt, Jake thought, he must have been shot or stabbed. Looking up and to the right Jake had a clear line of sight to a hill and some bushes and rocks. Everywhere else he saw trailers.

People were mumbling; the group of curious had grown to seven.

Wally Archer was the closest. "What happened?" he asked.

"Dunno," Jake answered, mystified. "Maybe Buck's been shot."

"Shit," Wally mumbled and crouched beside Jake. He peered closely at Buck.

"Shit," Wally repeated. "Look at him, he's drippin' blood."

Jake saw blood trickle from the lips.

"Hey," Wally yelled as loud as he could. "We need some help here."

Then he whispered, "Is he dead?"

< 82 >

Jake's mind began to function.

"Find someone with a cellphone, Wally, and maybe you can find Quincy Preston, she's a nurse, or at least she used to be."

Wally had his bag of grooming tools and grabbed the strap as he stood up. Arturo took his place on the flattened grass. He touched Jake's shoulder and asked quietly, "Es he dead?"

Jake glanced up. "Dunno ... I think, must be ... could be that he was shot."

"We need a Doc," Wally said, and disappeared.

A young horseman from Sun Valley, Will, appeared, and helped Jake lay Buck out flat on his back. Jake thought he looked dead and felt for a pulse. Will did the same on the other wrist. Then Will tried with his finger on the edge of the jawbone. Neither found a sign. He glanced over and shook his head.

In about two minutes the small crowd had grown, including several with cell phones. Some voices reported 'no signal,' but at least two claimed to have had success, that help was on the way. And within five minutes the nurse, Quincy, had replaced Jake.

Jake had a little blood on his white shirt and assumed Buck was dead. He thought the shot had come from the little hill, the only open path to aim or shoot through. There were questions, but the present moved back into his mind. He squeezed through the onlookers packed into the small space between trailers.

When he found enough room, he bent, and unzipped his chaps, and put them over his shoulder. Then he went looking for Little Pete. Probably grazing in the shade. Jake knew the horse had probably stepped on a rein and broken it by now.

Some mounted cutters sat a little way off, just looking at nothing, talking in low tones. One held Little Pete's reins. Jake walked over.

"Thanks, Taylor," he said, as he hung the chaps over the saddle horn.

The conversation dwindled down, and Jake asked, "Did any-one call the cops?"

< 83 >

"Someone called 911," a rider answered. "I think they said Shane did it, or maybe Wally."

"I never saw a guy die before," said Jake to no one in particular. He noticed Little Pete still wore his white splint boots and absent mindedly squatted and took them off and fastened them to the rear cinch.

"I bet he got shot from that hill," someone guessed.

"Bet old Buck stepped into his trailer to take a leak and got shot dead when he stepped out."

"Who'd wanna shoot Buck anyway?"

That was the question everyone asked that day.

Word had spread to the arena, and the cutting contest had stopped. After a quiet discussion between the ranch owner, the judge and some board members of the Idaho, Montana, and Utah Associations, it was decided to cancel the rest of the contest.

The atmosphere at the J Bar M had been overhauled. Anticipation and optimism flipped to a sober reality. The grass that seemed so golden in the early light appeared gray and dry. The cool invigorating air became hot and stale. The hurry up and wait of competition was replaced by questions, and confusion. Spirited fellowship became somber distraction.

The secretary turned on her microphone and spoke clearly. "We're canceling the cutting. I'll be here all day, to settle up. Sorry everyone. Please drive safely."

They had finished two days of a three-day event. So she settled in to write checks and close her books. The videographer returned to pack his equipment and pull his buried wire out of the arena dirt. His wife, Cee Cee, a girl so nice they named her twice, was available to anyone who might want a video.

The judge, suddenly free of responsibilities, went to the lodge to consider his options and get a stiff drink. Later he went fishing.

The ranch owner sent a couple of cowboys to turn the cattle out.

Jake knew he should wait for law enforcement, but he felt weird, just hanging around. He unsaddled and watered his horses.

< 84 >

They still had a little breakfast hay spread in their panel stalls, so he left them and walked around, talked to friends, asked the same questions.

Jake thought about the drive home. He had no idea how long it would take for officers to come. Island Park was far from everywhere, and the remote ranch was even farther.

He went to find the secretary. There he picked up checks for his winnings. He had shown two horses in three classes, winning the non-pro once, third once, and had a third and a sixth in a novice horse class. Because the five novice was a huge class and since there was added money in the non-pro, he had managed to cover expenses and be about nine hundred to the good.

Repeating conjecture seemed useless, so Jake saddled Starlight, and went for a little ride up that hill. Jake was looking for answers or clues but saw nothing until he noticed a highway patrol car's flashing red light slip under the huge log arch that welcomed visitors to the J Bar M. We are probably disturbing evidence up here, he thought. So they headed down, toward the crime scene.

Jake gathered his buckets, making sure he hadn't forgotten anything. He was hooked up and ready to go. Just load the horses and step on the gas. Once out of here, he had about a six- or seven-hour drive. At least.

Only then did he walk over to where the body was.

A patrolman was looking, walking, and talking to a collection of cutters. As Jake joined them, another patrol car followed by a doctor in a Bronco pulled in.

By 12:45, about two and a half hours after Jake had held the dying man, the first official car had arrived. But in the next twenty minutes, there were two more highway patrol cars, the doctor, two unmarked but official cars, a county sheriff deputy, and an Island Park volunteer fireman. The doctor left when he determined his patient was gone. Finally, an ambulance from West Yellowstone rushed in.

Jake told his story. Over and over, he repeated it patiently to

< 85 >

each new official.

Gradually, cutters hooked up, and loaded horses. Most didn't seem anxious to rush off, but almost everyone faced a long drive. It was go or stay overnight.

The cutters assumed Arturo would take Buck's rig and horses home. He was a good-natured guy and had worked for Buck several years. No one there really knew him very well. Jake thought he lived on the Francis place but didn't know if he had a family. He had come up with Buck, been here through the cutting, loped horses and done chores. But as people were leaving, Buck's horses started looking lonely as the panel pens all around them emptied. Arturo's absence began to be noticed.

"He was here this morning, and I saw him when Buck was shot," Wally observed, as he started to leave. "But I haven't seen him since."

"Where is Arturo?" became another popular question.

The group dwindled down to eleven cutters, a family member or two, Jim and his family, and some members of the law. Buck's remains were in the ambulance. A discussion centered around Arturo, and Buck's horses.

The lawmen wanted Buck's truck and trailer to stay where they were, so they could be examined properly. The first officer to arrive had looked inside. All he'd found was a mare in the forward slot, tied; the panel that separates her had been swung open.

He also found a floor covered with rubber mats, pungent shavings, and manure, evidence that at least five horses had ridden some distance, and had pooped in there, each probably more than once, and trampled it around a bit. The mare, tied at the time of this inspection, had pooped since the shooting, and her manure was warmer than Buck.

The inspecting officer also noted that she had nickered at him in a friendly manner, and not tried to bite or kick.

In the shavings on the floor the patrolman also found a well-used red and white lead rope, a smashed coffee can, a long latex

< 86 >

glove, and a cheap hoof pick.

Since no one could say which way Buck was facing when he was shot, the officer suspected that the shooter had probably been on the hill, and shot him as he stepped into sunlight. No shell casings were found in the shavings. They would, the officer said, inspect the shavings later with a fine-tooth comb, just in case. At any rate the truck and trailer were staying put.

Buck's horses could stay on the ranch, until the widow sent for them. Or ...

One cutter from St. George had room for two more horses and volunteered to take a couple. He would go down Interstate 15, and it would be easy to drop them at Buck Francis's place, south of Salt Lake City.

Another cutter lived near Buck and had space for one. Mark Brown would take one and keep it at his place and take it the rest of the way later. Will, going home to Sun Valley, had an empty slot. He'd feed it until he found it a ride south.

Someone scouted the panel pens and announced that Buck had only five stalls, so all his horses were accounted for. That just left the mare still in the trailer.

Jake had two horses here, and a three-horse trailer, so he agreed to take the last horse, the bay mare.

Jake reviewed his statement with an officer and left his name and phone number.

He gave the three horses another chance to drink, and jumped them into his trailer, the big bay mare first, then the two smaller ones.

Then Jake hit the road. Except for two Texas cutters and one from Oklahoma, he was the last to leave. To drop off the bay mare would add at least another two hours to his anticipated seven hours on the road. And, he thought, Buck's poor wife would have a lot to deal with for a while. He might as well keep the bay mare with his brood mares a few days, then call her and find out what to do.

< 87 >

As Jake drove, he left the radio off, letting his mind sort through the day's events. Strange having a man die in your arms. He and Buck had been friendly for years, always horse related. He'd met Buck's wife at a banquet somewhere, but she'd never been to a cutting that he could remember. Jake hoped she'd be all right. He was relieved that it wouldn't be his responsibility to break the bad news.

In about two hours Jake stopped in Blackfoot, Idaho, for a Wendy's chicken sandwich. He parked and opened the trailer windows so three horses could stick their heads out. He chewed chicken and watched them.

A new question snuck into his mind. They had been cutting for two days, and today was the third. All the horses had been spending nights in the panel stalls, presumably the bay mare also. Then why was she tied in the trailer? If she was being saddled, she'd have been tied on the outside, near the trailer's tack room or saddle compartment. Was Buck loading to go home early? Not likely. Had he kept her overnight in the trailer? Also not likely. Besides, hadn't someone checked and found Buck's name marked on only five stalls? She hadn't wanted to drink much, so she probably had been watered earlier. Indeed, she'd probably had a big bucketful in her pen all night like the others. But with names on every pen, whose pen had she slept in?

Jake decided to give his mind a rest. Let the cops figure it out. He shut the trailer windows, pulled onto the southbound highway, punched a button and the voice of Canadian rancher, Ian Tyson, sang to him.

"You know, it's a funny thing,
About this cuttin' game,
A man gets hooked,
He's never the same,
All he wants to do is ride,
and hunt a cow.

< 88 >

So he'd better have an understanding wife
And keep it all together in his business life
If he wants to be cuttin'
A couple of years from now

Aw, but there's magic in the horses' feet
The way they jump, and the way they sweep
It's an addiction, not that hard to understand ...

< 89 >

Darcy

Thinking about getting a coffee to go, Jake went into the Kamas Kafe. Darcy Lightfoot was at the counter with a pencil, some papers, a map and a cup of java in front of her. She looked up and smiled.

"Hi, Darcy," Jake said.

She gave him a warm smile.

"You're a sight for sore eyes," he said, and moved to stand beside her.

"That's a greeting from the last century," she said. "I haven't heard it in forever."

Jake knew she recognized him, but thought she wasn't coming up with his name.

"Jake," he said. "Jake Oar."

"Jake. Of course. It's been years," she said warmly.

She was turning toward him on the stool, reaching out and hugged his hips, without really getting up. She seemed shorter than he remembered, with thick brown hair and a pretty face. She smelled good. Like lavender. Subtle, not sweet, like the color purple, if colors had odors. Her eyes seemed to sparkle and penetrate in a way that suggested a firm sensibility behind them.

"I bet it's been fifteen years since we actually talked," Jake said smiling. "But I saw you at the Land Conservancy Fund Raiser. And you were great, by the way."

"Oh?"

"I wanted to say 'hi' but you were too popular."

"Yes, that was a busy night. Couldn't escape till pretty late. As a fund raiser it was a great success."

Animated now she rose to her feet.

"Thanks for coming."

Standing she was shorter than average, but with a presence that seemed bigger. He decided she was long-legged.

< 90 >

"I was mighty sorry to hear about George," Jake said quietly. "I was in Texas when I heard. Hmm, five years ago?"

"Seven. Took a while to get over it. I'm finally used to being alone." She seemed comfortable enough as she spoke. "But you know about that," she said.

"Yes," he said.

"Have a seat. I'm meeting someone but I'm about forty minutes early." She patted the stool next to hers. Jake sat.

A full-bodied blond dressed in a white with a name tag glided up behind the counter looking at Jake. Trixie grinned.

"Just a coffee, please," he said.

She was back in a flash with a mug in one hand, the pot in the other, and filled both cups. She flapped her elbows and spun away, a puff of white, gone.

Darcy smiled at Jake and touched his shoulder. He looked at her gently chiseled features and smooth skin. Any wrinkles there were good ones, he thought.

"Really good to see you. Time goes so slowly, and then it goes too fast," she said.

Jake nodded.

"I agree on both counts. I started thinking about you after your presentation. Not the quiet shy wife anymore. You looked plenty comfortable handling that audience. Smart as a whip, too." Jake paused.

"I'm not much different than I ever was," she replied. "More confident maybe, the job has done that for me. But I like the time alone just fine, and I like getting out and looking at land. I see a lot more nature than I ever did before."

"Are you still living in Heber City?" Jake asked.

"No, I have a small condo between Hideout Ranch and Park City," she replied. "Moving was part of the process for me," she hesitated and looked at Jake. "I went back to my maiden name, too."

"I noticed. I like the sound ... Darcy Lightfoot."

They both sipped their coffee as memories awoke.

"We had some good times back then," she remembered, "and ..." her voice drifted off.

"Our lives merged a bit," Jake agreed, and they both sipped, thoughtfully.

"How about you, Jake Oar. What are you up to?"

"Pretty much the same, I guess. Running some cows, fooling with some horses. Still on the same property and still alone, if that's what you're asking," he said. "Got a real good dog though."

"You were just starting with the cutting when Mae died. Killed on her bike by a drunk driver."

"Yep. Helped distract me some, when I needed it, I think."

They talked some about the old days, when they had been two couples with overlapping social circles. People with their lives and dreams in front of them. At a time when optimism was in the water they drank, and the air they breathed. Was it because of their ages, and their friends? Everybody was young, then. The whole world seemed young. They were ready to go, and going.

Or maybe it was the place. America, still gleaming on a hill. It valued truth and had a moral compass in those days. Idealism ran everywhere. Idealism and optimism. It was a special time in the land, before greed and tribalism took over.

"Remember those evenings at Alyssa's? The social center of our group."

"Sure, gosh, haven't thought about those nights for a long while. She was a party girl in a major way. Too much wine, and always interesting guests from Switzerland or somewhere else. A good cook but supper was always really late."

"The more she drank, the slower she cooked."

"Good conversations, those days."

"Here's a thought." Jake said. "My dad had an old folk music album by Bud and Travis, and part way through, Travis tunes his guitar for a moment, and says, 'If I can ever get it in tune, I'll have it welded.' In those days I thought my life was all laid out, just

< 92 >

how I wanted it, and I was ready to weld it in place. But life doesn't work like that. Life is always throwin' curve balls."

"We had our lives planned, and our ducks in a row," Darcy said. "Or so we thought."

"Yeah. Funny, at that age we knew everything."

"Well, it was interesting what can happen to the best-laid plans," she said.

"Seems like when you're young, plans are made without considering fate ... or bad luck ..."

They both sensed this conversation should be left for some other time. Or, maybe, never.

Life is lived one step at a time. So they talked about the changes in the economy and in real estate, over the years. And they were starting to share news of people they had known. What is Alyssa up to now, they wondered.

When Darcy's date arrived, a rather elegant looking older lady with a colorful scarf, Darcy introduced them. Jake got up to leave, putting a dollar bill under his coffee as a tip.

"Can I call you sometime, Darcy?" Jake asked.

She gave him her card, and said sincerely, "I'd like that."

Jake headed for the cash register.

< 93 >

Funeral

Six days after the death of Buck Francis, Jake went to the funeral. It was one of those beautiful late summer days, with suggestions of fall in the air. He drove down through Heber City, around the Jordanelle Reservoir, reflecting the majestic Mt. Timpanogos. Then he curled into Provo Canyon, one of the most spectacular drives in America. The Wasatch Mountains standing steep and rugged on both sides, with the highest aspens starting to turn yellow. The highway followed the river as it got pinched between vertical stone cliffs and finally popped out between the cities of Orem and Provo.

The elevation is fifteen hundred feet below the Kamas Valley and Jake could feel the air fifteen degrees warmer, as he stepped out of the air-conditioned truck.

The service was at a Latter-Day Saints Ward House. Jake spotted four cutting friends—Taylor, Brent, Ann, and Boyd sitting in a row, and joined them. Four black Stetsons, somber cowboys, and a slim chestnut-haired cowgirl under a walnut tree.

Buck Francis lay in a fine casket, looking peaceful and still. But he just didn't look right without his hat. Jake was curious to see if Buck wore a trophy buckle but resisted the urge to push the jacket aside. He would have had several to choose from. Jake guessed that Buck was in Mormon Heaven, quietly waiting for his wife, sons, daughters, and grandchildren to join him again, like they had, year after year, on his Christmas cards.

After the service and viewing, Jake stood in a line to meet the widow. She was small and subdued, and, Jake thought, seemed a little older than Buck.

"I'm so sorry for your loss," he said, knowing full well it was a worn-out cliche. It served the situation, and he had decided earlier to go with it.

< 94 >

"Oh," she said. "Thank you." A strange look crossed her tired face.

"Weren't ... You're Jake Oar ... Aren't you? ... They said you were with Buck when he ..." her small voice trailed off.

Jake nodded.

"Oh." A pause. "Thank you."

She seemed pretty strong, Jake thought, considering what she'd just gone through. Was going through. Her life must be pretty confused right now. Jake looked into her eyes.

"Thank you," she whispered again, a little stronger this time.

Jake paused, then said quietly: "I brought one of his horses back from Idaho. It's in a pasture at my place just now, and it's no problem. I'll keep it till you tell me, then I'll bring it wherever you say."

"Thank you," she murmured. "Yes, keep it, and I'll call you. I'm ... I don't know what ..."

"Don't worry ... If there is anything I can do, please let me know," and he moved past her, to make room for others in the procession of grief.

On the lawn outside, he stopped next to Taylor, standing alone in the shade of a Big Tooth maple.

"Nice service," Jake allowed.

"Yep," said Taylor, usually a man of few words.

"Have you heard any news from the law in Idaho?" Jake asked.

Taylor's wife, Helen, made up for her husband in the communication department, and she usually knew all the gossip in the cutting community.

"Helen called the sheriff in Island Park, to handle logistics on Buck's outfit. Apparently, they're still investigating." Taylor paused. "The bullet was some sort of nine-millimeter, and the angle was slightly down, but almost straight on."

"So, the shooter was near the bottom of the hill?" Jake asked.

"That's what they think," Taylor replied. "Bottom of the hill, or somebody standing in front of him."

"There are a couple of cabins at the top of the hill," Jake remembered. "I guess the angle of the bullet in the body might depend on the height of the shooter, but also, on the position of old Buck's body when he's getting shot." After a pause he continued, "I got there right away, with Arturo and Wally, and none of us saw anybody leaving."

"That's probably right," Taylor theorized.

"Somebody could have ducked between trailers, I guess."

"Uh huh."

They both looked at the shadows at their feet.

"Anyway, he sure is dead."

"I wonder who did it and why."

"Buck probably don't care, where he's at," Taylor said in a tone that suggested he was much less curious than Jake. Dead people seemed to depress him.

"You're planning to take your three-year-old to the Gold Coast?" Taylor was changing the subject.

Jake went to the graveyard. The group of mourners was reduced in size, and the Taylors were among the missing.

"Ashes to ashes, dust to dust ..." and Buck rode his shiny new casket down into the hole.

Strolling toward his pickup, Jake spotted Wally, and caught up with him.

"Strange," Jake observed. "And sad."

"Yes," Wally answered, "hard to figure."

They stopped and faced each other.

"What bothers me is, who and why anyone would kill old Buck," said Wally.

"Exactly. Me, too."

There was silence a moment, then Wally tried humor.

"You know his horse was good, but he wasn't unbeatable."

Jake sensed Wally was sorry he said it. Jake smiled, thinking it was typical Wally.

< 96 >

"Sorry," Wally said, "bad joke."

Jake spoke then. "Something has been bugging me."

Wally looked at him.

"Where was Arturo?" Jake asked. "I can't remember when I last saw him."

"Gosh. He was at the trailer," Wally remembered.

"Hmmm," said Jake thoughtfully.

"He was there when everybody was standing around, and Quincy was looking Buck over. Then he wandered off, I guess."

"He was there as we got there at first," said Jake, "but I don't remember seeing him after that."

Wally appeared to be thinking.

"I suppose he just hung around like everyone else."

"Are you sure?"

"Sure, I'm sure," Wally said. "Pretty sure, I'm sure." He paused. "He was just looking at the grass, and looking at the hill, same
as all of us. Just wondering what to do, what just happened. He'd just lost his boss."

Jake was silent for a moment.

"But then he disappeared."

"Well, shit," Wally sputtered. "He's a strange guy in a strange land, he's probably illegal, his boss just got shot, he can't hardly speak English, and he thinks that the cops will be coming. I guess anybody'd disappear."

Jake was quiet, and then he said, "I guess so. I wonder where he is. Where'd he go? How'd he get out? We were probably thirty miles of gravel road from the highway."

"Shit," Wally repeated. "He could be hiding under a stump or bush still ... but ... most likely he snuck into somebodies' trailer; the tack rooms are always unlocked, so he crawled under some blankets or into a gooseneck, till he got where he was goin'. Easy to sneak a ride to Montana or Sun Valley if he wanted to spend the winter skiing, or he could head for Texas where the Mexican

< 97 >

food is great. All he has to do is check the license plates and the world is his oyster."

"I guess," mumbled Jake.

"Shit, he knew everyone, sort of, he could of asked for a ride, if he could find the words ..." Wally was into it now. He thought a moment. "Me rido usted trailer, por favor, amigo. Comprendo?" Wally grinned, proud of his mastery of Spanish. Jake grinned, too.

"What about the plastic glove?" Jake asked. "Maybe that's a clue?"

"Shit, Buck probably took a horse to the vet a month ago. Who knows? The shavings weren't fresh, probably been there all summer. He just picks the shit out after each trip. I expect there's a lot of strange stuff under those shavings."

They thought a moment and gradually headed for their vehicles.

"Hey Wally, are you going to the Gold Coast next month?" asked Jake.

He wondered why everyone had all the answers, but him.

< 98 >

Bay Mare

Jake loved the dawn. Without it, if for some reason he missed it, he felt like an important piece of the day was wasted. No matter what problem had been turning over in his mind falling asleep, the first morning light swept the trials away, or put them in perspective. It brought a sense of anticipation and freedom. Solutions seemed just around the corner.

The sky was beginning to color as Jake took his coffee and headed for the barn. Buster, the self-appointed captain of ranch zoology, waited by the door. The dog was dressed formally, as always, in black with a white collar and four white gloves. He seemed to float forward and upward as the door opened. Then he stood at attention, only his tail moving.

The horses nickered as they entered the building, and Jake spoke to each one. Buster zoomed around, checking the smells left by cats and mice during the night.

Jake inspected waterers, mixed supplements, and picked stalls. He climbed to the hayloft and dropped hay into each manger.

Then they walked twenty yards west, past the bushes and trees, to the edge of a ditch where he saw horses in the pasture. His coffee was getting cold, and he sipped the last of it studying the animals, looking as always for a limp, a suggestion of colic, or anything bothering them.

Buck Francis's bay mare was there, and she seemed to have made friends without too much fighting. A pecking order had been established.

As he watched, he heard a truck door slam. The sound came from somewhere on the other side of his house. Probably from his front yard.

Just before he headed back to see who might visit at this early hour, the bay mare made a move that caught his eye. She looked back at her stomach and bobbed her head. Colic crossed his mind.

< 99 >

He watched her for another minute. She looked like she was going to pee, widened her rear legs and crouched slightly, for just a beat, and then took a step and went back to grazing.

Jake headed for the house at a fast walk.

"Hey Bud."

"John. You're up pretty early," Jake said, as he glanced at the knurled hand holding a Big Gulp container. "Want some fresh coffee in there?"

"Sure, Bud. Any news on the crime wave you're witnessing?"

"None. No news," Jake answered. "Some speculation at the funeral, is all."

They entered the kitchen. The coffee maker was working hard at its job, next to a lazy sleeping television.

"I can dig up some cream and sugar."

"Nope," said John Farnsworth, "I'm a purist. An actual connoisseur. Not many of us left anymore."

John looked like he'd enjoyed some hard living, hardworking, and his face suggested some of it might have been recently.

"Let's watch the sun come up," he suggested, and they moved to the porch. Jake's house was small, and the living room was cluttered. Jake liked it that way, but he was aware that almost everyone else preferred the porch in summer, and his office in winter.

"You takin' a pony to the Gold Coast?" John asked, once they were seated.

"I've got a Derby horse that could go, but my Futurity prospect would fit better in Wyoming, so I think maybe, if I go out of town that week, I'll go north."

"Hmmm ... Two Futurities with dates overlapping?"

"It happens. But not often. Anyway, that Gold Coast's gotten awfully big, tough, and expensive. All the Texans and the Californians will be there. The added money is huge."

"Better to be a big fish in a small pond, huh, Bud?"

"Yep," Jake paused. "I'm a little pinched, and I think the fees

< 100 >

in Wyoming reflect my bank account better."

There was a little silence then. John pulled out a pack of cigarettes, shook one up, touched his lower lip with the tip of his pink tongue and looked at Jake. John made a slight shake of his head. Then he lifted the pack, touched the extended white cylinder with his moist lip, then both lips pinched it like a trap. His hand lowered the pack, and his lips moved the cigarette around and around. Then the lips held it centered, a second, and an unseen tongue made the tip move up and down three times. He seemed to be thinking as he performed these tricks. He then fished in his jacket pocket, and came up with a worn gold lighter, which he examined.

"I've been scheming on a waitress at the Kamas Kafe," he announced around the cigarette.

"Unusual for you not to be there this time of day, isn't it?"

"She was mean to me this mornin'."

"Mean?" Jake asked.

"She gave me some shit about my Big Gulp cup, said maybe I preferred gas station coffee to hers. Hell, I've had that cup forever. It's a part of me."

"Mildred?"

"No, Bud. The other one. Mildred prefers younger handsome cowboys."

"Well, John, I always thought Trixie was looking for a trucker."

"Can't be sure, but she's got cute ways, and I'm mesmerized by her eyes."

"Mesmerized?" Jake repeated. "Have you been readin' the dictionary lately?"

"About once a month, she'll come in heat, and she'll flirt all over me, tell jokes, touch my neck, pinch my ear. I drool for her, like a high school kid. Then she cools off, like today, and I guess she don't wanna old, wasted, cowboy after all."

They sat silently a moment, both picturing the waitress.

< 101 >

"Maybe I'll go back to Oklahoma," John said.

"I once heard a story," Jake announced, "about old Buster Welch at the NCHA sponsors' cutting in West Texas— a bizarre mixture of cowboys, cutters, and important city slickers. They let 'm cut some old slow cows, go on a roundup, eat at the wagon, sleep in tepees, or under the stars. They want to make everyone pals, you know, trying to raise sponsorship money. Some feller plays guitar, and everybody sings *Home on the Range* in the key of C. And I guess there's been some cocktails flowing. Buster telling stories about cutting horses in the old days."

The dog looked up at Jake and cocked an ear.

"Not you, doggy, the other Buster," Jake whispered.

Turning back to John, he continued, "So, somebody that knows enough to know that Buster and Matlock competed about the same time, but doesn't know they hated each other, asks Buster about Matlock Rose, who's from Oklahoma. Buster says, 'Well, we were never very close, but it reminds me of a story ...

"There were two guys talking, and the subject of Oklahoma comes up, and one guy says 'Hell, nothin' good ever came from Oklahoma, 'cept whores and team ropers.' Then the other guy takes offense. 'Just a damn minute here, he says, my wife's from Oklahoma.' So the first fella, real quick says, 'Well, did she head or did she heel?"

John smiled. "Very funny," he said in a straight tone that suggested the story was not the best he had ever heard. He looked at his gold lighter for a moment. Then he popped it open and it burst into a rather excited flame. He lit the cigarette and breathed deeply. He looked at Jake a moment and let the smoke out through his nose.

"No, I'm serious," he said. "Jane's been on my ass. She don't like the way I run the ranch. I guess she knows more from Beverly Hills, than I do out leaning on a post, lookin' straight at the damn cows."

"What's Roy say?" Jake asked.

< 102 >

"Dunno."

He puffed on his cigarette and created more smoke.

Jake sort of liked the smell. Some smelled sickly sweet. John's smelled like real October, outdoors. It was kind of nice.

"I can't talk to Roy very easy anymore. It's a circus to try to get through to him, guards, time to call, time not to call. Spend half your life on hold. It's never convenient for them to fetch him. Mostly it's a busy sign anyway. I can smell the walls, wires, and guards, right over the phone."

"I can imagine," Jake observed.

"Jane's no use to me either. I don't think she likes me talking to Roy."

He puffed some more, as the sun started to peek over the mountain.

"Hard to run a ranch long distance, for a woman trying to sabotage you at every turn, married to my genius brother, who's in the can," John said sounding grumpy. "The damn tractor broke, and I need to take it to Jared for a fix, but she wants me to do it myself, 'cause she don't wanna spend any money."

Both men were squinting at the sun.

"I think part of Roy's deal with the feds is two years in the slam, but he's also gotta pay back the money. To who? I guess to the insurance companies, who are crooked also as I see it. And the feds are after him to sell the ranch, and maybe Jane wants to, also. But I'm pretty sure Roy wants to keep it, but I'm not sure, 'cause I can't get straight information out of either one of them."

Another long puff. With the sun glaring at them, Jake tried tipping his chin down, until the brim could shield his eyes. John reached behind his head, and thumbed his Stetson forward, his eyes totally inside, looking at the sweat band.

"We're gonna have some necessary expenses before winter, and I've gotta get Jane to release some funds, no two ways about it."

Tired of looking at the darkness in the hat, he stood up and turned his chair to face Jake.

< 103 >

"Probably I should just go back to Oklahoma and see my mom. She's about ninety." He thought a minute, smiled, and said, "I think she roped the heels."

Serious again, he said, "I could get out of here before the rain and snow and cold come, and let Jane come up here and feed cattle in the mud, we'd see if she likes it then."

"I wonder if there's a way you could buy the place?" Jake asked.

"Me and what bank?" He puffed another cloud of smoke. "Property this close to Park City is too valuable to ranch. It'll sell to some developer. What you get for ranching, even in the best years, with the best cattle prices, everything ideal, gosh, you just can't make the figures work out. Price of land is just too high. Price of cows too low. Ranching couldn't make the bank mortgage payments. The only way to court a bank would be to disguise myself as a developer, and I'm sure they all gonna go to hell. God must be pissed off about what they're doing to the country He created. I'm not a religious man, Bud, but I'm getting where meeting Him ain't that far off, and I'd sure rather not find Him in a bad mood when I ride in."

Jake thought about that.

"Do you remember Wes Riley from Oakley, who used to rodeo some?" Jake asked.

"This valley produced a lot of dang good rodeo cowboys over the years, and I think I remember 'em all."

John admired some smoke. "Use to go a little myself, back when it was doggin' and calf ropin'. Yes, I think I remember Wes, doggin'."

"Well," Jake said, "Wes was a steer wrestler in high school and college and held a PRCA card for a while. He manages the Zions Bank in Kamas, and he probably speaks your language.

"Maybe Roy'd give you the ranch for an old-fashioned price, you being his brother and all, enough to get him out of debt with the government. You borrow the millions from the bank, then you

< 104 >

sell off a juicy corner, close in and with a great view, to some developer for enough millions to pay off the bank and cover the cost of a new tractor ...

"You got the ranch, or most of it, some new neighbors, and Roy and Jane can live happily in Hawaii or Florida."

They both sat quietly a rather long while, sipping cold coffee.

"Hearing you talk about millions ... it's pretty scary. But I suppose that's how your cuttin' horse pals talk ... like money ain't nothin' but numbers on paper."

John stood up. "I'll think about it, but I may be too old for such big plans."

He flipped his cigarette off the porch, onto the tired old lawn.

"Let's see your Futurity horse," he said.

Buster stood and wagged his tail.

In the barn they looked, but her nose was in the hay. Then they went in the stall and admired her long hip and short back. She swung her head around and looked at them, ears up, eyes bright. Then they visited the Derby horse, a blue roan with a coon tail.

"I wish he had more withers," said Jake.

"There's some things you give up, for cow sense and quickness," John said. "I'd like more size for climbing these mountains, if he were mine."

"You're right. I have different horses for that," Jake admitted.

They talked about breeding horses for sport, and interesting outcomes, and then John wanted to see Buck Francis's mare, so they walked toward the pasture.

"She's the tall bay, near those trees," Jake said, and pointed.

She stood grazing, but as they watched, she threw up her head as though something was bothering her. Then she looked like she wanted to urinate, but she didn't.

"She acts like, maybe she wants to colic, Bud."

"Or she could be comin' in heat."

< 105 >

"Nice built mare, it looks like."

Jake got a halter from the barn, and they entered the pasture, Buster leading, in charge, as always. They walked to the mare.

"I wish I knew her better," Jake lamented. "Horses are all different, with their own quirks. She's not young, I looked at her teeth. Built more like a racehorse, if you ask me. She's got the size."

They haltered her and led her to the barn.

"She seems kinda nervous," Jake observed, it was a comment and a question.

"Something strange with her," John agreed.

They put her in a stall and watched her for a while. John collected an ash on his white cigarette, knocked it into his hand, then carefully put it in his pocket. The bay mare seemed relaxed and normal.

He spoke, "Well, I'm outta here, Bud. I'm gonna check if I can find a waitress who'd like to see Oklahoma."

"I think I'll call the vet," said Jake, and he and Buster walked John to his pickup.

About three that afternoon, Jake hooked up his trailer and drove the bay mare to the clinic. The examination brought nothing to light, until Doctor John put on a long plastic glove to explore the vaginal cavity. There was a tiny stitch, a Caslick, which he snipped, then reached inside where he found a package, sealed in plastic, about six pounds of something white.

"I bet it was put in there, at a racetrack in Mexico," Doctor John guessed.

The sheriff said it was probably heroin.

< 106 >

Irrigation Ditch

The sun was sliding lower, and it definitely smelled like fall. Wood smoke from far away, but certainly a presence, combined with the pungent odor of disturbed earth. The warmth of the day was pushed aside by an autumn coolness. Jake was in a ditch, trying to reposition a large irrigation gate; a culvert with a square frame, and metal slider, welded to one end. When in position it could block most of the water that might be flowing, or, the slide could be pulled up, letting the water pass on through. Sometimes these dams would work trouble-free for years, and sometimes they leaked, and eventually washed out annually, as water found its way around the metal.

Jake's tractor was at his back, reflecting some of the day's warmth as he struggled with the awkward dam, shoveled dirt, and tamped it tighter. Jake hadn't felt the cooler temperature and didn't need the heat. He was plenty warm from his efforts and perspired lightly.

Buster lay where he had been sleeping, but was awake, head and ears up looking intently toward the west.

Although it had not rained much lately, the bottom of the ditch still held mud puddles, and Jake was in one as he worked. His rubber footwear stuck in the goo and every time he needed to move his feet, it took a serious effort. The boots were slightly large and comfortable but kept trying to come off as he attempted to get them unstuck.

He wanted to have this gate planted and tamped in before dark. And he wanted it packed so tightly that this time water couldn't find any way around it.

One thing about flood irrigation he had come to realize, it was a war with water that you could not win. Water was an uncanny foe, persistent, determined, an unrelenting enemy of amazing

< 107 >

strength. Blocked, it had the ability to find a way. Free, it took everything with it. It played a game with only one rule: it goes downhill.

Jake pushed on the shovel, sighed, and suddenly noticed that far down the ditch to the west, some one was walking toward him. Jake squinted at the figure. It was too far away to recognize. It would disappear into willows that grew next to the little canal or behind some trees, but reappeared larger each time. There was no road or structure in sight. Someone must be coming to see him. It was unexpected and a little disturbing. A long walk for an unannounced visit. Well, he thought, eventually we'll find out who and why. He went back to work, but kept an eye peeled to the west.

Finally, Buster stood up, watching intently.

When the newcomer was about thirty yards away, Jake felt a chill. He thought he recognized the movement, and the outline of the figure against the bright sky. It struck him that the visitor was Arturo. Jake froze, watching him.

Arturo walked toward him, the sun at his back, just a dark shape, probably armed. In his pocket Jake had a small folding knife. His hands were on a shovel, and his feet were anchored in mud.

Jake waited as the man came close, stopping about twenty feet away. Arturo above him, on dry ground. The sun was right behind him and although he squinted, Jake couldn't read the face. There was nothing to see, just an outline of a man in a hat.

"Good afternoon," Arturo said carefully, his voice giving away nothing.

"Good afternoon," Jake replied, holding the shovel tightly.

"Amigo?" It was a question.

"Arturo? Are you OK?" Jake asked. Then in Spanish. "¿Como estas?"

"I am troubled, Sir," Arturo said. "¿A me comprendes?"

"What kind of trouble: Ques este trouble?"

< 108 >

"Usted habla Espanol?" Arturo asked. It could have been a joke, Jake thought, he knew his Spanish was pretty bad, and he was sure Arturo could tell. But he said:

"Si, we may speak in Spanish, if you please."

"No gracias, Señor. We are in America now, and I speak English. In English, please."

Jake nodded, and Arturo continued.

"Señor Buck's murder is very bad, you know." His voice sounded less confident now.

"Yes," Jake said, "Si," and he relaxed a little.

"Police think I am the murder."

"Maybe I think so, too."

"I am not the murder."

"Hmm," said Jake. He wanted to get out of the ditch. He felt vulnerable and was getting tired of looking up. But he remained still.

"I am not murder," Arturo repeated, and his body seemed to slump slightly. He removed his hat and brushed his fingers through his hair.

"I cannot go home. I must live in my truck. Police are looking for me always. I do not know where to go."

"I expect so," Jake said. He took a breath and tossed the shovel onto the grass and loosened his feet in the mud. Then he climbed out of the ditch.

They moved to the tractor and sat on the bucket, side by side. The sun lit them from a more neutral angle, and both seemed more relaxed.

"Tell me what happened," Jake proposed. "Do you have a green card?"

"Jess Sir, a green card."

"So, what happened?"

"I was with the mare, you know."

"We found heroin in the mare," Jake interrupted.

"They wanted me to put package in the mare. They wanted me

< 109 >

to get package out of the mare. The mare, she was go to Canada. I think, maybe they want to kill me, like Buck, you know."

"Who killed Buck?" The sixty-four-thousand-dollar question.

"I do not know who killed Señor Buck."

"You were there."

"Yes I was there, Señor, but in the trailer with the mare, and Señor Buck, he was coming in and saw what I was doing with the mare, you know, and I say nothing, but I got the glove on, so I look at him, he is lookin' at me, and big bang, and he was fallin' out the back, and I was gettin' out of there, and guys comin' and we all lookin' at Buck who is gettin' shot. I'm getting scared, you know, and Buck gettin' shot ..."

"But did you see who shot him?"

"Somebody shot through the window, you know. Maybe somebody behind da trailer, maybe, I could not see. I was with the mare, and it was very crowded, an her jumpin' around, an I don't want to get stepped on, or get kicked, you know. So I'm not gettin' a good look, and do not know, where to look, the big bang, who shootin' ..." Arturo's face reflected the memory.

"Then all those people coming out, everybody, crowd around, we want to see Buck, you know."

Jake thought about the story. The windows of a parked trailer being open is not unusual, but it would be hard for a man on foot to see in, much less shoot accurately. The mare fussing about with Buck coming in, and the business with the plastic glove, and a gun shot, you'd expect the mare to freak out. Arturo probably had been lucky he didn't get hurt. The tale could be true, he thought, but on the other hand, Arturo had plenty of time to think up his explanation. Jake wasn't sure what to believe.

"How did you get out of the trailer?"

"Hid behind the mare. Then everybody was comin', lookin' at Señor Buck. I, you know, and I was standin' by the people, feelin' very bad, an then I jess came out an went away. I am worried about the police, and I am very sad. Señor Buck and I, amigos,

< 110 >

you know. Police think I was the murder."

"Yes," said Jake. "Yes, they probably do."

Arturo seemed a pathetic figure, sitting on the edge of the steel bucket. He looked like he could use a bath.

"Where are you staying?"

"I am sleepin' in my pickup." His eyes darted toward the hills.

There was a pause. The dog sat looking at them, anticipating something.

"I cannot go to Spanish Fork; 'cause police want to find me. It's no good there. I cannot go to my sister, or my friend, you know."

He moved some dirt with his foot.

"I think murder after me, too. I think I will get killed."

"Who does the drugs?" Jake asked. "Who deals, who gives you the package for the mare, tells you when to put them in, and take them out?

"Drugs from Federico or from Prince, I think. I mostly take drugs out, cuz they mostly get put in, in Mexico. Diz I hear. I don't go to Mexico."

"Those are the only names you know?"

"Jess, Sir."

"Don't you know full names?"

"No Señor. Sir."

"Do you know where they live?"

"No Sir. Only Prince in Salt Lake City, maybe, West Jordan, somewhere, and Frederico, I'm pretty sure, he is in Lehi, but stays with his cruel friends, in Spanish Fork, you know, but I never been to their house."

"How do you contact them?"

"I never going to contact. They come see me at my sister's, or at Señor Buck's, but when Señor Buck is gone, mostly."

"But," Jake asked," if you had to, could you contact them?"

"I have a phone number, teléfono, but it is at my sister's casa, you know. I no contact, police listen to my sister's teléfono. I am

< 111 >

in very much trouble, Señor."

"Can you ..." Jake started but Arturo interrupted.

"I do not wanna talk to these guys, they want kill me, I am sure."

"Have they tried to kill you?"

"Well, I know they are going to kill me."

Arturo sounded pretty convincing, and Jake found himself starting to believe the story.

"Let's go tell your story to the sheriff in Coalville," suggested Jake, thinking maybe Arturo could get protective custody. "He's a friend of mine, and he'll know what to do."

"No Sir, No Sir." Arturo got up to leave. He put on his hat.

"Hey," Jake said. "Would you like a shower at my house?"

"No, no Señor; gracias, but no," Arturo replied. "Going."

He put his fingers to his hat in a strange salute.

"Let me tell your story then. We'll figure out something."

"No Sir."

Arturo was backing away in the direction he had come. The sun had just tucked itself behind the mountain top, and things generally seemed much less sinister now.

"I will find you again, you know, soon," Arturo said.

He stopped and stepped back toward Jake and held out his right hand.

"Amigos?" he asked.

Jake took the hand slowly, searching Arturo's somber eyes. Looking for something specific, an answer maybe, that was not there.

"Amigos," he said quietly.

They paused a second or two. Then Jake asked, "Arturo, do you have any protection?"

The Mexican's face under the black hat seemed confused.

"Do you have a gun or a knife?"

Arturo smiled broadly, showing white teeth in the dark face. He reached into his jacket pocket and pulled out a worn forty-five

< 112 >

pistol. It was quite large. He pointed it toward the ground and opened it to show the shells. Then he snapped it shut one handed and tucked it back in his pocket. His face was serious, and he turned without a word and walked back along the ditch, into the remnants of the western sunset.

Jake stood for a long moment, then looked down at Buster.

"Arturo," he whispered to the dog.

He might follow, see what kind of vehicle had brought him, maybe check a license plate, but he thought better of it. He jumped back into the ditch. When he lifted the spade, it felt heavier than he expected. His perspiration had evaporated. His momentum to finish by dark had left him.

"I'm an old geezer and you're an old dog," he said to Buster, and the tail wagged.

< 113 >

Breakfast with the Sheriff

S ummit County Sheriff's Office," said a rather officious sounding voice.

"Bertha?" asked Jake.

"She no longer works here, sir, may I help you?" she replied
in a sour, icy tone.

Jake had hoped, and assumed, he was going to get Bertha,
a woman he had known for years. He paused. Then:

"Yes. Is Marvin Thompson around?" he asked.

"Deputy Rivens is here, sir," the voice again. "Can I connect
you?"

"Uhhh, no," Jake mumbled. "I need to talk to Marv."

"Is this official business?" asked the frosty interrogator.

"Well, yes and no. I guess, well I guess, no, ma'am."

"Well, he's not here sir."

"Do you know how I can contact him?"

"He won't be checking in till noon at the earliest. I can
contact him if you're having an emergency, sir, but deputy Rivens
is right here."

Jake wished he'd planned his request better, this woman
seemed to be getting a little hostile.

"No thank you. Please, just have Marvin buzz Jake Oar,
783-5378, when he has a moment." Politely.

"Won't be till afternoon, at the soonest, unless it's an
emergency, sir."

"That'll be fine."

She repeated the number and name.

"Can I tell him what this is regarding, please?"

"No, just ask him to call."

There was a pause. The dispatcher was having a slow day.
Finally, she said, "Thank you sir." And hung up.

< 114 >

At seven thirty the next morning Jake sat in the back booth of the Kamas Kafe. That booth was free standing, between the back door and the restrooms. The restaurant was busy, and Jake wished he'd arranged for later, when the regulars would have gone.

Mildred poured his coffee, and he was glad because Trixie seemed to be in a bit of a mood.

"You waitin' for someone?" Mildred asked.

"Waiting for Marvin Thompson."

"Well, honey, you ain't waiting for long, 'cause I saw him makin' an illegal U turn just now."

She smiled at him. The smile was a gift, like a Texas dawn. Her uniform was sparkling white, and she had white tennis shoes. Her black hair was pulled back from her face. Her earrings were large hoops, orange and very visible.

The front door opened, and Marvin strolled back. He was in his sheriff uniform, brown with gold trim, but no hat.

"Hi Jake," he said.

"Marv."

"We crushed North Summit, huh," said the sheriff.

"Hmm." Jake hadn't heard, but if Marvin thought so, it was probably true. He didn't care either way.

"It was a hell of a game. You shoulda been there. Fred Barbor's kid caught an impossible pass, and it was all downhill from there. Coalville didn't have a chance." Pause, he went on, "A little different than when we were kids."

"Yep," Jake agreed. "We had the beef, but not the skill. All our brain surgeons were in basketball and wrestling, as I recall."

Mildred brought Marvin a cup of coffee.

"You geezers gonna order a breakfast, or just drink mud?" she asked with her famous grin.

"I'll have some eggs, but you'll have to ask the cowboy what he wants."

She looked over and raised her eyebrows at Jake.

< 115 >

"OJ please, and eggs, I guess," he said. "Thanks, Millie."

Mildred left, and Trixie cruised by. Her hair was tangled, but, at this early hour, her makeup was still impeccable. She smiled at the booth. Jake thought she had a pretty face, and the only time she looked hefty, was when she stood next to the teenage waitresses. Skinny twigs that came to work at three.

"Morning, gentlemen."

Jake said, "Howdy," and they both grinned at her.

"Heck," Jake said, "I thought you looked kinda crabby this mornin', guess I was wrong." He gave her a quizzical look.

Trixie bumped his shoulder hard, with her hip.

"Looks crabby, but I ain't."

Jake slid the length of the seat, to the safety of the wall, and put his back against it, turning to face her, all in one smooth move.

"I'm glad," he said. She stood smiling at him, so he asked, "Ever been to Oklahoma?"

"You tell that John, should you ever see his stubbly little ass, that the only way I'll ever go to Oklahoma is in a Mercedes-Benz or in the hearse, and I know he's got neither."

"OK," said Jake. "I'll tell em', but I sure don't wanna be the one to squelch something beautiful."

Trixie pretended to bop his hat with her rag.

"Sheriff, you get a grip on cupid here, or he'll be wearing his eggs home on his hat."

She stormed off theatrically. Jake smiled to himself.

These women in their white uniforms could take the loneliness out of a cup of coffee or add personality to the eggs and hash-browns. They were, he thought, the sisters he never had.

"Well, you didn't invite me to breakfast to discuss high school sports. Lemme tell you what I found out."

"Yes," Jake said. He had lowered his voice.

"The murder you saw in Idaho," Marvin said quietly, "is being investigated by the Fremont County Sheriff's Office. An officer

< 116 >

named Ray Whorton is in charge. He's not real open with his information, but since he remembers you as the guy with the victim's blood on your shirt, he shared a little.

"The drug aspect of the case gets the Salt Lake County law enforcement community involved, so there's a small jurisdiction squabble going on. Anyway, he's a little hesitant, but we have a couple of mutual friends, and so he opened up some."

Jake was sitting square at the table, no longer frightened of Trixie.

He leaned forward, elbows on the table, hands around his mug.

"All right." he said.

"The lab found six point two pounds of H in the bundle, no fingerprints on the plastic anywhere."

"Yes?" Jake, interested.

There was a pause, the sheriff was thinking.

"Who smuggles shit in a horse?" a little joke.

Jake stared at him.

Marvin went back to business.

"Anyway, the murder weapon was a nine-millimeter pistol, not recovered," said the sheriff, serious.

"The guy was shot at pretty close range. The slug went through his heart, and they found it in his shirt later. It went through him but didn't have the energy to go out the back of his shirt. Interesting."

He thought a moment. Then looked back at his notes.

"It came out on the ground when the medics cut his shirt off.

"In the trailer no drugs or paraphernalia was found. They discovered the plastic glove, six inches of bailing twine with frayed ends, lots of manure, rubber mats, lots of shavings, a cigarette stub, a couple of small rocks the size of gravel, and that's all. A lead rope and hoof pick had been collected earlier by the first patrolman to arrive."

Marvin put the little piece of paper back in his pocket.

< 117 >

"You asked me about the Mexican that worked for the victim. They want to talk to him. They theorize he might be the perp, but they're keeping an open mind. They've tried to get in touch with him. His name is Arturo Hernandez, and he lives in Spanish Fork with his sister. Like you said, he had worked for the victim for about four years. He had another job washing dishes in American Fork at the Red Lion, a steak house, I guess. I've never eaten in American Fork, to the best of my recollection.

"So, he's not with the sister, anymore, in fact she claims not to have seen him since the killing. She acted scared, Whorton said, when they talked to her, she said she hadn't talked to Arturo. Period. Whorton didn't say, but I expect they probably tapped her phone. I'm guessing, but I'd bet on it. His clothes are gone from her place, but she said someone must have got them when she was away at work. She's a maid at the Econo Lodge in South Salt Lake on Interstate 15."

Marvin took a big breath and continued.

"This Ray Whorton guy thinks Arturo is still nearby some-where. I guess he visited Spanish Fork and asked around. He thinks Arturo hasn't left the state, but he's not sure. His truck is a tan Toyota pickup, nineteen eighty-four, license plate WJF 238."

Marvin was consulting his notes again, and Jake knew Marvin had given this some serious thought. When he resumed, he looked at Jake's eyes and spoke in low tones.

"He could, of course, have left the state," Marvin continued, "could be anywhere. Whorton's concerned about some connection at the cutting contest."

Jake looked slightly puzzled.

"They think someone at the cutting may be involved. They don't think Jim Mitchell or the ranch, or his family, were involved. They speculate the drugs were supposed to get removed from the mare, and changed to another horse or somebody's glove compartment, or wherever, and were headed on, who knows where. Maybe some other cutter brought the bay mare. They

< 118 >

think, from manure piles in the trailer, that only five horses came up in Francis's trailer, and that he had only five panel pens with his name, but at a cutting, there is no record of how many horses a cutter might bring. Or take away, for that matter. Competing horses we know. Practice horses, turn back and helping horse … no record."

"Right now, that guy Arturo is their best lead, and they really want to talk to him, bad. Some informants in South Salt Lake, and in Utah County, suggest he knows some real mean Chicano dudes. I asked him to be specific if he could, and Ray said specifically, a Frederico Juarez, and a Jesus Menudo known as Prince, and Enrique Gomez known as Heavy, all known gang bangers and sometime drug smugglers. Unsavory characters, all … armed and dangerous, as we say."

Marvin again glanced at his notes.

"Oh yeah. And a Ronaldo Coutier, currently residing in jail at the point of the mountain for armed robbery and drug trafficking. Gomez is wanted for a drive-by in West Jordan, and all are wanted for questioning in this case and others."

They looked up, because Millie's smile was beaming down at them, over a coffee pot. "Eggs coming soon," she announced.

"Hmmm hmmm," Marvin murmured to her.

She filled their cups, wiggled her butt, and twisted away. Marvin continued his narrative.

"So, what this Ray Whorton wonders, is, was someone putting drugs in the mare or taking them out, was that Arturo, and, if so, … or if not … why and how did he disappear, and who was gonna get the drugs and if any cutters were involved. Who, how and why? They are assuming the drugs are originally from Mexico so they're doing some checking at racetracks in Ensenada and other places.

"They said there is a couple they want to talk to but won't tell me who just yet. They have a cop coming back down, Ray says, as soon as the jurisdictional matters are settled. They probably want to talk to you again. Maybe."

< 119 >

There was some silent coffee sipped.

Marvin leaned forward and fingered his moustache.

"So, you said you had something interesting to tell me."

"I saw him," Jake said. "Arturo. He found me fixin' a ditch and scared the hell out of me."

Jake started the story over coffee and completed it over mouthfuls of eggs. When he finished, they sat quietly for a few moments.

"One thing for certain," Marvin allowed. "You better get a cellphone and keep it close, and call me if he turns up again. And he just might, because he's probably got nowhere to go, and somebody'll spot the tan Toyota, sooner or later. If he don't get himself killed first, that is. Ray says these guys, Prince and Frederico, are the worst, meanest, bastards you can imagine. As soon kill you as look at you. They're hooked into a gang that eats folks like you for breakfast."

Jake contemplated that, as he looked at his empty plate. Smeared with the remains of eggs and A-1 sauce, it depicted a bloody little crime scene.

"He probably won't show again," Jake said.

"I'll bet he does. If he tries to contact you in any way, you call me right away. OK? I'm seven eight three four eight seven three. Remember it. I'll be waiting for a call. That's my cell. You can always get me, unless I'm in the mountains."

Marvin dug in his pocket and drew out a brand-new business card and wrote his cell number on the back.

"I'm not in the Coalville office anymore. They moved me to the old office, here in Kamas, just me and a dispatcher, who is my assistant. Just two of us."

"You got promoted?" Jake guessed.

"No. They wanted me out of the County Courthouse. I was too close to the seat of power. I think they wanted to get rid of me, can't fire me, but stick me over here and out of the way. There's been this old sheriff office here for decades, but it hasn't been used for thirty years. Got two cells and an office. I love it."

< 120 >

Marvin sounded sincere. "So, I'll be waiting for your call. Gassed and loaded."

"All right."

"Be sure." Marvin was very intense.

"Stop what you're doing and call. Don't give us any Lone Ranger shit. You call, I'll be right there."

After a while Marvin continued. "Do you have a handgun?"

"Course not. What would I want a pistol for?"

"Keep your voice down a little," Marvin said in a low tone. "It might not be a bad idea. These gangsters have baggy pants, and deep pockets, and there's a loaded pistol in everyone.

"I'm surrounded by paranoia," Jake said, and Marvin looked at him intently.

"At least keep your damn deer rifle loaded, and in your truck. I know you and Arturo are chums after the confab in the ditch, but I'm worried about the gangsters. If they think you know something, or saw something, you could be toast."

"But I saw nothing, and Arturo only told me what I told you, which is basically nothing new."

"Yeah, well you were at the murder, holding the feller's head, and everyone wants Arturo, and you're the only one who's seen him. Maybe somebody thinks you know more than you do."

"We're a long way from Spanish Fork."

"We're not much over an hour," Marvin interrupted.

"Damn it, Jake, if Arturo could find you, I'm sure that a Chicano gang can find you, if they want."

Jake looked thoughtful. "Maybe you're right," he said.

They thought for a moment, and the sheriff spoke first.

"I'll think some more, and keep my contact with Whorton, and the other authorities, and you get a weapon, and keep it close, and get a cell phone right away.

I'm sure that little Mexican's gonna contact you again. I can feel it ..."

There was another pause.

< 121 >

"Jake," Marvin said suddenly. "What's my number?"

"Seven eight three, forty-eight, seventy-three," Jake mumbled.

"Good."

Jake reached for the bill, but Marvin grabbed it quicker.

"Save your money for that cell phone. I'm not kiddin'."

Jake and the sheriff left together, and as they stepped into the sunlight, Trixie turned to Mildred and smiled.

"Cupid and the sheriff," she said.

Jake walked Marvin to the patrol car.

"I'm serious, Jake, watch your back, and get a pistol."

And he drove away.

< 122 >

Dallas Airport

Darcy Lightfoot had to change planes in Dallas. A late flight from Atlanta had caused her to miss a connection to Salt Lake City. She'd been at an environmental conference and was feeling relaxed. The pressure gone; she was glad to be on the way home. Waiting on stand-by was never fun, but time alone to just sit and think seemed to fit her mood. She watched the passing crowd; far more diverse than the largely Mormon population she saw at home. She was wondering if she'd have to spend the night in Texas, when she noticed a silver belly Stetson, coming in from a recent landing at a Delta gate. She recognized the face under the hat. It belonged to Jake Oar.

She trotted up behind him and touched his shoulder.

"Hi cowboy," she said.

They stopped and slipped out of the rush of moving bodies.

"You're a sight for sore eyes," Jake grinned.

"You're stuck with that old line, I guess." She was smiling, too.

"Old people hate change," he said. "If you're not in a hurry we could go over there and talk." He pointed.

"Let's," she said.

When they were seated Darcy shared a quick overview of the circumstances of her trip, and why she was now here. Jake said he was on the way to Weatherford to look at a horse and visit some friends in Boyd. Actually, he corrected himself: several horses.

They were in a food court area, with travelers coming and going, bags on seats saving space for their hungry owners. Realizing they were in the way, and since neither of them was in a hurry, Darcy had a suggestion.

"Let's go to the Delta lounge for high-rollers. I've got a new membership through my office."

Jake agreed, and carrying coats and their bags, Darcy's on

< 123 >

wheels, they went in search of the lounge. Once checked in there, they found a quiet corner and parked themselves. Jake placed his Stetson upside down on the low end table, got two cups of the free coffee, and they relaxed and chatted.

One subject rolled gently into another. The drought in Utah evolved into global warming. Politics, a dangerous area, turned out to be safe enough, and led to environmental conservation, a controversial subject in rural America. Jake had a personal interest, being a landowner and rancher, and Darcy was returning from a conference on the subject. She was bright, articulate, and well informed.

"You are really a woman who is looking into the future. And not just talking about it. You are the future," Jake said, meaning it.

The conversation had been thoughtful and slow, so instead of an automatic and polite 'Thank you' she paused and said, "Hmmmm."

"You, you are in the future, a large contrast to me; I'm living in the past."

"How so?" Darcy asked.

"Ranchers like me are dinosaurs," he said. "We get smaller and smaller. Huge corporate ranches take us over or developers buy us out. My retirement is in the land. And since I love ranching, I don't know what else I'd do anyway. Even my hobby is focused on reliving the past."

Darcy was a little confused.

"Well, in cutting we celebrate a special kind of horse that was once used as a tool to separate one rancher's cattle from another's. In the days of the open range this was a serious job, and horses that were smart enough to read cattle, and athletic enough to outmaneuver them, those horses were held in special esteem. Today that job is done in chutes, pens, and alleys, but as an esoteric sport, or as an art form, it has thousands of dedicated followers and participants."

When Darcy's interest didn't seem to fade, Jake told the

< 124 >

story of the first cutting for prize money. It was held in West Texas in 1898.

That story led to a discussion about the need to look to the future, while remembering the past, and how two people with such diverse viewpoints could thoroughly enjoy such widely ranging discussion, for five and a half hours, in an airport lounge. And, that realization led to thoughts of food.

"We could get an early dinner and beat the crowd," said Darcy.

"All the places I know are west of Fort Worth," Jake said. "Near the Will Rogers Coliseum. But the freeways can be a monster. Probably we should stick close to the airport."

"We can let Über find us one," Darcy said. "Where are you going to sleep tonight, anyway?"

"When we finish supper, my plan is to rent a car and get a room in Weatherford or call my pals in Boyd and sleep there. Probably go west and see Lew and Sue later," Jake said. "They know I'm coming, just don't know exactly when." He was thoughtful for a second or two, then he said, "I'll get a car here, at the airport, after supper."

As they waited for Über, Jake asked, "Are we looking for white tablecloths?"

"Not for me, that's all I've seen for the last three days."

The driver dropped them at an Applebee's. It was still early, and they got a booth with no waiting. After supper, another driver found a motel near the airport for Darcy. It was a brick three-story building with white trim and juicy landscaping. She told the young fellow she liked it just fine.

"Come on in for a minute. It's too early to call your friends; they're probably eating supper," was Darcy's spur of the moment offer.

A nice invitation, Jake thought. He knew he may, or may not, call his friends that evening.

< 125 >

"OK," he said.

The room was on the third floor, above the landscaping. Out the window was the eastern sky above the treetops, and not much else. The space was smaller than most, but neat, efficient, and clean. It had a modern bathroom, a chair, a built-in shelf for the TV with drawers below. There was a king-sized bed, with a tiny table and lamp on each side.

Darcy looked around, put her bag on the shelf by the television, and tossed her coat on the chair. Jake felt slightly uncomfortable, and a little old, and thought he should have stayed in the Über. He put his bag by the door, his jacket with hers, and his hat on his bag. Darcy sat on the edge of the bed, and when Jake glanced over, she patted the space beside her.

He sat, and they both smiled. Jake lay down, his legs bent at the knees, feet on the floor, and she did the same.

"I remember one time I was with some gals in Billings, and we had to get a room ..."

When she finished her cute story, Jake countered with one about a fishing trip, and the conversation went on from there. An hour later the comfortable talk slowed down. Shoes and boots were off, feet no longer on the floor. Darcy and Jake were crosswise on the bed, side by side, looking at the ceiling.

It's probably time to leave, Jake thought, but he said nothing.

"It's hard to beat Texas barbecue," he finally said. "Next time we should go to Riscky's."

He reached quietly over and unbuttoned the top of her blouse.

"If we ever get to Houston, I know where we can get all the crayfish you can eat," said Darcy.

Jake wondered if she'd noticed the careful unbuttoning.

"Don't think I ever ate a crayfish," Jake said. "Didn't know they're edible."

"They're pretty good."

"We usta catch something like that when we were kids. Crawfish, crawdaddies, mudbugs, or mountain lobsters."

< 126 >

"The place was huge, with a parking lot big as a football field," she said.

The room was quiet a moment. Then Jake reached for the second button.

"It was packed with every ethnicity except white."

"Oh yeah?"

"Mostly African Americans, with huge stacks of crayfish on big plates."

Jake reached for another button.

"It's sort of Chinese architecture, and named The Star. You see it from the freeway."

Jake said, "Uh huh," and waited.

"You know that crayfish don't give much meat?" she asked.

"Didn't know that," reaching for the fourth button.

"Eating crayfish is like wrestling a tarantula for about as much meat as you squirt on your toothbrush at bedtime," Darcy said to the ceiling.

"If you ever get back to Utah, I'd like to take you to the Snake Creek Grill; it's got white tablecloths," said Jake as he reached for the last button.

He turned toward her and raised up on an elbow. He looked into her eyes, trying to read her mind.

"This has been the nicest day I've ever spent on stand-by," she said.

He gently reached over and opened her shirt.

"Those crayfish were really good, huh?" he whispered, "if your plate was big and you ate enough?"

She rolled on her side away from him, and scrunched toward him, getting her shirt out of the way.

"I'm curious about eating them on a toothbrush," he said.

"Crayfish, good ..." she claimed.

"Stacks of crayfish?" he murmured at work on the bra clasp.

"This damn thing is high tech," he muttered.

"Need more practice," she suggested.

< 127 >

"A beautiful back," he said.

They were both on their backs again, looking up. There was a fan up there, resting. Waiting for summer.

The huge bed was lit by the warm bedside lamps. Light from the window was almost gone now. Soft light seemed to suggest soft voices and soft skin.

He touched her shoulder, as if it were a baby kitten.

"Those crayfish."

"Yes," she purred."

"They're all you can eat?"

He was looking at her breast. Beautiful he thought. Just like her face.

"Toothbrush?"

"That Riscky's you mentioned," she asked quietly as she partially raised herself on an elbow. "It's yummy?" and she begun to unbutton his shirt.

"Yes, yummy."

The first button was loose.

"We're talking bar bee q?" she asked, and another button was opened.

Her breasts were lit from the side. As she turned toward him, the nipple cast a little shadow. Nice view with a tiny surprise. He caught a slight whiff of lavender.

"Texas style, I suppose. Since we're in Texas."

"Yes. Texas."

"Have you experienced Memphis style?" she asked, and another button was opened.

"Only in Heber, at the Spin Cafe. I think theirs is Memphis style."

Another button released.

"Try their pulled pork spaghetti." Another button.

"I know two Texas natives, who claim Riscky's Texas style is the best you can get, short of your mama's." Another button gone.

"Let's get these shirts off," she suggested. And they did.

"I do like barbecue," she said, and gently touched the crotch of his Wranglers.

"It's getting crowded in there," Jake said.

"Is Riscky's a chain or only one store?" Darcy asked, as she tried to unzip his pants.

He really was feeling crowded, and very uncomfortable, so he helped her with the zipper, and then pushed the pants down, and focused on her skirt. Their underpants and panties were quickly gone, and they soon became a collection of body parts, mixing and mingling and moving, in the soft bedside light.

Much later they curled together quietly, and gradually fell asleep.

The huge bed was in a dark room.

Jake awoke with a start and wondered where he was. It was absolutely pitch black. He moved a little and felt something soft. Darcy responded with a tentative touch of her own. For a long time, they explored each other with gentle fingers. She found his arms, the shape of them, his chest with just a hint of hair. She felt the bones at his sternum, his back and shoulder blades, legs and groin. His softer places, and his hardness.

Jake, too, was examining the feel of her, and the fitness of muscles. Her breasts and belly and her back. She felt beautiful everywhere his hands roamed. Gradually the searching in the dark concluded with another tangling of bodies, a fitting together of parts, a coupling, and afterwards, they fell back into sleep.

The huge bed was in an orange room.

The space that had been so black hours earlier, was saturated by a grayish orange half-light that seemed to infuse the entire room. Predawn light, filtered in through a thin filmy red material over the window. Viewed from eye-level at the surface of the bed, it created a fantastic world of wrinkled sheets piled into little mountain peaks, and pillows into hills. It was a small panorama

< 129 >

on a king-sized bed.

Darcy's eyes opened slowly, and she found herself a part of this miniature world where some valleys included human skin, hairy, wrinkled, or smooth.

Jake stirred. As he opened his eyes, he found Darcy's toes were close at hand. One of us is upside down he thought. They were part of the dim orange landscape that existed here alone, in a room, on a bed, floating somewhere in space.

Slowly they merged together and became one, again. And that's how they drifted back to sleep, in an orange world.

The huge bed was a festival of lines.

Jake awakened in bright light an hour later. The thin film of material was no match for the Texas sunlight streaming directly in through venetian blinds. There were parallel shadows across the wall. Moving his head slightly revealed Darcy's nude body, covered by those linear shadows, like a topographic map. Her curves, mounds, shapes and dips, all seemed to be diagramed by a cartographer. As he watched, she stirred, and the shadows made joyous moving designs that camouflaged the breasts and torso and shoulders and face. What a beautiful morning, he thought, as he allowed his eyes to close.

Much later Jake's eyes popped open. Confused, he lay still, searching for his bearings. There was a tangle of brown hair and some smooth skin nearby.

He sensed she had been awake for some time, waiting for him.

When he found his watch, it said 10:03.

He lay next to her. They felt like old friends as well as lovers. Their arms found each other and although he felt another stirring begin, they got up. There were the faint sounds of maids and their cart working their way up the hall.

They showered and got dressed.

After a late breakfast at the airport, they said goodbye,

< 130 >

separated, and resumed their real lives. His life, Jake thought, had a solid new dimension.

Silver Slippers

Jake thought of the cutting in Island Park as his last show of the year. There were still Futurities, Derbies, but why not take this winter off. Maybe go skiing, and relax a little, give the horses a rest. So he had Clint take the shoes off the shod ones and trim them all. The bay mare was with the others in the pasture, so she was included. Mrs. Francis said the mare had not been one of Buck's, and she did not know whose it was. Jake had ridden her a couple of times. A nice saddle horse, he decided, but definitely not a cow horse.

When Clint came, Jake said, "Let's do her first. I'll hold her. We'll find out if she's easy with her feet."

Pretty soon Clint had a shoe off, and then another, and she presented no problem.

"Interesting," Clint noticed. "She's wearing aluminum shoes. I don't see that very often."

That evening, Jake called the sheriff.

"Hey Marv," he said. "We may have a clue. That bay mare was wearing aluminum shoes. We pulled 'em off today."

Marvin's next day started slow at the office, so he made some phone calls to farriers in the area and had the best luck with Dan King in Lehi. His was a large shop where people brought their horses to him. All the others worked out of a truck, or trailer, and traveled to the customers.

Dan's shop usually had horses scheduled all day. In cold weather a blazing fire warmed people waiting their turn. There was a metal calf, and ropes everywhere, so ropers or children would practice with it. A skittish horse might cause the shoer to demand a temporary stop to roping. He was a team roper himself and you were always reminded of that if you shook his hand: his

< 132 >

right thumb was missing, a common roper's souvenir caused by a mishap with the rope and the saddle horn.

Business there was often a social event.

"Sure Marv, I've seen aluminum shoes. I've got some here, somewhere. Nobody wants 'em, too expensive, I guess. You might see 'em at the racetrack some, I guess, but not much need otherwise."

"Have you sold any in the last two or three months?" Marv asked.

"Yep."

"Well, Dan, I'd like to visit you if you'll be there."

"I'll just be here workin' all day. I haven't seen you in ages. Come on."

With nothing to do but paperwork around the office, Marvin decided to leave Molly in charge and take the hour-long drive to Lehi.

When Marvin arrived, they talked as the farrier worked. Dan had never seen him in uniform and admired the new look. They gossiped about friends from twenty-five years ago. Marvin picked up a rope and threw some loops on the dummy calf. Then he demonstrated a little back hand trick shot from his childhood. Holding the loop draped on the floor he stepped out to his right as he brought the loop back and with a flick of the wrist spun it in front of, then onto the patient metal calf.

"Big deal," said the blacksmith without enthusiasm. "Heck, I can do it myself."

"About aluminum shoes?" Marvin asked finally.

"A lady came in about a year or so ago. She had a barrel horse; I had been shoeing for some time. She said she wanted aluminum shoes; did I have 'em. I did, but I said; "What do you want aluminum for?"

The horse shoer put the foot down he had been working on and stood up. Then he stretched his back and continued.

"She said, 'You know in a barrel race nowadays the difference

< 133 >

between first and second can be a tenth of a second, and we need every break we can find. I think the lighter shoes might help.'"

"So, I said, 'Why don't you just lose twenty pounds?'"

Dan bent down again and pinched the horse above the ankle. The animal lifted his foot, and the blacksmith slid into position to hold it.

"I hope you knew her pretty well," Marvin said.

"I thought so, but she never came back."

"So tell me about the last time you sold aluminum shoes," the sheriff asked.

"I guess it was about two months ago. A guy comes in with a bay mare. A nice horse, as I remember. I don't think I could pick it out of an official horse lineup, but it was nice to shoe. Calm, didn't lean on you like some of 'em do. Stood still, no fussing."

"Anything you remember about the guy?" Marv asked.

"I didn't know him, but I recall thinking, I'd seen him before. You know like at the grocery store. Or maybe he's a team roper, and maybe I've seen him at some ropin's. Hard to remember. Didn't seem like a roper though."

"Any distinguishing characteristics?" The sheriff side of Marvin coming out.

"Nothing. Regular sort of height, I don't remember a moustache or anything."

Marvin was about to say goodbye, but Dan said, "I think he paid by check."

"Do you have a record?"

"The accounting is at home, but I record stuff on an unofficial ledger here."

He was looking toward his little desk in the corner. He had put the horse's hoof down, and his eyebrows were frowning.

"I think it was a Friday and old Wallace was the first customer. He had several horses, and then there was this new guy. The afternoon was empty 'cause we were ropin' after that. Might not be that hard to find. Give me a couple minutes to finish this horse ...

< 134 >

and I'll take a quick look for you."

Marvin was grateful and felt lucky and said so.

The check was from a Fred Markowitz, and because he hadn't known the man, the blacksmith had noted the address. Marvin's luck continued. It was in Palmyra, only a twenty-minute drive south and Markowitz was home. Marvin found him working on a fence behind his house. When he saw the patrol car and the uniform, he appeared to tighten up.

Fred's eyes darted around as he talked. He'd taken three horses to a shoer on a Friday a couple of months ago, but he didn't remember where exactly, somewhere in Lehi. Yes, he did ask for aluminum shoes for one horse, but it was for a friend of a friend. He didn't remember why aluminum. He said he didn't ask. His friend's name was Willie something. Couldn't remember the last name. He didn't know the name of the friend's friend.

This guy can't remember much, Marvin thought.

"Anything you can remember, please call me," Marvin said, and gave him his sheriff's card.

"Yes sir, I will," said Fred. "Yes sir, I sure will."

"I don't think that guy even has a clue. At least that's the message he hopes to deliver," Marvin said to himself as he started the patrol car.

"Clueless."

The Girls' Plan

Karen Kelly and Carol DeClaire were having lunch in the Kamas Kafe when the subject came up. Carol looked clean, fluffed up, combed, painted, and glamorous. That's exactly how she always looked. She had a salad in front of her. Karen looked a bit weathered but had a clean shirt and a mouthful of the pastrami on rye.

"Maybe," Carol began, "we should revive the All Girls' Over Night. It's been over a year, and we always manage to laugh our little asses off."

"If you mean like when we went bowling in Evanston, and spent the night in the no-tell motel, and drove home the next day with a cranking hangover? That, my lovely Carol, was three years ago, and I remember that oil linesman that followed us to the motel and how you finally got rid of him." Karen and Carol were both laughing. "I bet Tina is still cracking up from that scene."

"She peed her pants so bad, Sally went to Walmart and bought her the diapers," Carol continued the thought, "and we had the official presentation at the bar, toasting her bladder ..."

"Remember the fat bowler in the next lane with the red shirt? I think you had a bet with him and had to pay off with your big gulp full of Scotch."

"He had been bowling strikes but when I got through with him, he was all gutter balls," Karen giggled.

"His balls were in the gutter, you mean," Carol squealed.

"Get rowdy and talk dirty, that's us."

They calmed down, realizing they had been causing a little scene.

"So watcha think, girlfriend?" Carol asked.

"I'm all in, but can we go somewhere else? Wyoming, been there, done that."

"I'm ahead of you. How 'bout Las Vegas?" Carol asked.

"A better class of drunken oilmen down there."

"That, and they never run out of booze," said Karen.

"That, and what happens in Vegas, stays in Vegas," said Carol.

"And I had another idea too, give you a choice," Carol smiled like she was telling a special little secret. "A Mexican cruise."

"It would be fun, but when do you plan to do this all-girl night out? Cruising sounds complicated."

Carol pouted and gave a tiny groan. She was a cruise kind of girl.

"Another thing is a cruise; you've got to select the right girls. Narrows our choice substantially ... for example, as funny as she is I'm not spending two or three days with Adele, and truth be told, I don't think Ruthie could afford it."

Then Karen added, "Vegas gets my vote."

"Who shall we invite?"

"Holy cow, girlfriend, we'll get all our regular pals," Carol said. "Maybe add a fresh one or two ... more the merrier."

Now, with the serious planning done, the conversation moved to more mundane topics and they focused on their meals.

A few days later they met again in the booth by the window to revise their plans. They were joined by Tina, Becky Smith, an outdoor type who had a van named Travelmobile, along with Sally Randall, a software designer and photographer in her spare time. She was the youngest of their group of regulars.

Trixie came by with the coffee pot in her hand.

"Hang on girls, I'll get some cups," and she disappeared in a blur of white.

"Well, girlfriends, we've got problems," Carol announced seriously.

Trixie spread coffee cups around.

"You all eatin' today, or just drinkin?"

"Dang girl, are you developin' an Oklahoma accent? Is that what I detect?" Carol asked with a big grin.

< 137 >

"Better leave that rocky romance alone. Cowboys are goin' out of style," Trixie replied. "Gonna eat?"

"Let's start with coffee," said Karen. "Then we'll probably eat somethin'."

There was a sense of agreement all around. The waitress went for the coffee pot and the ladies braced themselves for bad news.

"Vegas is out," Carol announced. My honey, and two other husbands nixed it. Sally's said too expensive, and I think Ruthie's hubby doesn't trust her with those male strippers. I tried to explain they're all gay boys, but he doesn't care."

There was a long pause.

"I haven't been to San Francisco for a long while," Karen said.

"Still probably too expensive. I kept picturing the drive to Vegas, all of us packed in Becky's van ... That would have been a party ... But any farther we'd have to fly."

Other cities were discussed but nothing stirred excitement.

"If we wait a month or two, we could go skiing in Vail or Sun Valley," Carol offered. "Actually, we have friends in Sun Valley with a condo we could probably use if we avoid weekends."

"There's also Steamboat, a reasonable drive," said Becky with some building enthusiasm. "Five hours in the van is all."

Becky was an excellent skier and could be their guide. A discussion of ski resorts followed. They all liked to ski with the possible exception of Sally, who felt timid on the slopes. But they soon realized this line of planning eliminated several women who did not ski at all. And besides, this puts the outing into February.

Something that could happen right now was needed.

And so the discussion turned into a nature hike.

"How about a pack trip, with llamas carrying our overnight stuff?" Sally suggested. "Francie would love that idea. She has the animals."

In her mind Carol pictured scenes from the movie *Deliverance* where the city boys are terrorized by nature, hillbillies, dueling banjos, toothless rednecks, and raging rivers.

"Llamas are spitting creatures," said Carol.

"Maybe something with less walking and more drinking, Karen thought.

Then came a discussion involving horses. Too complicated. Hiking, too strenuous. Four-wheeling and mountain biking, too dangerous. Most sports seemed to leave someone out.

"Maybe we can find a place in nature where we can picnic, and watch the beavers play," suggested Tina. "Watch the sun go down and sleep in warm bags under the stars. It's up Weber Canyon, then up the north side of Hoyt's Peak. A tough road that peters out and takes a while."

"I know places like that, but closer," said Sally. "Everything but the pond. It's off Mirror Lake Highway."

"As a nature photographer, I bet you do," said Karen, getting on board with the idea. "I'll set up the bar and we'll have a nice evening."

"We'll get shot by hunters," Carol worried. "Aren't the mountains filled with the orange army?"

"Deer season is over, the hunters are home, their freezers full, and the deer are free to wander around again. They've put the guns in a closet, they're all watching football now, hoping nobody asks 'em to do the dishes."

"Well, I guess that might be the plan. But we'd better do it quick, before the weather gets bad," Carol said. "You ladies think we should invite any newbies?"

"One I've been thinking about is Darcy whatshername from the land conservancy. She seems nice, and I'd like to know her better," said Karen.

"She is very nice," said Becky. "I know her quite well ... recommend her highly."

Tina said, "I'm for it. She works for conservation and all the global warming stuff we should be worrying about, and she's trying to save open space. I bet she'll be interesting ... Her name is Lightfoot."

< 139 >

"Is that a description or just a name?" asked Carol.

"I don't know exactly, kind of early middle-age, and pretty. She could be light on her feet. Bet she probably is."

"Sounds good to me," said Sally.

"We agree then? Want me to call her?" Becky offered.

< 140 >

The Dance of Death

Buster had been dreaming. Lying on his side he let out some little bird sounds, like squeaks, and they were accompanied by little leg jerks. It seemed as if his body was inhabited by Mexican jumping beans. His tail, built for wagging, lay still.

He sat up and growled ...

Buster got up and trotted to the front door and growled again. Jake put down his magazine and they looked at each-other. Jake got up and they both went out on the porch. At first everything seemed quiet, but then they heard it.

Agitated voices, coming from way down the driveway. Probably near the mailbox 80 yards away. Listening carefully, it sounded like a fight. Pretty unusual in this valley, he thought. Feeling a strange sense of responsibility for his property, Jake headed toward his truck, but on the way, he paused to call his friend Marvin, the sheriff.

"I think someone's fighting in my driveway," he said.

To the dog, he said, "Stay."

Jake drove the farm truck toward the noise. He glanced at his watch, and realized it was bedtime.

The driveway meandered, following an old irrigation ditch, lined with cottonwood trees. He drove slowly, lights off, in the cool glow of a nearly full moon. Rounding the last curve, he saw dark figures in the road. Pausing there he tried to assess the situation.

He snapped on the headlights, revealing a fight scene. A small pickup had crashed into a tree and was half in the ditch, and another vehicle, a sedan, was blocking the driveway. The activity had been in moonlight until Jake's truck lit everything. Four guys in the road were staring like deer in the headlights. There was a fifth man, folded up like a pile of bloody laundry on the ground.

Jake reached up to make sure the dome light was switched off,

< 141 >

then got out of the truck slowly, taking his rifle with him. He cleared his throat, stalling for time.

"Hold up there folks," he said, calm and serious. "Do not move."

He stood behind the open door positioned behind the headlights where he imagined they couldn't see him well. He reached in the truck and turned the engine off, but left the head lights on. A few moments of silence followed, and Jake cocked the rifle. In the quiet night air, the metallic sound was loud enough that it gave some authority to his words.

"So, what's goin' on here?"

He sensed these were not local kids. They looked like big city ghetto gang bangers, baggy clothes, chains, and at least one held a baseball bat. It didn't seem like a gang war, more like a massacre, and the pickup wreck in the trees didn't seem accidental.

"What happened to your friend there on the ground?"

His question was answered by silence.

"Is he OK?"

Nothing. Then a cough.

"Fuck off, dude, this ain't none of your shit," said one of them.

The figure on the ground moved a little. He was moaning. It began to dawn on Jake that these people were probably armed. Someone was holding a knife, and they all had pockets that could easily hold pistols. He could feel his adrenaline and hear his heart pounding.

One of the men whispered to the others in Spanish, followed by some low tones back and forth. Jake cleared his throat again and moved a little.

I'm way over my head here, he thought. He was holding the rifle, but the bullets were in a box in his bedroom.

"It seems we're at a Mexican standoff here," he said. "Tell me what's goin on."

"Tu hijo podrido de un perro inmundo. Fuck off." was one

< 142 >

reply, another was: "Ain't none of your business, old man. Back the fuck off."

The little group started to spread out slowly, carefully, hoping to create four little targets, out of one big one.

"Stop moving," Jake demanded. "Stand off," he said again. "I hear the cavalry coming."

He was awfully glad he'd called Marvin.

Sure enough there was a police siren, but it sounded far away. Everyone heard it, and as it turned off of the state highway on to Boulderville Road, it suddenly seemed much louder and closer. They all seemed to freeze and listened as it turned onto Democrat Alley. Louder yet.

The fellow farthest to the left suddenly darted into the cottonwood trees and disappeared in the darkness. There was a wild scramble, as the three others sprang for the car. With the doors open the interior dome light showed a glimpse of a head in a red bandana, a bald head and a knife. Then darkness hid everything.

They sped backwards into the road spewing gravel, shifted into drive, and threw more rocks as their headlights blinked on and they headed west. The taillights were disappearing as the sheriff's headlights and rotating red roof light came rushing in from the east.

The scene was soon lit by headlights from both sides and attention was on the body in the driveway.

"Sure glad to see you," Jake said. "Assailants split, one into the pasture and three away in a car. Mean little fellows."

"They killed this guy, or did he die in the wreck?" Marvin asked, looking toward the little pickup in the ditch.

"I think he's alive, Marv."

The sheriff called dispatch for an ambulance as Jake bent over the bloody body. It was a mess of torn clothes with a mangled face. The entire head was badly broken. Jake tried to look in the eyes but where were they? The nose was not where it should be, and the jaw was twisted impossibly. It struck him that this was someone familiar. Or had been. He looked closely. The head was so messed up, he couldn't tell. He glanced at the pickup in the ditch. It could be tan, but it was too dark to be sure.

... Inside the broken skull the space was filled with great pain and only slight consciousness. Death and Pain were dancing cheek to cheek, waltzing through a gooey mess. The beating had stopped, and someone new was here, but the pain pushed everything else away.

Then the hurting slipped aside, replaced by a quiet fever dream that was not really quiet at all. It seemed humid, near the ocean of long ago. The air felt very heavy. Weighted. Air that couldn't fit in empty lungs. Faces were everywhere. There was mariachi music, but it wasn't music, just a pounding. A rhythmic screaming. Moving faces were everywhere. Most wore masks or had been painted to resemble skulls. Black and white. They seemed to be crowding, pushing through a graveyard. The stones were everywhere now. Floating. Faces of skulls and skeletons moving, dissolving together. It was the Day of the Dead. The faces were not human. They were the faces of rats.

Then inside his broken shell the pain came dancing back, and men were asking him nonsense questions. Darkness enveloped him, the outside voices faded away and a dot of white light appeared. He moved towards the light. He floated in that direction. It had the most beautiful glow he had ever seen. It brought a peace that engulfed him.

The dance had ended. Pain said thank you to death ...

Crouching by the dead man, Marvin said the obvious. "They really wanted to hurt this guy."

The remains were lifeless, no longer human. Inert.

While they waited for the ambulance, Jake explained what he knew. And he kept an eye out for the fellow who had run

< 144 >

into the pasture.

"I can't imagine four more vicious fellows," Marvin said, and it was exactly where Jake's mind had been. They were doing a lot more thinking than talking. Neither one wanted to examine the ruined corpse.

Two volunteer firemen arrived with the ambulance, and they examined what they could of the victim. A collection of parts, once held together by muscle and bone, now resided loosely in the bloody clothing. With their fingers in plastic gloves, the volunteers felt their way, trying to put the pieces in proper order on the stretcher board. Both men lost their suppers.

Finally, after the ambulance left, and Marvin had carefully gathered the baseball bats—there were two, and a knife he found—and put them into evidence bags, he announced that tomorrow morning, he'd come back and search around some more. The damaged pickup would rest where it was until then.

As he was leaving, Jake stood by the driver's side as the window rolled down and Marvin looked at Jake.

"See you in the am?" It was a question as much as a statement.

"Marv, I think that guy might have been Arturo," Jake said.

< 145 >

Jake Gets a Hand

The oldest building on the place was the barn. Although the house was the first structure to greet visitors, the barn was the centerpiece. It looked rather grand. The roof could be seen from a mile away, if you knew where to look. Stalls were on the dirt floor, and a huge hayloft sat above. It was a style of architecture popular all over the West, until the huge round bales came in vogue. The hay doors at each end were designed for loose hay and work fine for the traditional bales. Although Jake remodeled the ground floor layout several times, the shell always remained original. There was fresh paint when it was needed, and a new roof or two, but that was all. The barn and Jake's grandmother were the same age, but the exact year was argued among family historians.

About five thirty Jake started his evening chores in the barn. Five horses, supplements from the grain room, a scoop for each one. Then to the hayloft. At the foot of the ladder, he looked up. One of the cats was looking down at him through the opening.

Up the ladder he went, but when he stuck his head through the floor the cat had disappeared, and he was getting a cat's eye view of the hay storage. He climbed out into the large space. The floor was mostly covered with scattered loose hay. Behind the opening in the floor were six bales of suspicious alfalfa; the bottoms looked and smelled moldy. Three bales high, two stacks end to end. Someday soon he planned to drop these bales down the ladder hole and feed them to the cows.

On the far side of the open space stood the good hay, about 80 bales of alfalfa on the left and about 200 bales of grass, neatly piled on the right. There was a four-foot-wide space to walk between the stacks.

Jake's mind had slid back to the brutal murder again and again all day. At first there was no getting past the viciousness of

< 146 >

it. Then gradually he began to wonder who were those sinister thugs, and why was the attack in his driveway? Were they trying to get information, or was it pure hate? And why? There was the question about Jake's own involvement. An innocent bystander? Could they recognize him on the street?

Feeding the horses was a calming ritual, except in those rare cases where something was wrong, a scratch, a limp, a stomachache. As he was dropping hay to the horses, he heard Buster outside acting like there was a visitor.

Jake froze, listening. He had not heard a vehicle drive up. His mind was racing. The deer rifle was in the house. The only weapon here was? What? There was a pitchfork with four tines sharp enough to pierce a man's flesh. But where was it? Out of sight somewhere, probably between the big stacks of hay. He was near the hole at the top of the ladder, and there was the hatchet that he used to break open the hay bales. It had been sharpened two days ago. And it was lying on the stack of moldy bales.

He picked up the hatchet.

If it is a friend or neighbor, they will knock on the house door, Jake thought, or perhaps call out. Strange he hadn't heard a car. He was listening to every sound now. Time passed, at least a few minutes, with nothing to hear but horses chewing and moving. Maybe his mind had been playing tricks on him.

Nothing unusual.

And then he heard the barn door open, and someone moved around below. He listened as each stall door was opened, then closed. He heard the tack room door and the feed room, open and close. Someone was searching for something.

Jake threw his hat toward the walking space between the two big stacks of hay, thinking it would get the attention of anyone poking his head up at the top of the ladder. Then he moved, as quietly as possible, behind the small six-bale stack next to the opening. He stood silently a moment, then dropped to his knees, hidden, he hoped, behind the waist-high stack. His tentative plan

< 147 >

was almost no plan at all. If an assailant arrived and saw the hat, he might assume his victim was hiding between the stacks of hay. There might be a chance to escape down the ladder. Trapped, that dumb plan seemed better than no plan at all. If the head that appeared was a friend, well let's hope that it was.

Then came a noise from below, mumbling and complaining as someone started up the ladder. Focused on the opening in the floor, Jake saw an orange bandana-wrapped head pop up, stop, then slowly rise till the eyes could see out over the floor. The visitor was looking at the hat, and the hay stacked beyond. Then the wrapped head twisted around and saw the moldy hay close by, then swung quickly back to the hat, and paused. Waiting. Jake thought he might be satisfied with an empty hayloft and leave.

It wasn't going to be that easy.

The newcomer carefully rose another rung on the ladder, head and shoulders above the floor now, followed by one arm, and then the other. His elbows and hands rested on the floor, as he watched the hat and the space between the stacks. One hand was about ten inches from Jake's knee. And it held an ugly pistol, finger in the trigger guard, pointed at the hat.

Without thinking, Jake's hand flashed down, and the hatchet chopped the hand clean off. There had been fear, even terror behind that swing, and maybe some revenge for Arturo also.

There was a yelp, and a commotion as the orange head disappeared. Someone slid bumping down the ladder and fell to the floor. Howling, and thrashing around, he gathered his wits, and struggled to his feet. At least two more voices entered the barn. There was some frantic jabbering in Spanish, and the sounds of people scuffling around, and finally leaving. A vehicle started in the distance, grew louder, then maneuvered around, car doors slammed with more swearing, and then sped away. Buster was barking excitedly. Horses snorted.

Jake sat down where he was, trying to get calm. His heart was beating like a gorilla on a pogo stick.

< 148 >

But the severed hand lay quietly and didn't seem sinister at all.

The spotted yellow cat appeared and came close to smell the strange hand and dangerous gun. A nine-millimeter Smith and Wesson. Black.

A fter a while Jake gathered himself and went down the blood splattered ladder, past a puddle soaking into the hard packed dirt floor, and into his house. He poured a Bourbon over some ice and picked up his phone.

"Hey Marv, I can give you a hand with the murder case."

Jake had been thinking about how to present the evidence to the sheriff and that was the best he could come up with. Marvin didn't understand it, of course. Silence lasted a couple of seconds.

"Jake, is that you?' Marvin asked. "Your voice sounds funny."

"You should check with the hospitals to see if a gangster comes in with a hand missing." There was a pause, and Jake added, "I've got it here, in the barn— and his gun too."

"Left or right?" Marvin asked, all business.

"Right, I think. I hadn't really thought about it."

"Stay put. I'll be right over," Marvin said.

"There'll be a handful of fingerprints for you, Sheriff." Jake said. He had used up all the humor he could muster. Picking up the glass again he noticed his hand was rattling the ice. Shaking.

After a long sip of Bourbon, he relaxed a moment, then went with Buster to finish feeding his livestock.

< 149 >

Quick Exit

Cookie's fall from the ladder was nothing compared to the missing hand. He was stunned for a few seconds, his mind trying to deal with reality. Blood was squirting like a sonofabitch, and he was freaking out. Panic, terror and confusion.

"My hand is GONE," he screamed. "Help, shit, shit, TJ, help!"

Hurting and panicked, he tried to drag himself away from the bloody ladder. Crawling and moving had not worked well. He felt desperate to create distance. Something up there had taken his hand. Helpless. He resumed yelling.

"My fucking HAND!"

In a minute TJ was there, helped him up, and then quickly laid him down again. In a flash Armando Cruz arrived with a "Qué pasó?"

"Find a tourniquet, quick, brother," TJ said holding the bloody end up. "Hazlo rápido."

"Shit. Look at his fucking hand, it's not there …" screamed a stunned Armando.

"A tourniquet," TJ yelled, still keeping the arm elevated. Blood was squirting up and out, splattering everywhere. "Look around."

Armando seemed to have lost his senses.

"Armando, conseguir un control. Remember in Boy Scouts we learned about a motherfuckin' tourniquet."

"Shit."

"Gotta stop the bleeding. Any piece of shit, to wrap around his arm."

"Agarra un alambre, cuerda, ensarta algo para atar la sangre," said TJ, "Rope, wire, string, grab something, we gotta tie off the blood."

"His fuckin' blood is squirting out," Armando said, trying to grasp reality.

Cookie was blubbering, howling, and moaning.

< 150 >

"There's a clipper on the fucking wall with a cord on it," TJ yelled. "Grab that thing quick." Then, "Sacas el cable del cortador."

Armando tied the clipper cord tight around the bleeding arm.

"Tighter," TJ, examining the squirting blood.

"Where's fuckin' Pedro? Fucker'd be tarde a su propio funeral." Then, "Get the fuckin' car down here, we gotta get Cookie to a doctor. The little bastard could die on us."

TJ ripped the clipper off the cord and tossed it in a corner, and Armando went for the car. Running, it still took a little while; it had been parked down the driveway behind some trees.

As TJ was loading the bloody boy into the car, Pedro appeared. He'd been admiring the horses, he said. When he saw Cookie, he said "Oh shit. Mierda."

As the car sped down the driveway Armando spoke.

"So, we're goin' to the hospital. And where is it, TJ?"

"Hell no. Hospitals attract cops. We'll take him to Doc Martin."

"I think he's dying here. He looks white to me," said Pedro seriously.

"It'll take an hour to get to the Doc, TJ, ain't nobody closer?"

Talk stopped for a few moments, except for Cookie, who kept fading out, and then would come back yelling and moaning.

"What we gonna do about that asshole in the barn, TJ?" Armando asked.

"Fuck him, let's focus on Cookie for a while," TJ replied with his man-in-charge voice. "We can kill him later."

"I say we burn down the fucker's barn," Pedro suggested.

"With him in it," muttered Armando, who was staring at the speedometer.

"Don't get a ticket, TJ, you're goin' damn fast."

"And maybe we'll get a police escort, get there even faster," TJ said. "Cops look in, see we're with the wounded, say nice job on that tourniquet, I see you bad boys are Boy Scouts, so let me

< 151 >

fuckin' help you with a police escort at ninety miles per fuckin hour. Sireeeeen and red lights whirlin'." TJ cracked himself up with his own humor. The others mostly didn't get it.

Doctor Martin treated Cookie in an older house in a residential area near the freeway in Lehi. The doctor, well past middle age, looked tired. He wore little glasses on a big nose. He had rather long ears that seemed to flop when he spoke.

"What have you gangsters done this time?" That had been his greeting, but when he saw Cookie, very pale and only semiconscious, his tone changed. He became all business. He thought the boy would die.

But when the doctor was finished, he was a little more optimistic.

"I don't want to know what happened, but you'd better be careful. This boy will have to stay here for a while so I can change bandages and shit, but you better stop your freelancing. Prince told me to tell you little shits to stop it. There are fuckin' bigger fish to fry, and you assholes are causing a distraction."

The little old doctor was scolding some rather vicious men, the biggest and baddest being TJ. He stood six foot six and was all muscle. Even Pedro was six feet of pure meanness. And they all carried pockets full of weapons.

"One of these days I'm tellin' Prince to fuck off," said Pedro.

"Pedro, shut the fuck ta hell up," demanded TJ, as he grabbed him by the shirt and shook him hard. "Nobody is telling Prince shit. I'll fucking kill you myself and feed your intestines to an alligator."

"You know I'm gonna have to tell Prince," Doc Martin said. "He'll shit a brick and run it up somebody's ass. Probably yours, TJ."

"I know."

"If I were you, I'd take Prince seriously, and stop your free-lancing," said the doctor looking at them all, then turning his eyes

< 152 >

to TJ. He said, "You are going to get killed. All of you."

When the three fellows left Doc Martin, they were silent a while. Then Armando spoke.

"My fuckin' car's a bloody mess.

"You'll get a new one," TJ said. "Don't worry, we'll dispose of this fingerprint covered automobile."

"We oughtta kill that fuckin' asshole."

"That may be beyond our skill level," said TJ.

"Wouldn't be hard, he's just a hick farmer."

"I'd like to burn him in his fuckin' barn," said Pedro.

"I dunno, maybe we should sit low a while. Prince is gonna ream my ass and besides, we don't even know what the fuck he looks like," said TJ. "We could be eating a Big Mac next to him and not know it's him."

Armando glanced out the blood splattered window at the dark sky and town lights.

"We do know what his truck looks like," he said quietly.

< 153 >

Trucks

Jake, like many ranchers, had two trucks. His ranch pickup was an old Dodge Ram with fading paint and some rust starting to show up like bruises on a banana. It had dents and a major scrape on the right rear fender. It was always referred to as the Ranch Truck and it did the working-class jobs. It normally sat beside the barn resting, waiting for Jake or Simon to take it somewhere to do something.

The Dodge had a lot of personality, rather like a raccoon in a hollow log, grouchy but ready. Its faded exterior sported three colors, green and white from the factory, plus reddish brown from the rust. And it was useful in another way: it always had what you might need, from tire tools to chains for snow, other chains for towing, extra coats and hand tools, a huge bundle of used hay string, nuts and bolts. It could seat six people if you moved the coats and tools over. It had a two-year-old engine, four-wheel drive and a new battery. And though it looked old, it usually acted young.

The other truck was a six-year-old Chevy Silverado 250 with a Duramax transmission. It could pull Jake's three-horse trailer up the highway like it didn't even notice. And it had four doors and easily held five people. It was a common color: a metallic grayish gold. Jake kept it fairly clean and used it to meet Darcy at the restaurant in Heber City.

Separated by a white tablecloth, Darcy asked for a glass of white and Jake ordered a Coors Lite. The Snake Creek Grill was locally famous as a source of fine dining, and great service. It had been the 'go to' restaurant whenever a extra special place was needed. Darcy and Jake dined there often enough that the staff begun to recognize them as a couple.

"I've forgotten what we're celebrating tonight," Jake said.

< 154 >

"Each other," she replied.

"So, what's new with you?" Jake wondered. He hadn't seen her in over three days.

"I have been invited to an all-girl all-night picnic." Darcy grinned. "Other than that, it's just the usual, meetings and more meetings."

"All girls?" He smiled.

"All night," she said.

"Any girls I know?

"Probably," she said. "Karen Kelley, Carol DeClaire, Sally Randall, Becky Smith, Tina Valentine, Ruth Hanson, Somebody Hicks, but we're losing girls one by one. A conflict here, a gotta headache there. I think it'll be Karen, Carol, Becky, Tina, and I. Maybe Sally, too. Know them?"

"Everybody knows Karen, and I cut hay for Tina. I've met Carol."

Darcy explained the details. How they would go up the Mirror Lake Highway about twelve miles, turn north on the dirt road along Shingle Creek, and in about a mile and a half, make a left over a cattle guard and follow two tracks up and around the corner of a mountain, and it will suddenly reveal the Kamas Valley, far below.

We'll have our folding chairs and sleeping bags, and sandwiches for supper. Karen is in charge of setting up a bar. We'll watch the sunset and sleep under the stars."

"Have you ever been up there?" Jake asked.

"I'm not sure. I may have been. The Conservancy had interest in the old Champion Ranch, and it was on the west side of Shingle Creek. I saw a lot of it, but I don't think that's exactly the place. Becky's been there, she's our guide."

"After the cattle guard the two-track is terribly rocky. Not just rocks, but boulders," Jake said. "We'd unload the horses at the cattle guard and ride up." He paused, remembering, then continued.

< 155 >

"Old Greg Alexander takes a tractor with a blade up there every few years to get out some of the boulders. I think he's the one with the grazing permit."

Jake let her think about that, and then said, "I think you'd need a jeep to get up that hill. Something with big wheels and four-wheel drive."

"Oh."

"I could loan you my old Dodge farm truck," Jake offered. "It's been up there before."

"OK."

"Be sure to take a cellphone, If you get stuck you can walk on around the corner of the mountain and when you can see the valley, then you can get cell service. Call me if you get stuck."

Jake, thinking about that steep primitive little road, remembered the scary part. A long fall if you thought about it. More frightening than dangerous. Give the girls a little thrill, he thought, and decided to let it surprise them.

He had two more pieces of advice.

"Do not go if the ground is wet ... when is this all-girl, all-night event anyway?"

"Thursday, unless Carol reschedules. But winter's coming, so I think Thursday," Darcy responded.

"Do you have a gun?" Jake serious, but trying not to alarm her.

"No." The way she said it was not a hell no, nor was it a timid little no.

"Well, I've got a new pistol and I want you to take it with you. No worries, I'd feel better if you had it. Have you ever used one?"

"My dad gave me a little lesson when I was just out of high school. I think he was getting me ready for the big bad world, off to college and all that."

"Good," Jake said.

"We were in an old quarry and shot beer cans with our neighbor's rifle and pistol. The rifle was kinda fun if you like noise, but I couldn't hit shit with the pistol ... gosh, that's a long-

< 156 >

lost memory from the distant past ..."

"That's settled then, I'll gas the truck and put the gun in the glove box. Put it in your sleeping bag in case you encounter a cougar or a weirdo."

After a delicious meal they walked to Darcy's Subaru.

"Let's sleep at my place tonight," smiled Darcy.

"I'll check in with Simon, make sure all is well, and follow you home."

< 157 >

The Lexus

Pedro, Armando, and TJ were sitting in TJ's Lexus parked in the empty lot by Dick's Drive In. They could see cars passing the stop light on SR32 and everything that passed on the Mirror Lake Highway. They could drive through Dick's if they got the munchies. They were three young men settled in for a day of chilling out in Kamas.

For the past few days, they had been doing some illegal odd jobs for Prince and had today off. Their original idea had been to go to Armando's mother's house, lie around, smoke some weed, maybe do a little coke, relax. But they had started talking about Cookie and decided they could smoke and chill in the Lexus up in the Kamas Valley just as well, and maybe catch the farmer and eliminate him. Snuffing him out would be sport. Sport and revenge. Anyway, thinking was getting hazy in the car full of fumes.

"Hope the motherfucker shows today, before we get pulled off this project," said Pedro.

"We're not on this fucking project, asshole," TJ said, talking in his serious voice. "If we cap the farmer, it's for Cookie, not for Prince, don't you forget it. Nobody's business but ours."

"Wish Cookie was here," said Pedro from the back, where he was lying down on the seat with his feet up. "He was expert bashing heads with that fuckin' bat."

"Where is that bat now?" asked TJ.

"Dunno."

"How about you, Armando? Seen it?"

"Nope."

"Has anybody seen it? I mean them? There was two, when we whooped on Arturo in the driveway?"

TJ was starting to get hot now.

"You assholes are gonna get us real fucked up. We need a lot more attention to detail around here. I sure as hell hope Cookie

< 158 >

remembers where he put the fuckin' bats because it's probably got our fingerprints all over 'em. Cops would have a motherfuckin' heyday with that shit."

TJ fumed a while, then he said, "Shit."

"How is Cookie anyway?" TJ asked.

"He's at his mama's," said Armando. "She said his arm is bigger than shit. She's pissed at us, thinks it's all our fault. Poor little fucker is really fucked."

Armando let that ride and then said, "His mom said she's gonna make him go to church."

"Oh shit, Armando. Look, is that our asshole?" TJ asked as he started the engine.

They followed the truck, but not closely.

"Lay back, that fuckin' truck screams asshole from a distance!" said an excited Armando. "Green and white piece of junk, ugliest truck I've ever seen."

"What's goin' on?" asked Pedro, sitting up.

"We're following the farmer," said TJ.

"Are we gonna burn him in his barn?"

"I dunno, Pedro, we'll decide when we get him."

They followed the truck, staying way back as it left town on the Mirror Lake Highway, and when it swung north on a tiny road, they let it get out of sight before TJ made his U turn, went back and followed it, headed north. Here they kept their distance, TJ driving like a man who didn't want to get his Lexus dirty. Even if they couldn't see the truck, dust hung in the air showing exactly where it had gone. They saw when it stopped and turned west and bumped across a cattle guard.

"Where in hell is he goin'?" TJ mumbled.

They followed two tracks across a grassy area, with much less dust. They gained elevation and maneuvered through trees, and finally turned steeply up into a very rocky area. Here the going was very slow. Twice, TJ stopped and got out to take a walk and examine the tracks ahead. Then he'd get back in for a few more

< 159 >

minutes of thumping and bumping up through grass and rocks. There were scraping sounds as the pan or differential crossed boulders, and soon it was too much. They quit, hung up on a big stone that wouldn't let the front wheels touch the ground.

"I'm wreckin' my car," said TJ, staring glumly out of the dirt-covered window.

"We're done," he announced. "Fuckers' truck may be ugly but it's amazin'."

All three got out and listened to the sounds of small creatures moving through branches. Tall pines and aspen blocked out much of the sky, their deep shadows competing for space on the ground. A slight breeze tickled the treetops and made their shadows seem alive on the forest floor.

Thirty yards farther up the hill a tall skeleton of a long dead spruce stood against the vast blue yonder. A Red-Tailed Hawk sat on a high branch and annoyed two noisy small birds who flew around and scolded him. Pedro pointed his trigger finger at the large bird and mimed shooting it with his thumb. It stretched up and spread its large wings, gliding into the sky, looking free and flying easy.

"I'd need a rifle ..." Pedro muttered.

The boys looked at the trees, the impossible road, the clear blue sky. Somebody said "Shit." and they all got back into the car.

"Fuckin' amazing," TJ said reverently. Armando assumed he meant the road and the truck ahead. Pedro thought he was talking about the beautiful natural world and lit up a fat joint.

"Gimme one," said Armando, and both he and TJ reached their hands behind their seats, toward the fresh smoke.

For a while they relaxed. Just gangsters on holiday. At least that's how Pedro saw it.

Armando thought about the farmer. He went up this road, and he'll probably have to come down the same way. We could cap him in his green and white truck, let the cops find him in the spring.

But TJ was trying to figure out how he was going to get his

< 160 >

Lexus out. High centered on a boulder, they were stuck. If they did get loose, there was no obvious way to maneuver around. He'd have to back a long complicated way. He looked at his cell phone. No service.

Can't call the Auto Club.

< 161 >

All Girls All Night

On the mountain, aspens had been changing color. Green to lime, then yellow and finally gold. The scene that welcomed the all-girl, all-night group was foliage at its most spectacular. Wildly festive, the moment was fleeting and precious. The next storm would leave many of the trees bare.

Scattered at the white trunks of the quakies were the early fallen leaves looking like gold coins tossed on the dead grass.

The women had arranged five sleeping bags so everyone had a nice view of the valley, a clump of aspens close beside them to the north, and a large grove of trees not far to the south. The ground sloped west toward the view. The truck was about twenty yards above them in an open meadow, turned around, pointed home.

Karen had arranged a cluster of five folding chairs next to her 'bar on a blanket', just below the sleeping bags. There was fine wine of course, three bottles of scotch, two of vodka, and some water. The cooler with melted ice still contained a few exotic alcoholic punch drinks in cans, and some lemonade. For backup there was most of a container of Makers Mark, and for dessert, a bottle of peppermint schnapps. When it came to booze, Karen thought it better to bring too much than to run out.

They had consumed the supper of croissant sandwiches stuffed with chicken salad made with grapes and nuts. It had been served earlier, as the wine was uncorked, so it wouldn't interrupt the sunset, which Carol predicted would be excellent.

The all-girl group had eroded with the calendar and now was down to Carol, who would rather be in Vegas, Karen, Darcy, Becky, and Sally, who were all quite happy here.

As the sun started to get noticeably lower, the air cooled a little, the women started to put their jackets on. Darcy was cool and her jacket was in the truck, so she slipped into her sleeping

< 162 >

bag for warmth. There had been a little hiking earlier, and a couple of rather silly games, but now they all were calm, and reflective. Conversations were getting more serious. Karen and Carol were on either side of Darcy's bag, facing the view. Becky and Sally were below them, in chairs angled so they could talk. The actual sunset was still an hour or two away.

Sally jerked around when she noticed something or someone moving near the pickup. She jumped to her feet.

"Who's there?" she said loudly, and then louder yet "Who is there?" All the girls were looking up toward the truck, and they watched three large men coming down through the grass. When they were close the largest one spoke.

"We do not want to scare you folks. I am John an diss is Paul an George." He looked closely at them all.

"All women," he said in a rather surprised voice. "Muchas mujeres bonitas."

"You are a Mormon family. We are here to meet your husband."

An awkward silence enveloped the group while everyone tried to understand and evaluate the situation. John seemed in charge, with the other two glancing around, watching the ladies, and checking the woods. Sally and Becky were out of their chairs now and looked ready to flee. Darcy sensed a disadvantage looking up at everyone from her bag on the ground.

"We want to see your husband," the biggest man repeated.

"Gosh," Carol said lightly. "I sure hope we're not double parked?"

He gave her a hard stare and said, "Where is that man?" He continued to glare at Carol. Then he seemed to relax slightly, focused on the other women. He studied Karen, and then Sally. He squatted down and spoke to Darcy.

"One of you is going to tell me where that man is."

Carol was moving around, trying to put a little distance between them.

"Pedro, grab that bitch." He pointed at Carol who made a

< 163 >

quick move to escape as Pedro grabbed her wrist.

"Hold her right there next to that tree. Armando, grab the fuckin' twine outta that ugly truck."

"Take off her coat," he said.

Then they pushed her back against a tall aspen and tied the hay string around her right wrist. Carol was terrified but tried not to show it. Whatever she wanted to say stuck in her throat. They seemed almost polite and concerned with her comfort when they tightened the knot. It was tied so it would not loosen, or tighten, if she struggled. It was a bowline.

"He was a Boy Scout, good at knots," said the big man. "You comfortable?"

Then they tied her wrist to the tree, shoulder high, putting the final knot on the other side, where it would be hard for her to reach.

"She was trying to leave," the huge fellow said. "But we mean no trouble. We jess wanna talk to the husband. Understand? Comprende?"

... In her sleeping bag Darcy had found the cell phone and the pistol, a Sig Sauer 250. With her fingers she moved them next to her hips. Feeling them helped her realize the special responsibility that was hers alone. Her position in the bag did not feel quite as vulnerable as it had. She needed to be careful and think clearly.

Darcy lay still and hoped they would forget about her. At least one of these guys had a gun, probably all of them. If they knew about the pistol, she would be their first target. Toast.

"Is the husband hunting for deer? Does he have his gun," asked the biggest man, John.

He was looking all around as he talked. "What's all this shit? You ladies having a party?" He picked up the half empty bottle of scotch. "What's this?" He took a big swallow.

He ambled downhill a ways, still holding the bottle, and had a little meeting with the other two. They spoke Spanish in low tones. Darcy took that moment to send a quick text message to Jake.

'Deep trouble, send sheriff. We are on mountain where we planned', it said.

She was pretty sure the little pistol was loaded, the safety on.

Soon the three men stomped back up.

"Well, you nice ladies, we'd like to party with you, but you gotta tell us where your man is."

"Well big boy," Carol had gotten her voice back," my husband is going to be awfully mad when he hears you tied me to a tree. He'll have your ass."

"Big talk for a lady in a tree," he smiled. "Where is he? We'll let you go."

He turned to the other women.

"Do not try to leave. You can see what happens if you do.

"Now we will wait for the man to come back, and my friends would like to be friends with you. Amigos. We can eat and have drinks ... all together ... Amigos."

Pedro came close to Sally. "I want dis one," he said.

"First, I want you to take some more of the string, and tie dis one in her bag, so she won't run off while we are not lookin'."

Pedro got the twine, and straddled Darcy. He felt her legs and feet through the nylon and padding, wrapped the twine around the bag at the ankles and pulled it very tight, then tied it off. He patted her thigh as he moved off, smiled, and stood looking down at her a moment.

The wad of string was beside her. Since it had been cut from bales of hay, it was in eight-foot lengths, yellow, with a few red exceptions. Pedro mounted her again, took another string and wrapped her once more, this time just above the knees.

"That's one we won't have to worry about for a while," the huge guy said. "We can use her later."

Pedro moved back to Sally and tentatively put his arm around her waist.

"You are very nice," he said to the terrified girl. She didn't speak but snuck glances toward the trees, waiting for a chance.

< 165 >

Picnic Gone Wrong

The sky was beginning to change, and a slight breeze slipped by tickling the golden leaves. A hint of coming winter was in the air. The atmosphere on the mountain floated from suspicion and fear toward hostility. The sense of trouble was rolling into terror.

With Carol and Darcy disabled, the other three glanced often at the trees. Karen, old enough to be the boys' mother and past the age of running, tried to lighten the mood.

"OK boys, drinks are on the house," Karen said, and began mixing alcohol for her uninvited guests. She could have used one herself but decided no more today.

Pedro took Sally to the bar-blanket and they sat down. Karen noticed he had a pistol in the pocket of his baggy black pants. She looked closely at the weapon. It seemed like it could slide out if he got careless. A thoughtful bartender.

"Now that we're all amigos, you can call me TJ like my friends do."

"My husband is gonna call you worse than that," Carol said.

TJ moved very deliberately and slowly into Carol's face.

"What did you say? ... Bitch?"

"I said my husband will have your ass," she replied.

"Where is this mysterious madre chingado asshole husband?"

His face was inches from hers and she flinched away from his strong breath.

"Pedro," he shouted. "Get some more fuckin' string."

TJ's grip was very strong and he squeezed her free wrist as Pedro tied the knot. They pulled the arm out straight, and they had a couple of tree choices. They picked one and tied the wrist there. She was not exactly uncomfortable, but certainly felt vulnerable. She decided to be quiet.

"Dis girl is a lesson for you all," he said.

He followed Pedro to the bar where Karen continued making

< 166 >

drinks. Everyone seemed to be trying to keep the mood as light as possible. The three men got rather loud. They were enjoying themselves, but the all-girl, all-night group remained quiet. An hour of drinking passed with some long conversations in Spanish and a few short ones in English, mostly with Karen about the quality of her drink and her unique recipes.

"I hope you girls are having fun," TJ said.

With time ticking by, the sun was sliding west, and TJ's voice was sounding slushy. "Come on ladies. We rrr habbbing fun herrr."

Karen had been noticing the more Pedro moved around on the blanket, the more often the pistol appeared at the entrance to his pocket. One of these times it would be out. She watched carefully. The men's movements seemed to be slower than before.

Someone else noticed the sluggish behavior.

Becky had quietly moved into the aspen grove, and she suddenly split at a fast run. She burst into the meadow below in big ground covering strides. She was a large girl, athletic, and had youth on her side.

At the first instant of her departure Armando sprang up with surprising quickness and leapt into pursuit. The others watched as he headed down the hill. They were about sixty feet apart, and Becky seemed to be stretching her lead. Armando was showing great speed for a city boy on a very uneven surface, but the girl was losing him as they disappeared into some pines.

After what seemed like a long time, but was only eight minutes they reappeared, marching back up. Becky was barefoot and walked gingerly.

"She crashing on a log and I caught her," he said proudly. "Had to show her my gun to make her to come with me. Took her shoes so she can't run anymore." He held the shoes up like a prize, but nobody cheered. Armando was breathing hard, and Becky had some scratches on her cheek, a rip in her pant leg and a tear in her eye.

"Here's a drink," Karen offered.

"In jesta minute."

He took a hold of Becky, and twisted her arm up behind her back, forcing her to her knees.

"Pedro, get the twine."

She begun struggling and screaming. She was much stronger than she looked, and freaking out. TJ joined the fray and they held her down. Pedro was slow, and when he finally arrived, they rolled her on to her stomach and pulled off her coat. She wrestled against them all the way. Finally, when they had her hands tied together behind her back, they stood up gasping for air. Becky finally stopped yelling.

Calmer now, everyone was looking around.

Pedro was in the aspens throwing up. He looked terrible. And Sally was missing.

"Shit, we lost one," said TJ. His words sounded more like "Shed we sloshed un."

"Well, fuckin' summovitsh," Armando mumbled. He looked at his trophy on the ground, face down, wrists up. Her fleshy little fingers curled and uncurled. He sat down next to her and said, "Hey girl, I hope you're not cryin' ..."

Tenderly, but with some effort, he rolled her onto her back and bent close to see her eyes. She spat in his face.

"You bitch," he said and grabbed the collar of her shirt and ripped it open. There was a bra, and he got his knife and cut it off. He stood up, moved to the bar and sat down hard on the blanket.

"That will let her cool off," he said. "She's not going any-where."

He needed to sit a minute and catch his breath.

The sun was lower, and the sky was starting to color a bit. The temperature was dropping.

Darcy, her hand clasped on Jake's gun, lay quietly in her bag, watching.

< 168 >

Karen, too, was watching.

Pedro was somewhere near, in the trees, but his gun now rested near her knees, hidden under the edge of the blanket.

Carol was wishing she had her coat.

"Hello TJ," she said politely.

TJ was sitting on the bar-blanket ignoring the Vodka-Scotch-special standing beside him.

"This is really getting fucked up," he mumbled to himself. "¿Cómo llegamos a esta estúpida situación?" and then he heard Carol.

"Hello. Hey TJ, hey, I want to ask you something, please."

"¿Que? What now?" TJ groaned. "Damn it all anyway." He got up carefully.

"Si?"

"TJ, I'm cold. Do you think I could get my coat?"

He looked at her, then slowly reached in his pocket and pulled out a long switchblade knife, with a very unusual shape, brass knuckles and strange design on the handle. It looked like some kind of gangster weapon. He held it before her eyes a few seconds.

Then he moved it to her throat and cut her UCLA sweatshirt from the neck to the bottom. Slowly and methodically, he cut along the tops of the arms and the gold and blue cloth slipped to the ground. Her natural reflex to cover herself caused her fists to tug at the bonds, but the only result was the twine biting at her wrists. She clenched her teeth and glared at him. There was no bra and he smiled. The sudden cold caused her to shudder, her pink nipples as hard as dried raisins. Carol stood still, frozen.

He moved behind her then, reached down and grabbed an ankle and jerked her foot up behind her, then pulled off her shoe. She hopped one-legged, trying to regain her balance. TJ switched feet and repeated the procedure.

In front of her again, TJ unzipped her jeans and bent down and grabbed the cuffs. He locked eyes with her for just a moment, then suddenly stood, pulling her pants off, jerking her feet out

< 169 >

from under her. She momentarily hung suspended by her wrists, the strong hay string pressing into the flesh. She scrambled to get her feet back for support.

TJ took out his unusual knife again, and cut the black silk panties away, revealing the thick patch of dark hair.

Armando got up and moved close to see the naked lady. TJ mumbled something to him in Spanish, and he responded. Slowly, deliberately, TJ took off his pants and shorts. His movements almost suggested he was performing a secret ritual. Then he folded them into a little bundle and tossed them aside. Armando did the same, his pants landing near the foot of Darcy's sleeping bag.

Karen stood up. Darcy sat up. Their positions offered a side view of the action about fifteen feet away. They saw Carol squirm a little as TJ moved toward her. He was erect. He paused then, and started to bend, as though reaching for her ankles.
Bang.

The sound was loud and crisp, like the crack of a bull whip.

It seemed to elevate TJ into the air, spinning him, and when he hit the ground, it was like a man without legs. His leadership was replaced by pain and confusion. Totally out of gas.

Carol did a quick little dance to keep from touching the thrashing man at her feet.

It took a few moments for Armando to realize what had happened.

"Fuckin' farmer's back ... where?" ... he muttered. Unsure where the shot came from, he lunged for his pants and gun.

"STOP!' Darcy screamed.

His face reflected a mind turning over options. On hands and knees, he was about five feet from his bundle, seven from the muzzle of the gun pointed steadily at his face.

"Just give me a reason and you'll be dead," she yelled, trying to sound calm.

He was gathering himself for something ... when a chair slammed down on his head.

< 170 >

Karen had hit him with the heaviest of the folding chairs, not one of the new plastic kind, but metal, built to last a lifetime. He rolled on his side, grabbing at his head, and she smashed him again. She ducked away but was back in about six seconds with the gun from under the blanket.

She crouched near him, and poked the pistol into his knee, and pulled the trigger.

Click.

"Damn," she said.

"The safety," Darcy said.

"No," Armando said.

Karen glanced at the gun and moved the little lever.

"Don't do it you crazy bitc … Yeoooooshitfuckkk," howled Armando, grabbing his ruined knee and rolling in pain. "Why? Tu horrible criatura podrida."

Karen jerked the pants away before Armando could decide what to do next. She dug in the pants and found his gun. She then pointed both at him rather theatrically.

"You dirty que nuestro Señor te envíe a vivir con el diablo."

"Shut up, party boy," Karen ordered.

"You shot my knee you rotten old mother."

"Pedro's gun shot you. I just touched the trigger," she said. "Are you listening?"

She moved where she could look the moaning fellow in the eye.

"You can keep on your whining, if you like, but if you say anything, anything at all, to any of us, I will shoot your other knee." Karen let that sink in. "I might just shoot it anyway."

Then, for effect, she shot a hole in the wad of pants.

"OK, Darcy, you got all the guns," Karen said as she put them above the sleeping bag.

She found the fancy knife in TJ's wadded pants, and another gun. She added the pistol to the pile by Darcy and cut the strings holding her legs with the knife.

< 171 >

Then Karen cut Carol loose, then Becky.

Carol stretched, rubbed her wrists, and looked down at the struggling man near her feet. He seemed to be trying to get his elbows under him to get up but was having no luck. She kicked the elbow out of the way and let him flop on his side. She squatted and tried to pee on his head. The effort was only slightly successful, with his squirming, and her dodging his attempts to grab her ankle, but she made her point.

Carol pulled her pants on, trembling, got her shoes and went for her coat. She was shivering like a wet puppy on a cold porch.

Darcy found the pile of twine and they helped Armando crawl and drag himself to a tree and tied him there. He was upset, still dangerous, and at one point Karen used her chair on his head again.

"Surprised I had to do that," she said. "I thought you'd be pretty hammered by now ..."

She looked at him closely. "Oops, I think you have a bloody nose."

They all tied him, with his back to a tree, hands together behind it. Each one participated, twine over twine, and they carefully inspected each other's work. Armando looked like he might be getting sick. A semi-naked fly trapped in a golden web.

"We may be cutting off his circulation," Karen observed.

"Hell, yes you are ..."

"Shut up," said Karen as she picked up the heavy chair. "Do we care about circulation?"

No one cared.

Finally, they focused on TJ.

"I tried to shoot his pecker off," said Darcy. "I guess my aim was off."

"No wonder you missed, girlfriend, the little tiny thing's wigglin' around, hard to see, and doesn't make much of a target, that's fer shure," said Carol, getting her revenge in bits and pieces.

TJ muttered something no one understood, but Carol smiled,

< 172 >

knowing he'd acknowledged her opinion.

"It seems to have missed any arteries, the wound only dribbling a little blood. What a pussy," Carol said, stepping back and folding her arms.

But her examination had only included the entry wound.

The other women used a three-foot stick to examine him, poking and prodding to turn him over and test his reflexes. The nine-millimeter bullet had gone into his hip and left a small ugly hole, but on the other side the damage looked much worse. It had taken some of his hip joint bone with it as it ripped its way out. That side was bleeding into the remains of Carol's sweatshirt, turning the blue and gold material brown and black. There was substantial blood, and he was conscious, but weak and sick. He looked terrible. Getting weaker and sicker, he was writhing in pain. The ladies all stepped back as he began to vomit.

"What shall we do with him?" Becky asked. Her shivering and shaking had subsided a little and her mood was much brighter. It was the question on everyone's mind.

"I could shoot him in the other leg, that way, he'll stay put a while." Darcy sounded deadly serious.

"We can tie him to a tree if there's any string left. That hay string is tougher than nails," offered Carol, "I should know."

"Problem with that is, he's a mess. I don't think any of us wants to touch him," said Karen, holding the stick.

"True enough."

"If he had pants on, we could pull him by one leg."

"But he doesn't." A new voice, and they all looked at Sally.

Of course they all hugged. Grateful. She hadn't gone far, she said, just hid back in the trees waiting to see what was going to happen.

"So, what did we decide about TJ?"

"Let's keep an eye on him, and if he tries to escape, I'll just shoot him some more," said Darcy.

"If it comes to that, I'd like a turn," Carol said. Her shivering

< 173 >

had begun to recede.

Look," she added, "we are about to get our sunset ... But first, let's tie up Pedro. He's passed out next to that tree ... and Karen, is there anything left to drink?"

Asthe orange ball slid down into the Wasatch Range, and the leftover light had passed pink on its way to yellow ochre and headed for gray, help arrived.

The scene that greeted Marvin and Jake was not what they expected.

Darcy and Becky were in coats and lawn chairs, Darcy with a pistol in her lap. Carol, her red coat zipped up to her ears, peeking out of her bag, Sally and Karen in their bags half in and half out. They had moved their sleeping area about ten yards up the hill. Their prisoners had started to stink.

Three other chairs were strewn around where the bar had been, along with empty bottles and some piles of baggy pants. It was very calm, the ladies watching the western sky changing colors.

When Darcy saw Jake, she yelped.

"Wow. A sight for sore eyes."

"That's my line," Jake said.

There were hugs spread around, some tears of relief and joy, and everyone got their share—except, of course, the captives. Marvin was glad to finally put his heavy backpack down.

Then they began to chatter like chipmunks, slowly at first, then more excitedly until the sheriff said hold on, one at a time. The adventure had been complicated enough that they all agreed to meet at the sheriff's office, tomorrow if possible, and debrief. Meanwhile, under the heading of first things first, and since they were rapidly losing their light, they gave Marvin and Jake a quick guided tour of the scene.

"Here is a pile of weapons, three handguns, and a very unusual specially decorated sharp knife." The primary narrator

< 174 >

was Karen.

"TJ's pride and joy," said Carol.

"Stepping over here, you see a passed-out young gangster tied to a tree with a hay string. And moving over this way, here we have an unhappy captive with no pants and a sore knee, tied to a tree with more string. Perhaps he should be handcuffed, 'cause I notice his string may be too tight. Just look at those little hands.

She checked his face, "You OK, honey?"

"Moving on. Between those two trees there is another gangster with a bullet hole in his butt."

"He's pretending to be unconscious, 'cause he thinks Darcy is going to shoot him some more," said Carol as she poked him with her toe. It may have been more a kick than a poke. "He seems to have lost his erection."

"It looks like he's missing his pants, too. You ladies pretty well have this handled," Sheriff Marvin marveled.

"But we have a problem. The road down there is blocked by the car these guys came in, and I need a wrecker to tow it out, but he can't start till morning. Jake and I came up from the blocked area, and it's a long dangerous hike from here. Probably impossible in the dark. So, I don't see how we can get you home tonight. I'm very sorry."

"That's OK," Carol said. "We sort of like it here. Right, girls?"
There was a less than enthusiastic yes.

Marvin had a small first aid kit and did the best he could with TJ and Armando. He had handcuffs, so the bad boys got spaced far apart hugging trees.

There was some sitting and talking, shaking and a little sobbing. As night rolled in, they were soon in their bags, watching as the stars began to appear, trying to sleep. Marvin poked around with his flashlight and did what he could.

Darcy was one of the last to go to bed, and she invited Jake to join her, but it looked way too crowded and didn't seem right, so

< 175 >

he curled up in the grass with the blanket that had been the bar. His pillow was some gloves he found in the old green and white truck.

Carol's voice whispered in the darkness, "Are you OK, girlfriend? I hear you murmuring."

"That was the Episcopal Lord's Prayer from my childhood. Haven't said it in decades." Then she added a little louder, "Thank you for protecting us all, in Jesus' name, Amen. And the Great Buddha's name. And Muhammad's. Just covering my bases here, Lord. Amen."

"Amen," Carol repeated.

Jake could hear the ladies talking low but couldn't tell what was said.

Thanks, God, they're all right, crossed his mind.

About to fall asleep, Jake heard some rustling noise not far away, as Marvin lay down. Jake let him share half the blanket.

"This is the all-girl, all-night group?" Marvin asked the sky.

"Yep."

"Wow. Don't tell Kay I spent the night with 'em."

Above, the heavens were alive with stars, so thick they filled the entire night. There was no room left up there for even one more.

< 176 >

Marvin the Sheriff

M arvin's office in Kamas was tiny, compared to the Forest
Service headquarters, which was small enough. And although
he went to the police academy, his law enforcement style reflects
more of his cowboy life than anything very official. As for keeping
up with the latest investigation techniques, he preferred logical
thinking and intuition to labs and scientists. Years fighting crime
had made him older, wiser, and a bit bulkier. His moustache had
turned from dark brown to gray.

His office phone was usually answered by a woman with a
voice like a valentine. Her name was Molly. Not tall, but with an
athletic body and almond-shaped green eyes set in a comfortable
mocha-colored face, she didn't look old enough to have teenage
children—but she did.

The morning after the night Marvin spent with the all-night
girls everything got hectic. It started at first light when a family of
magpies began their wack, wack, wack, presumably discussing the
previous night's party. Meadowlarks and the others with pretty
voices had gone south to sing, but these black and white birds
hung out all year-round.

Trapped on the mountain with magpies, Jake, and the women,
Marvin had to work on the cell phone.

In the office the phone did a lot of ringing:
… "What do you mean, you slept on the mountain all night?"
asked Molly.

Pause, listening.

"OK I'll wait, but I want all the details."

Pause, listening.

"OK, yep … OK, got it … Right away … I'm writing all this
down … helicopter? OK got it!"

That was how the morning went for Molly.

< 177 >

On the mountain Marvin did what he could, but, limitations on him were causing frustration. The helicopter would come, but when? Prisoners needed medical help badly and must be fingerprinted and interviewed. We need to get the Lexus out of the way and get these ladies back to their homes, lives, and husbands. We have to get evidence bags up here and try to preserve what we can.

The ladies must be interviewed, preferably with Molly present, maybe with a mental expert as well, one at a time. Marvin's mind was buzzing.

Marvin tried to talk to the ladies, one by one, informally, offering comfort, and looking for signs of PTSD. He knew Karen, of course; everybody knew Karen. A self-sufficient woman who expressed her opinions and made decisions. She'd be fine, he thought. But the others? He wasn't sure.

As he paced around feeling the pressure, he would think of things, and call his office.

"Molly, write this down." He was driving her crazy but could not help it. She understood; she was his unofficial psychologist, confidante, and compass.

"Molly, can you find somebody with a high center big wheel vehicle we can use to haul these girls out? Maybe we can hire Billy to do that."

Or: "Hey Molly, it's me, call Finkelstein, when he goes to get the Lexus ..."

"He's on the way, Marv," said Molly.

"That's great, thanks, but if you can call and stop him, please. He won't be able to get that big flatbed thing with the winch up through those trees. I think he needs an old-fashioned tow truck and tell him to take a chain saw with him."

"OK. Marv."

"Thanks, Molly."

Jake had volunteered to do anything needed, but Marvin couldn't think of anything that didn't require a two-hour walk to

< 178 >

the Lexus and the patrol car, and then a two-hour steep uphill walk back.

"Molly it's me. Make sure to give the dupe keys to the patrol car to Finkelstein, because I think I'm blocking him, and hey, by the way, Molly, I'm gonna try to wean myself from calling you, cause my cell battery is gettin' low."

"I'll surely miss you, boss," she said sweetly, and hung up.

Waiting, walking, socializing. Marvin chatted with his prisoners a little. He had them handcuffed, hugging large aspens, so far apart they would have to yell if they wanted to communicate. He wanted to get them behind bars and question them, but on the mountain, there might still be things to learn.

Pedro, the youngest, seemed mean and vicious. Behind the anger, there was a sort of innocence. No morality in him, but maybe there's something to learn, with a little time.

Armando was a hard case. He didn't even enjoy the sunrise. Marvin had pointed out how the peaks seemed to glow just before the sun appeared. He asked nothing about the night before, just a happy guy in a sheriff shirt, peeking around the tree, acting friendly. Actually, he was killing time, waiting for the chopper. Finally, Armando got serious.

"Hey man, could I have my pants?"

"Wish you could. We have to keep those pants as evidence."

"Mother assholefucker," Armando said.

"Listen, Armando, I'd like to keep that ugly little thing covered as much as you do, because it's causing a lot of wisecracks among the ladies."

"Fuggoff."

"How's the head, Armando?"

"Fuck you asshole."

"That older lady packs a wallop, I guess."

"Besa mi culo."

"I see you are bilingual. That's something to be proud of," said Marvin, giving him a friendly smile, and making a mental note to

< 179 >

have a bilingual officer present during the interviews with these guys.

"Why dat bitch shoot my knee? Son of a bitch hurts. She had no fuckin' reason ..."

"She explained to me you were quite a track star, specially runnin' downhill. Thought you might run off before they were done with you," said Marvin, glancing at his simple bandage. "You're lucky, I think, she missed serious bone. I'm no doc but she could have hurt you much worse."

When he looked and smelled TJ, he didn't expect much. TJ was on his back, looking at the treetops. His hands were above his head, handcuffed, with the tree that had held Carol's left hand between his elbows. His legs were out flat. The bleeding had stopped, but he looked very pale. When Marvin squatted beside him, he tried to speak.

"Man, I'm really fucked," he whispered.

"We have a helicopter coming to get you. It'll be here soon."

"That's not what I mean," he said quietly. "This shit was a big fuckup from the beginning. We should of stayed home. Don't know what we were thinkin'. Hell, obvious we weren't thinking. Acting like idiots."

He tried to get his breath. "I been shot before, ain't nothin'. I'll be fine."

He groaned and looked at the sheriff. "How we got here, one fuckup after another. We didn't plan nothin, shit just happened, one fuckup after another."

"Are you saying it's not your fault? An innocent bystander as fate hands you lemons?" Marvin asked. "Interesting story. Let me know if you get any believers."

TJ rested for a couple of long minutes, then he spoke again, "Do you think I could have my pants?"

"I'm not a doctor, but I think your hip is messed up by a bullet, and I really don't want to move you at all, till medics come in the chopper."

< 180 >

Talking about the pants reminded Marvin about the fancy knife.

"How do you feel?" asked Marvin.

"Man, I really feel shitty. Hurts like a sonofabitch, and I've got a real headache, too. That old woman can make a drink that gotta kick like a cement mule."

"I wish I had something to give you ... hang on, the medics will come soon."

A moment passed, and then the sheriff said casually:

"TJ, can I call you TJ? ... That knife you had was very unusual."

"It's my favorite possession," he whispered.

"It looks like it's brass knuckles and knife, all in one," said Marvin, straining to hear what TJ was saying.

"Part brass, part pure silver," he muttered very softly. And then a little louder. "That fuckin' knife is my best friend, I never leave it ... only the knuckle part is brass, rest is steel and silver ..."

He's fading away, thought Marvin. "Who made it, TJ? I'd like to get one."

"I been told dare's only ten in the whole world. Can't get no more."

"Who made it?"

"Got killed, that guy."

And then an important question, thought Marvin.

"How did you get it, TJ?"

"A guy, I swore not to tell," he coughed a little, and Marvin could see, and smell, that TJ had been sick in the night, about three hours earlier. TJ was the only prisoner that hadn't been moved, and it was a mess of dried blood, trampled grass, ripped sweatshirt, and human body waste.

"It had a beautiful design tooled into the silver," Marvin prompted.

"Yeah," said TJ. Marvin could hear the noise of the chopper, far away, but approaching fast.

< 181 >

"What does the design mean, TJ?" Marvin asked.

"Very secret. Special society ... no ... group ... yeah, you could call it a special society, gonna ... change ... the voice was obliterated by the throbbing rotors.

A helicopter landing close by grabbed everyone's attention.

The rest of TJ's message, actually any conversations, were drowned out by the chopper which parked just above the pickup truck in a huge cloud of dust and debris. Marvin pictured the wind from the props blowing possible evidence away.

EMT personnel clamored down trying to hurry with their bulky equipment, the rough terrain challenging balance and coordination. From below they looked a little like the Three Stooges on vacation.

Where the bar-blanket had been, they began preparing the prisoners for travel. Marvin uncuffed them and stepped back to let the medics do their work.

He talked a moment to an EMT, reinforcing the victims' status as prisoners and the importance of keeping them shackled and separated, where they can't see or talk to each-other.

"I'll visit them later," he said. "Both are super-dangerous, so be very careful."

Carol or Becky might have gone with the chopper, being the most traumatized, but they declined, claiming that the all-girl, all-nighters, all stick together. That and the fact the captives were very smelly.

The sheriff got on his cell phone again.

"Molly, it's me. Two of our hoodlums are in the chopper goin' to the hospital. Park City, unless they change their minds. I suspect they're assessing the wounds as they fly, and may decide to go to the University Hospital ... Please call the County and make sure we have some law there to meet 'em. Impress on them these cats are a serious danger."

Within another hour, the rocky trail got unstuck, and pretty

< 182 >

soon everyone was gone, including Pedro, cuffed and sullen, leaving only the sheriff Marvin, his growling stomach, and the magpies.

Billy acted as chauffeur, and then returned to act as a temporary deputy. They took pictures, filled evidence bags, and walked carefully around in the grass. Billy had returned with sandwiches, and a fresh cell phone so Marvin could keep in touch with Molly, the County, and his wife Kay. It was almost sunset when they were finally able to start down the mountain.

< 183 >

Pedro

G ood morning, Pedro," said Marvin. Pedro looked at the
sheriff but said nothing.

"Did you get a nice breakfast?"

"Si."

"Breakfast was made by the Kamas Kafe, and it's the best
breakfast in town."

Pedro was calmly sitting on the bed in his cell. Marvin was
quiet for a while.

"Remember yesterday, we told you your rights, that we can get
you a lawyer if you want."

"Where's Armando?"

"He's in the hospital in Park City," said Marvin.

"How come he's not here? You got two fuckin' cages."

"You ever been in jail before?" Marvin asked, changing the
subject.

"Fuck yes," he answered boldly.

"Ever stayed overnight?"

"No," a quieter answer.

"Not till now?"

"Si." Pedro looked at the sheriff. "Where's TJ?"

"He's in the hospital, Pedro. He got hurt pretty bad."

"What happen ..."

"While you were sleeping, one of the girls shot him." Marvin
decided to let this float around. He asked Molly to join them.

Pedro seemed surprised. "Colored lady?" slipped out of his
mouth.

"I'm a lady," she said, "and I'm black."

"Oh."

"Does that bother you?"

"No," Pedro said. "I seen 'em before."

After a moment's pause Pedro tried a pathetic little smile.

< 184 >

Molly and Marvin sat down on the little bench across from the cells.

"This is Molly, Pedro. She's here to help you if I'm gone somewhere," Marvin said.

"Hola!" Molly smiled.

"Hola," Pedro said. They were all quiet for a while.

"Which one?" Pedro asked. "Which one shot TJ?"

"I don't know, Pedro, I wasn't there," said Marvin.

"Was it Sally? Is she OK? Pretty girl."

"Sally's fine. She's home with her husband now," Marvin explained.

"Husband? Did that motherfucker come back? Did Armando kill the bastard? Fuckin' truck, damn farmer."

"The ladies were not Mormon polygamists, they were just ladies having a picnic," Marvin explained. "They were not waiting for some man."

"Jes ladies? Oh shit," he said. "Fuck me." He thought for a minute. "But then, where's the farmer that drove the ugly truck? Did he come back? Who killed him?" Pedro asked, his mind searching. He seemed a bit confused.

"Pedro ..." Marvin said. "He was not there."

The room was quiet, then Marvin said, "Do you want us to get you a lawyer?"

"Shit no, TJ will fix us up. No sonofabitch lawyer."

"If you want us to call one, just ask Molly ... OK?"

"Call TJ?"

"No, he's in the hospital. I mean if you want a lawyer, just ask Molly."

There was another pause, and Molly smiled at him.

"So, Pedro, what were you guys doin'? How did you find those ladies?"

"Shit, we were in the Lexus, jes hangin', you know, just restin'," Pedro said, wondering how much to tell. "We were minding our own business."

< 185 >

"And then ..." Marvin prompted.

"Then we saw the ugly truck, and thought we'd follow it, you know."

"Follow a truck full of ladies?" said Marvin.

"We didn't know it was ladies. We thought it was the asshole farmer."

"So why follow the farmer?"

"We don' like that farmer."

"So, if you caught him, what then?" Marvin asked.

"Shit, I don know. Ask TJ."

"He's in the hospital, so I have to ask you. What do you think would happen if you caught him?"

Pedro thought carefully. "Maybe we'd just fuck him up a little."

"Kill him ... you mean?" Marvin asked.

"Shit, I don' know. We don' like him, you know."

"How come you don't like him?" asked Marvin.

"Cuz he fucked up Cookie ..."

"How's that? What did he do to Cookie?"

"Cut his hand off, is what he did. Cookie is really messed up."

"I understand," said Marvin. "That's too bad. I hope Cookie will be all right."

There was a little quiet moment.

"Well," Marvin said. "We'll let you get some rest and probably get you a burger from Dick's for lunch. Do you like milkshakes?"

Pedro nodded, and Molly and the sheriff started to go, when Marvin stopped.

"Pedro, did you ever meet this farmer?" he asked. Pedro could not think of an answer.

< 186 >

Molly

Molly knew the sheriff wanted to talk to Pedro again after lunch. When she figured Pedro was through eating, she went down the little hall to the windowless cement room with the steel cells. Pedro was lying on his mattress studying the ceiling. The wax paper, paper boat for the french fries, and the empty milkshake cup were on the floor.

"Hello sweetie, how was lunch?" she asked.

"OK," he said.

"Are you feeling all right?"

"I wish Armando was here, you got two fuckin' cells."

"I can't help that. I'm sorry. I could get you some magazines if you want."

"Fuckin' police gazette? I don' think so."

Molly smiled. She wanted to say that our subscription to the Gang Bangers Journal had expired, but actually, in her most motherly voice said, "If you have a headache or anything, I have aspirin I could get for you."

"I could really use a blunt, just now," Pedro said.

Molly thought about that a long moment. Of course the answer was no. It might, however, improve Marvin's chances, when he interviewed the kid later. Where would she get it anyway? The evidence room, of course. There are five that were found in the Lexus.

"Pedro, please push your garbage over here under the bars so I can get it."

Molly saw the wheels turning in the boy's head. Nothing else was said, but soon the wrappers and paper cup were replaced by a marijuana cigarette and a match.

When Marvin returned to the office and sat down, he sniffed the air.

< 187 >

"How's our prisoner?" he asked.

"He ate his burger and he's resting now. He still had a little hangover, but I think he's ready to interview. And, by the way, boss, I think we miscounted as we sorted evidence yesterday. We recorded five joints in the Lexus, but actually it was only four."

"Are we talkin' code here, Molly?"

"Yes."

They interviewed Pedro then, making friendly small talk at first. There was a slight odor in the air. It was vague, but if you had parents who were cool in the 1960's it was recognizable right away.

When they gradually got to business, Marvin brought up the question that remained from the earlier conversation.

"So Pedro, that farmer with the ugly truck. How did you first meet him?"

"Man ... I don' know. Shit, I never really seen 'im."

"Was it with Cookie in the barn?"

"No, I wasn't even in the barn till all the shit about Cookie's got no hand."

"So then when did you first meet him?"

"Never met him, never saw him."

"So, Pedro, if I brought him in here, you wouldn't recognize him?"

"No."

"So you were going to kill a guy you'd never seen?"

"Maybe we wouldn't kill him, just whoop 'im up a bit."

"To a guy you'd never seen?"

"I'd seen him, but the headlight was in our eyes, so we seen 'im, he yelled at us, pointed a fuckin' rifle at us, shit, we seen him, but we didn't. You understand what I mean?"

So then, Marvin, keeping it friendly, said "So when you saw him, it was when he stopped you guys from beating Arturo."

"Uh huh."

"When you were with TJ, Armando, and Cookie, and Cookie

< 188 >

had the bat."

"We all used the bat, but Cookie was the best."

"Why did you want to punish Arturo?"

"I didn't give a shit 'bout him, was TJ said we had to do it."

"TJ hated Arturo?"

"No man, it was just a job," Pedro said.

They talked to Pedro for about an hour and then let him get a nap. And back at their desks in the office, Molly said, "I don't think he realizes that they killed Arturo that night."

And Marvin said, "So we only found four joints in the Lexus, huh?"

< 189 >

The Extra Special Knife

Something about that extra special knife bothered Marvin. It had a homemade spirit about it despite the fine craftsmanship. The switch blade aspect was not unusual but in combination with the brass knuckles it seemed designed for a street fight. Yet it was built like an art piece that could comfortably reside in a museum.

That knife flashed across the sheriff's brain at odd times, like a crazed mouse in dim light, never stopping in plain view, but darting past when it was least expected. Marvin would turn that knife over in his head whenever he had a spare moment. Sooner or later, he expected to remember something about it.

One day as he was patrolling around leisurely, he stopped at Jake's, and wandered around the barn. The smells and sounds of horses relaxed him and took him back to gentler times. Outside he leaned on the fence looking at livestock in a pasture, when it struck him. A memory and a shock.

He had heard a description of that knife thirty years ago. That was the memory. The shock was that he remembered seeing it. At Peter Ernst's house. On a green pillow.

Peter Ernst died on a hunting trip in the Wind River Range. At the time Marvin had a good pal who was a big game hunting guide working that area. Marvin had called him, and asked about the accident. They talked about a lot of things that day, but what he remembered was something about Peter's death. As Marvin remembered it, the story went like this:

"Your friend from Salt Lake City was above the tree line after a particular Big Horn ram. Trophy size. Two other guys had been with him. One was a guide I know, and the other, I'm not sure. Could have been a guide, too. Anyway, they were lower on the

< 190 >

mountain side, hoping the ram would go up rather than down into the trees. If it stays up in the rocks and snow, your friend could shoot him. Down, he probably gets away. Your friend had just crossed an ancient rockslide and was shot after he crossed it. He was shot with a big game rifle. The gun he carried was a Marlin 336, as I recall, and he was probably shot with something similar.

"They said it was a hunting accident, but nobody around here believes that. He was in plain sight with nothing anywhere near him. We don't get amateurs up that high. Somebody who knew what he was doing shot him. Dead center ...

The shooter could have been anywhere, behind him, across the valley, even above him. There were no clues at all, so they call it a hunting accident. Kinda cleans things up calling it that ...

"One thing interesting though; your friend, Peter, or whatever it is, was carrying the strangest knife you ever saw. Not a hunter's knife. Not anybody's knife. It looked part brass knuckles, and part dagger, made of brass and silver and steel. Really beautiful in an ugly way. There were pictures of it in the papers."

That was the guide's story as Marvin remembered it. He decided to have Molly find some phone numbers in Wyoming. Someone in law enforcement up there might remember the accident, or the knife.

Maybe they could find a photo of it.

< 191 >

A Chat with TJ.

You 're looking well," Marvin said.

"Where's my attorney?" TJ asked, peeking out of the white sheets.

"I understand you are making deals, and trading information, and all of that. After my initial investigation, I'm all out of the loop. You have your public defender, or attorney, and they have their DA. I just dropped by to see if you are all right."

"You notice my good leg is chained to the bed?" TJ offered.

"Other than that, are you feeling OK?"

"Yeah, physically. They installed a new plastic hip, thanks to the taxpayers. But it'll be a long fuckin' time before I feel anything but shitty."

"Do you remember me?" Marvin asked.

"Maybe. Weren't you the sheriff at the scene?"

"Yes."

"Wouldn't give me my fuckinmotherfuckin pants."

"Sorry about that, we had to keep 'em for evidence."

"You bastard, you embarrassed me."

"Yes, it probably was embarrassing, being exposed on a mountain top."

"How come you're here anyway? Bring me flowers? Wanna be pals?"

Marvin thought a moment.

"I brought you some coffee." He took it out of a paper bag and handed it to the patient. Marvin pulled up a chair and sat down.

"Have you had a chance to talk to your little friends?" he asked.

"Only with attorneys present. About impossible to have a real conversation, without some fucker tellin' us what we can't say and what we can. Those boys have their own defenders, and none of it makes any sense. Those two boys don't know shit about shit."

< 192 >

"I think they're going to be implicated in Arturo's murder," Marvin said.

"Yes, I know, me too. Go figure."

"Well, other guys are handling all of that. Want a donut?"

"Sure."

Marvin dug one out of the paper bag and passed it over.

"I want to ask about something you said on the mountain. Has nothing to do with the crimes, really, but it has me curious."

"Yeah?"

"You had an amazing knife."

"No shit."

"I've never seen one like that."

"No shit," he repeated.

"You told me there were only ten in the world."

"I did?"

"Yes."

"I musta been woozy, I was pretty messed up."

"Probably were."

"What else did I say?" TJ asked.

"You thought that the guy that made it had passed away and couldn't make any more. That you got it in a special ceremony, from a special group. A secret society, of some sort."

"That's all bullshit, I was out of my head."

"TJ," Marvin said, "I'm not investigating your crime, and I know you're making deals with various elements of the judicial system, and all tangled up with your various legal problems, but I'm only here to bribe you with donuts, and talk about your knife. I love knives, and collect them," Marvin lied. "Knives are my passion. And you told me on the mountain that knife was your best friend. I'm asking you about it, as one knife lover to another," Marvin paused, looking very sincere. "That was the most beautiful knife I have ever seen."

"So why should I talk to you? What the fuck I get out of it?"

"Your knife is in an evidence locker, somewhere, and I do not

< 193 >

think it is relevant to this case. It might be possible to get it back for you, once this is all wrapped up. I can't promise, but maybe I could get it for you. Maybe ...

"But before I try, I'd want to know everything about it."

"You think I'll tell you shit about it, on your stupid maybe?" TJ said.

Marvin stood up to leave. "It wasn't just a maybe," he said. "There was a donut and coffee, too."

"Brass and real silver," TJ said.

Marvin sat back down.

"So, who has these ten knives?"

"I'm not squealing on any guys, man."

"I'm not asking you to. There is no crime to owning a nice knife."

Marvin waited; he was in no rush.

A nurse came in, moved something and checked a gauge, made a note on a chart, and left.

"Tell me about the decoration on the silver, and the secret society," Marvin asked gently.

Gradually at first, the story came spilling out. Four young punks and a middle-aged criminal tried to form a secret crime business. One of their members was the designer and craftsman who created the ten matching items, part switchblade knife, and part brass knuckles, all in one. This was over thirty years earlier, when TJ was still in diapers, but he knew the story. In those early years, there was an occult ceremony involved. It included pledging allegiance to secrecy, and to the other members. Gradually, over the years, that aspect of the group had been neglected, but the bond among the original five remained strong.

Except, the five are now only three. The craftsman was killed in a territorial squabble with another drug gang, and another original member died in a hunting accident. And now, there are five newer members who also possess those knives.

"So who are the members with knives?" Marvin wanted to

< 194 >

know.

"I swore not to tell," TJ said.

"Well, we know you have one, now residing in an evidence drawer somewhere. And I expect Prince and Frederico probably have one, maybe one each," Marvin said, guessing.

"How do you know those guys?" asked TJ.

"Just guessing. How about Peter Ernst?"

"Fuck me. How did 'ja know that. Shit, he was one of the originals."

"Peter was a friend of mine," Marvin said. "I know he had one of those knives."

"Man, you're the strangest fucking sheriff I ever met."

"Call me Marv, TJ."

"This is gettin' weird, man."

"So, let's review. Prince and Frederico, two originals with knives. Peter, with a knife. You have one. Who else?"

"Man, you're freakin' me out."

"How about Buck Francis? Wally Archer?" Marvin was guessing wildly now.

"I'm done with your shit, man. I'm not givin' you any names. Your donuts are too fuckin' sweet anyway. I'm gonna get a sleeping pill. Preguntas estúpidas del molesto sheriff, sal de mi cara, idiota. We're done here. Shit."

TJ pushed a button on a white cord attached to his bed.

< 195 >

Tracking Knives

When Marvin got back to his office, Molly had fresh coffee ready.

"Good morning, boss."

"Good morning, Molly, thanks for the coffee."

"Where ya been?" The clock suggested he was a bit late this morning and her expression told him she had noticed.

"I visited our pal TJ in the hospital. Trying to make friends, kind of an unofficial visit. I was trying to find out more about his strange knife. I wish I'd taken you, that might have made a little softer presence. He's still mad at me for makin' him sleep without his pants."

"I never got to meet him," Molly said. "Is he nice? Would I like him?"

"No, and No. But we might have learned more if you were there."

"How's he feeling, being such a famous pervert, and all? Rumors starring his body parts are circulating. He must be proud of himself."

"What kind of rumors are you promoting, Molly?"

"Oh, I don't know. Maybe if his body part had been bigger, she'd a been able to hit it. Instead a missin', and hittin' his big fat ass," said Molly. "Stuff like that."

"Do I detect a lack of motherly concern?"

"Yes, you do."

"To quote him directly, he feels shitty. And that's how he looks too. Said they gave him a new hip, but he may be a bit confused about that. He's been fighting infection, and other problems, and the nurse said he's probably going to get a new hip someday. Anyway, he's got tubes everywhere, and looks pretty sick and hurt."

As they sipped the coffee, Marvin told Molly about the secret

< 196 >

crime club, and what he knew about who had those ten knives.

"I found out that Peter Ernst was one of the five original members. And, that a couple of the guys Ray Whorton talked about, Frederico, and Prince, were originals also. Founding members. And I think maybe Buck Francis."

"You think?" Molly looked quizzically at Marvin.

"I guessed, and his reaction seemed to suggest I might have hit a nerve."

"So you hope I'll get as interested in these knives as you are, and help you search for them."

"That is my hope."

"You probably think it would be a good idea to send pictures to all our law enforcement neighbors, and ask them to keep an eye out for those knives and contact us if they find one."

"It's like you're reading my mind."

"Your mind is easy reading." Molly smiled.

"And while we're on that subject, please see if you can locate TJ's knife. It's probably in some evidence locker, in the court-house in Coalville."

"Do you want it?" Molly asked.

"No, we have tons of photos, I just would like to know its location."

"I'll see what I can do."

"I told TJ that, maybe, we could find it. It's his favorite toy."

"I'll find it, Marvin, but we are not giving it back to that killer."

"Of course not, Molly, but wouldn't it be nice if I could give him a photo of it hanging on our wall with a tag that said 'PROPERTY OF TJ'."

"You do remember, your new best friend is a pervert, probably going to prison for life."

Marvin said he would remember.

And Molly sent photos to law enforcement with a note and took over the search for knives.

< 197 >

Chilling Out

At the top of Little Bald Peak, the view to the east includes the Jordanelle Reservoir and Heber City, thousands of feet below. Looking horizontally the spectacular Uinta Range goes into Colorado and disappears into the sky.

If you were a skier, access would be gained from the huge Deer Valley parking lot, up a lift to Silver Lake, then left on a simple trail, another lift, then a twisted blue run, then another chairlift, and there you are.

If you had come to Deer Valley from Kamas, you could have approached the resort from the Mayflower side, where parking was harder to find. Then you'd have gone up the Jordanelle Express Gondola, swinging high above a complicated network of interlacing roads, bridges, and ski runs, over huge homes of stone, logs, steel, and glass. The only way into these homes was a long, steep winding snow packed road, or ski-in and ski-out.

"What did you pay for this hideout?"

"Seven and a half million."

"Well, brother, it's worth it."

The two men were on a huge tan leather couch, their feet upon a giant log coffee table, looking at the incredible view. The snow was deep, fresh, and light, and the sky was dark blue, and pure as well. The huge fireplace was stone, from the floor to the high ceiling, two stories tall.

"Chillin' out. Man, this is the life," said Frederico Juarez. "Things get too hot in the city, we cool out on a mountain top, in four feet of snow."

He was in sweatpants and a white dress shirt, unbuttoned partway down, exposing a simple gold chain. He appeared relaxed and carefree, holding an unlit cigar between two fingers. He was barefoot.

< 198 >

Slouched at the other end of the long couch, was a tall man, in an expensive robe of intricate design with many bright colors, an elegant contrast to his olive skin. The robe seemed to enhance its owner's qualities of presence and importance. His name was Jesus Menudo.

"Are the ladies coming today?" Frederico asked casually.

"No. Maybe tomorrow or Thursday. They'll ski in. I think tonight we'll watch a movie downstairs. Order in some pizza."

"Suits me."

"Who knows we're here?" Frederico asked.

"Absolutely nobody ... except the girls. We just disappeared. They can't even track our cell phones; they're still in the city, in a drawer. The phone here is only for here, and no one knows the number. For the time being, we do not exist."

The tall man stood, moved to the floor-to-ceiling windows, and looked down. He moved like an athlete and could easily have been mistaken for a millionaire basketball player.

"No neighbors. Most all these houses are empty, except at Christmas. Maids and maintenance workers are all we have up here for company. If cops came in a car, we'd ski out the back. If cops skied in, we'd drive out the front, but cops never come up here anyway. Burglar alarm goes off, it's just a short circuit, and a rent-a-cop and an electrician answer the alarm."

Much later, after pizza, they watched "The Godfather" in the little downstairs theater and had a nightcap in the great room. They were back on the huge couch, with the room lights dimmed, so they could see the lights of Tuhaye traffic, far below, and the moon's reflection twinkling on the Jordanelle.

"Say brother, did you ever find out what happened to TJ?" Frederico asked as both men lit cigars.

"What I heard, was that somebody shot his ass off." Cigar smoke was drifting up. "I was kind of expecting him to try to get word to me, sort of hinting that he needed the help of our

< 199 >

attorney, but he got in trouble doing stuff I told him not to do—made a strong point of it, in fact, so I expect he's more afraid of me than he is of the law. He probably got stuck with a public defender. He'll be in deep trouble. He may still be in the hospital, trying to find his ass."

"Wonder what got him in trouble?" Frederico speaking, as he watched tiny traffic lights moving slowly.

"He was freelancing on his day off. His little pals were trying to kill the cowboy who chopped off Cookie's hand. They ran into some adventure in the woods, that ended with them in jail, and TJ in the hospital."

"Pedro and Armando, out on bail, maybe?" Frederico's voice reflected more curiosity than concern.

"I haven't heard, but I think they were being held for investigation in Arturo's murder. Armando was in the hospital too, with a sore knee."

"Hey Prince," Frederico asked. "Would you have helped TJ get a good lawyer, if he'd asked you?"

"I really don't know. I might have, but probably not. He picked his friends, so the buck stops with him. He used to preach attention to detail, but those guys were stupid as you can get."

The two men, relaxed, watched the world silently from their perch in the sky. After a long time, and some cigar smoke, Federico broke the stillness.

"We probably oughtta have that cowboy killed."

In the morning the house on Little Bald Peak woke up slowly. Prince left his bedroom first, wandered into the kitchen, and started the coffee machine. He had passed Frederico's door, which was closed, so he let him sleep. He was lounging on the couch when Frederico finally appeared and volunteered to scramble some eggs.

Two hours later they were struggling into their ski boots and stepping into their skis. Another bluebird day at hand, with three

< 200 >

inches of fresh powder.

Prince wore an all-black one-piece suit, a style popular twenty years earlier, and had long narrow skis. In a black helmet and goggles he would be hard to recognize. He started skiing with the most subtle unweighting and seemed to float off in a series of smooth effortless linked turns. His graceful style fit his persona to a tee. While his costume said old timer, nothing to see here, his skiing was elegant and beautiful.

Frederico, in a contemporary maroon jacket, black pants, gray helmet and yellow goggles, and modern 'shaped' skis, blended in with the tourists. He gave an aggressive push with his poles, and skied like a man looking for moguls, his movements decisive and deliberate. As planned, this looked like two friends having a good ski day. They rode the gondola up with a couple from Florida, and skied several runs before they were on a chairlift alone.

"Say Prince, have you heard anything about Cookie? Is he gonna be OK?"

"I think he lived with Doc Martin a while because it got infected. But I don't know where he is now. Probably with his mom. I imagine if he lives, he'll need a plastic hand or a hook or something. Too bad, they said he was a killer with a baseball bat."

"I heard the cowboy did it."

"I don't know. Nobody saw it happen, he just fell out of the sky, with his hand gone. But they were pretty sure it wasn't the farm dog chewing it off." Prince talked as he rocked his dangling legs. "If he lives, it'll be a good story to tell his grandchildren."

"He should probably get out of the murder business, I mean, if he wants to be a grandfather."

"We'll miss him. Have to trade him, I guess," Prince said flirting with humor.

"When we kill the cowboy, maybe we should kill the dog too ... you know, just in case. Coulda' been the dog."

Conversations on the chairlift generally end suddenly, and this was no exception. The chair closed in on the packed surface,

< 201 >

and when they felt the snow under their skis, they stood up and skied away. The chair made a sharp swing to the left and disappeared.

They skied two fast runs on Flagstaff Mountain, then skied west past the Montage Hotel, then up a lift to the top of Empire. The view from the peak was spectacular, and they made a few runs on that mountain because there was a huge mogul field for Frederico, and a long blue ridge for the stylish Prince.

Then they finally headed east for home. Their legs were burning and there were still many lifts and runs before they would be back at their hideout in the clouds.

Several days passed before the girls came. Prince and Frederico were beginning to get almost bored, as a routine settled in. Prince, responsible for coffee, Frederico for breakfast. They skied during the days, in the sun, in a blizzard, and in between. They had supper delivered, pizza or something from the Purple Sage where they tipped the delivery driver more than the price of the rather expensive meal. They would watch a movie, or play a game of pool, or sometimes lie around watching the view and chatting. They were enjoying their first real vacation.

But, sure enough, one late afternoon, the door to the ski run opened, and a commotion of banging equipment, stomping boots, giggles, and chattering announced the girls. Warmly welcomed and shown around, they loved everything.

The huge house had bedrooms for everyone, and a great room, living room, theater, game room, dining room, two small offices, and more. Bathrooms were everywhere.

Eloise O took ownership of the kitchen and ordered a huge collection of supplies from the Fresh Market to be delivered. The list was long enough it caused Prince to ask the girls how long they were planning to stay.

"Till spring?"

The only answer he got were a pair of cute smiles.

< 202 >

Eloise set a high standard in the kitchen, and, after supper and some brandy, the cigars came out. Everyone settled in the great room, in front of the panoramic view. Eloise curled like a cat on the tan leather, declined a cigar, and lowered her eyelids to half-mast. The girls had skied all day, and she claimed to be pooped.

Prince turned to Jenece Ocalla.

"So Babe, what's up in the city?"

"Where to start?" She smiled at him. "The world down there seems so far away. It's paradise up here."

"Well, we're very glad you two are here. I think we were starting to get on each other's nerves. Playing pool every night is driving us crazy."

"It's his house, so I gotta let him win, and it's starting to wear me out," said Frederico.

"See, we're bickering already. Too much paradise is eating us up," said Prince. "I think we're like in a cartoon, two guys stranded on a desert island."

They were all quiet for a moment.

"I guess," Prince smiled, "we are having fun here. What are we missing down there in real life?"

"Well, for one thing, moving drugs inside horses has its problems. For example, one mare recently gave birth to a bag of something, cocaine or heroin. Since it was unable to stand and nurse, they called someone, the vet, or a cop, and it caused a major distraction and problems. I think Ascension is going back to the tried-and-true methods. He's going to stop experimenting with horses for a while.

"Meantime, this law from up north, Ray Whorton, was back down with some local South Salt Lake or West Jordan law, tapping phones, and poking around some more. That's one reason we didn't come up here quicker. I was hoping we'd have a little more solid information about that, but legal news is slow to mature."

Jenece stood and put her cigar in an ashtray. She made a

< 203 >

horrible face.

"What an ugly habit!" she said, watching it struggle to death in its little metal coffin. The orange end turned gray, and the last gasp was a whiff of smoke.

"So, other than that, the drug business progresses, just about like you would expect. The murder business, however, is evolving, primarily due to TJ. We're not sure if he's cooperating with the DA or someone with the various investigations. I've got sources trying to find out. And if he is, how much is he talking? There are degrees to all this. His little gang of idiots are still in jail, one with a bad knee, so we don't know about them. I think they're getting linked to Arturo's murder through fingerprints and so forth, and, possibly some other killings, too. They may be talking some also, trying to make deals. But we don't think they really know very much, beyond their various little adventures."

"I wish I knew more about TJ," Prince said. "He knows more stuff that could be dangerous. I do think he'll stay as loyal as possible. At least I hope so."

"As for the murder business," Jenece continued, "it continues with the Polynesians. You remember Little Somba, and his band?"

"Yes," said Prince, "he had a good drummer named Flexo, who liked to kill people with a hammer, smashing skulls and chuckling."

"They mostly use guns now," Jenece said. "They've done three in the last two weeks, for the Lehi group. Nice clean jobs too."

"Jenece, if you can think of any creative way for me to communicate with TJ, please let me know," said Prince.

"I will. Nothing comes to mind right now, 'cause my legs ache, but I'll think on it," she said.

"Maybe it's time for bed," Prince suggested.

< 204 >

Murderous Plans

The foursome, side by side, poles in one hand, looking back over their shoulders, stood waiting. The fellow in the green uniform grabbed the chair, and it swung gently, chopping them off behind the knees. Four bottoms sat in unison, as the seat scooped them into the deep blue sky. The sensation was best expressed as 'Whoop De Doo.'

"So, we all agree, we'll finish the job for TJ, and his little pals," Prince announced.

"I think that would clean things up in a loose ends sort of way," Frederico agreed.

Eloise wanted to know if this guy was handsome.

"I hate to waste a good man," was how she put it.

"I don't think any of us have ever seen him," said Jenece.

"Basically, if he knew anything he would have gone to the cops, and we'd probably know. We have friends in the Summit County Court House. But assuming he can't cause trouble, is no guarantee. Letting him live is like waiting for the other shoe to drop. If we kill him, at least he'll be quiet from now on."

Prince was reviewing his thinking, out loud.

"TJ would recognize him, I expect. And Armando. And maybe Pedro, but there was some suggestion that he had passed out and missed the adventure on the mountain. So, TJ would have been perfect for the assignment, if he hadn't gotten himself shot up and caught ... and his team of clowns are probably gone forever. Which leaves ..." Prince turned his head and looked at Jenece, who said:

"The Polynesian Band."

"You liked their work?" Prince asked.

"We haven't used them yet, but the Lehi group said they were no nonsense, quick and clean."

"Little Somba, Flexo, and who else?"

< 205 >

"Little Somba, a large fellow called Turd Bird, Chico somebody, Flexo, and one more, I think," said Jenece.

They were watching skiers below as they talked.

"Little Somba must weigh three hundred fifty," said Frederico. "You said this Turd Bird is big, too?"

"Yes," said Jenece. "I'd guess six foot six, and strong, but heavy. Kinda huge. Flexo's skinny, the others, I don't know."

"I'm thinking the Polynesian Band will have a hard time blending in up there in the Kamas Valley," Frederico suggested.

"Good point."

"Maybe a lone wolf would be better."

"There was a guy from LA lookin' for that kind of work," said Jenece. "I didn't meet him, but I have a phone number."

"Is he a beginner?"

"I sure don't know."

They floated over another run, with skiers thirty feet below. A family went by, followed by a wobbly fellow who crashed. They were all quiet for a while as the chair took them into the treetops.

"Well, I guess we all know who we need," said Prince finally.

"Yes."

"It won't be easy you know. He thinks he's retired."

"I know."

"You want me to contact him?" Eloise asked.

"Yes," Prince said.

< 206 >

Wally

Wally liked good horses. He was working a six-year-old gelding he had hoped to show in the first spring contest, but he was starting to realize he wasn't going to be ready. The little buckskin was fat and saucy, eyes bright and pumped up. But Wally was finding him much too fat, and way too saucy. He had been on a complete four-month vacation, while his competition, horses from Arizona, Saint George, and Las Vegas, had been practicing all winter. They would be slick looking as seals, while the buckskin still wore his dull winter coat.

With a foot of snow melting outside, and no actual cows to work, Wally was in his barn, in a space he called his arena, with a mechanical cow. The black plastic creature was on wires that allowed it to go back and forth along the sixty-foot wall. It had three speeds and was controlled by a tiny box with buttons strapped to Wally's wrist.

The barn was cold, and the fake cow was performing on "slow." Wally's plan had been to try to keep things calm and quiet, but it wasn't working. As soon as he saw the plastic creature, the little buckskin's mind went into high gear. Quickly, he was hot and sweating. For every little move the thing made, he would make a gigantic sweep, and a huge leap. Wally handled the reins to slow him down, and the horse was getting resentful. The cutter's mantra, 'the horse's movements mirror the cow,' was not happening here. This practice was going badly, and Wally knew he should quit. He pinched the neck, the signal to stop working, and sat quietly in a cloud of steam rising from his sweating mount.

He suddenly realized he was not alone.

He rode slowly to the gate where Eloise stood and dismounted.

"Gosh, it's nice to see you," he said, as he pulled the Velcro off his wrist, and put the little control box on top of the gate post.

"You too Wally," she said.

< 207 >

He pulled a large green wool cooler off the fence and arranged it over the horse from ears to tail, saddle included. He spoke as he knelt and removed splint boots from the horse's front legs.

"I haven't seen you in months. How 've you been?"

"Been good. A bit of skiing lately," she replied.

"I'm thinking of gettin' up there some more, myself. I heard the snow was still pretty good."

"It's been great. Are you a skier, Wally?"

"I useta be fabulous, skied everyday as a kid, raced in high school and at the U of U, but I don't get up as often anymore."

He looked at his steaming horse.

"Walk with me, will you?" he asked. "I need to keep him moving."

So they walked, slowly, around the little pen leading the horse who was all ears up and attentive each time they passed the plastic cow. They chatted about some mutual friends, and how quick the snow turns to slop, once spring comes. Finally, Wally got to it.

"So, to what do I owe the pleasure of your company?"

She stopped and looked at him.

"Wally, Prince and Federico want to meet with you."

She let that sink in a moment.

"I retired from that shit," he said slowly. "They know that."

"They do know that, but hey, I'm just the messenger."

They resumed their walking. After a long pause, Wally asked, "How come they don't just call me on the phone? Are they all right?"

"They are not near their phones, they are on a vacation, incommunicado. No one knows where they are. Can't be reached. Can't be found. They have just disappeared. Period." She emphasized this with a nod of her head.

"They've disappeared, and I'm retired. I don't see how we're gonna' meet."

"Do you know your way around Deer Valley?" Eloise asked.

"Yes, I do."

< 208 >

"You know the warming hut at the top of Flagstaff Mountain?"

"Yes, I do. They call it a hut, but it's bigger and nicer, than my house. You can get a coffee or a hot chocolate for fifteen or twenty bucks. Nobody ever goes there except to pee or poo. Yep. I know it."

She gave Wally her best smile.

"Well, Prince wants to meet you there, next Wednesday, at ten thirty."

She was a little over half his age, but she put a motherly arm around him.

"You can have a very nice ski day, Honey," she said.

"Well, shit."

< 209 >

Meeting at the Summit

The tall, elegant man in the black one-piece outfit sat by the corner window with a view of snow falling through pine needles. A silent Christmas carol.

"Good morning," Wally said tentatively, and sat down. They shook hands and looked at each other.

"You forgot that I'm retired," Wally said.

Prince looked around the room. They were alone except for the opposite corner, where drinks and pastries were available, about forty feet away. At a cash register and tiny counter were two employees in forest green uniforms.

"I know you are, and I respect your decision. I'm reluctant to bother you with this problem ... but I must."

"My retirement is a firm decision," Wally said.

"Let's go outside and talk. I found a quiet place."

Three chair lifts unload at the top of Deer Valley's Flagstaff Mountain, right in front of the Warming Hut.

Prince and Wally stepped out of the quiet room, into a commotion of skiers going this way and that, sliding past each other, greeting one another, squeezing around and through the mob, checking bindings, and otherwise adding to the general confusion.

"Follow me," Prince said as they stepped into their skis. Down and to the right he went on a packed trail, winding past clusters of skiers of all abilities, dodging folks and gaining speed. Wally followed as closely as he dared. Visibility in the falling snow was a problem. The run widened. Prince hung to the left side, and suddenly sped into a narrow service road that cut left into the forest, and up. They maintained what momentum they could, but it was quickly dissipated and they coasted to a stop.

They took their skis off. The service road had been maintained only as necessary, and consequently had a packed surface under about six inches of fresh snow. Walking in ski boots, never fun, was not particularly difficult. Wally wondered where Prince was taking him, but after about thirty yards of gentle incline, the road leveled, and started down. There was nobody anywhere near, just silence and falling snow. Looking down through the trees there were glimpses of an uncrowded run fifty yards below.

Prince stopped and faced Wally. They were both breathing heavily, so they rested a few moments in the quiet wonderland.

"Wallace," Prince finally said, "we've known each other for a long, long time."

"That's right."

"I fully understand, and respect, your desires. But we have a little situation I want to explain."

"Well, you found a mighty private place to talk."

"I've learned this mountain pretty well," Prince said.

"Wallace, our regular guys have gotten themselves shot up, their hands amputated, their bodies locked into jail, and probably soon, into prison. And the heir apparent to replace those guys, is a Polynesian Band, who is efficient in the city, but would stand out like a sore thumb in a rural setting."

Yes?" Wally said.

"The mess we want to clean up, was created by our friend TJ, who's residing in the hospital while they prepare a prison cell for him. And to further complicate the situation, the guy we want to kill, is someone we have never met, or seen. We don't know what he looks like, have never seen him, and don't know where he lives."

"Prince. This is not like you. You don't know who you want to kill, and I think you hope to hire a retired gunman, to shoot somebody. Anybody. Have I got that right?"

"Yes, Wallace, you've got it right, except for one part. We might not know who to kill, but you do."

"I do?" Wally said. "I'm supposed to guess?"

"Remember when you shot Buck Francis?" Prince asked.

"Spur of the moment decision on my part," Wally claimed.

< 211 >

"Well, who was there when he died?"

"Arturo, his helper, and pretty quick a couple of cutters."

"We think Arturo visited and talked to one of those cutters."

"Might have," Wally admitted.

"Arturo was killed in the driveway of one of those cutters."

"I heard that."

"And TJ went to that cutter's ranch to kill him, and Cookie lost his hand."

"Heard that, too," Wally said.

"They were in Kamas again, trying to kill that cutter, when they all got arrested."

Prince thought a moment and continued. "You said there were two cutters there, as Buck Francis died. Do you think TJ was after the right one?" Prince asked.

"One was from Kamas, and he took the drug mare with him when he left, and the other one was from Texas, somewhere, going on to another cutting far away. So the one from Kamas is the logical choice, I guess. At least the handiest."

"So, Wallace, my old, old friend, you see why we need you?"

"I don't see why you need to kill anyone. If he knew anything, if he was a danger, I expect you would know by now. Why not let him be?"

"That would be nice, but it's gotten more complicated lately. Have you heard of Ray Whorton?" Prince asked.

"No."

"It doesn't matter. Whorton's a detective from Idaho, investigating the killing. Anyway, there are several jurisdictions of law enforcement poking around Lehi, Spanish Fork, West Jordan, and South Salt Lake, and they're tapping phones, acting closed mouth, and secretive. We are just trying to shut and lock any open doors, or loose ends, if you get my meaning."

"You want me to kill my friend?" Wally sounded astonished.

"Wallace, you've killed cutting horse guys before. You and I are real friends. That guy is just another cutter."

< 212 >

"No. I can't. He's a friend, and I'm retired."

"Wallace, you are the only person who knows this guy, you know his name, where he lives, his habits, what he looks like. Why, you probably know if his horse is any good. And you've got a dog in this fight; your ass is on the line too, you know."

Wally looked at the two pairs of skis and poles standing in the snow. Staring at the dense dark pines behind the falling white flakes, he seemed mesmerized. And the beautiful silence now felt heavy. Oppressive. He looked up at the sinister sky with the colorless dots falling down on him, melting on his cheeks and nose.

"Wallace, you know enough about me to put me in prison for life, and I know enough about you to send you to the electric chair. We know each other so well that we are friends whether we like each other or not. That, my old friend, is a fact of life."

The snow was coming harder and faster now, a blizzard. They were both looking down, watching their tracks disappearing into the white.

"Shit," Wally said. "Let me think."

Prince said nothing.

"Fuck," Wally said, "I'll get back to you."

"You can't contact me. I have disappeared," Prince said, "like our tracks in the snow. Disappeared. Period. Disappeared."

"Screwed," Wally said. "Shit."

< 213 >

Snow

Utah claims the Greatest Snow on Earth. It says so on the license plates since 1985, so it must be true. Its powder is so light, skies seem to float. The density is 8.5 percent. Winter tourists from the East freak out in the steep slopes and light white stuff. Assume a foot of new snow on a packed base, and drop a closed switch-blade knife from the height of your waist. In New Hampshire the 11.9-ounce object (338 grams) hits heavy wet snow and sinks in four inches. Maybe. If you were to pick it up and take it to Utah and drop it from a pants pocket, it would go all the way through to the packed surface a foot or two below. Lost until summer.

A powder day is one with 12 plus inches in 24 hours and Utah gets about eighteen annually. Anticipating one of these special days, the big house on Little Bald Peak got up early.

"No sleeping late tomorrow," Prince had said. "Let's make first tracks."

So, sure enough, everyone was suited up, buckled up, zipped up, and ready in the great room, watching the gondola sagging in the bright sky. When it wiggled they all cheered. When it started actually moving up, they all thumped loudly up the stairs and out the ski run door. Plastic boots across carpet and wood sound like an elephant parade crossing a covered bridge.

Skis were positioned and boots clicked in the bindings. Gloves were jerked out of pockets and put on and they all disappeared down through untracked powder, leaving twisting, curving, over-lapping paths.

And there was Prince's good luck treasure, silver, brass and steel, knifing down from his pocket, through the fresh powder, to rest on the packed corduroy a foot and half below the soft white surface. It had been set free by an entanglement with a wrist leash on a black ski glove. They came out of the pocket together, but only the glove went skiing.

< 214 >

Birth of a Legend

It was late morning in the Kamas Kafe. The owner was in the
kitchen, exploring a maze of copper tubing in the wall behind
a stove, but the front area was empty, except for John and Trixie.
She was in her white uniform, lookin' good, fresh lipstick, and
except for a coffee stain, two hours old, she appeared ready for the
lunch crowd. John may have had on a clean shirt. He was talking
geography while she might have been daydreaming. They were side
by side on the stools near the cash register.

"Oklahoma sunsets are the best 'cause there's no mountains.
Sun gets you up earlier and you go dark later, get an extra hour or
two on either end."

"Uh huh," said Trixie.

"Gives you more time to get stuff done."

"But I don't wanna do more stuff. I wanna do less stuff, and
get more night life," she said.

"How about, we go bowling tonight. Just you and me?"

"Are you courtin' me again?" she asked.

He pretended to think a long time. And then, as though it had
never occurred to him in his life, suddenly said, "Yes ... yes ma'am,
yes, I think I am."

They were two friends, sometime lovers, sitting on stools
in small town America. Playing familiar roles. Out of the cold,
content with the moment.

When in came a stranger.

Trixie jumped up quickly and became a waitress. "Sit anywhere," she said.

He looked around like a fox in an unfamiliar hen house, and
then sat on a stool near John. He had a confident air, a real
friendly guy. He wore a new red nylon ski jacket, with fresh snow
melting on the shoulders, and a long gray scarf. He took off black
wool gloves with leather trim. A Park City tourist, she decided.

< 215 >

"Coffee?"

He nodded. She poured and then, behind the counter, she found things to do.

"This is a sweet town," the stranger said. John thought the word 'sweet' sounded weird. It is not the word he would have selected.

"Uh huh," he responded.

"A beautiful valley, nice mountains, a quaint village. Skiing five minutes away."

"Well, a little more than five minutes," said John, the geography expert. "And the quaintness wears off pretty soon."

"Are you a native?" the stranger asked.

"I'm from Oklahoma, thank you, but I've been here a long time," John said, "maybe too long."

"I heard you had a little scuffle in the mountains," he said as he removed his red jacket.

"Oh yeh?" John asked, his tone invited more information, so the stranger continued.

"Yeah, I heard a local all-girls' book club got attacked, and terrorized by a crazed drug gang from LA."

John gave him an encouraging smile, and he went on.

"Apparently, these girls met in a secret location, far up on the mountain, and the gangbangers found out when and where they were meeting and trapped them there. I think the name of the secret society was, The All-Girls All-Night Long Book Club. Something like that."

Trixie was listening closely to the stranger's story.

"Incredible," she said.

"That's only the beginning," the stranger continued. "During the terrorizing, there were shots fired. Of course, the drug dealers were well armed, they always are, and in the melee, things went nuts. I can imagine the battle. These cutthroats attacking an all-girl book club. Anyway, after a while, when the police arrived, the gangsters were all tied naked to the trees, with string, and the girls

< 216 >

were in their lawn chairs, watching the sunset, discussing books."

"I wonder what they were reading?" Trixie said. "Must have been something spicy."

John looked at the stranger and said, "Yep. It's quite a story."

The stranger thought a moment. Maybe the story needed a stronger climax, so he gathered his courage, and said, "I was told one of the gangsters had his sexual organ shot off." He lowered his eyes, as he said that.

"Now THAT'S what I call real marksmanship," John said with gusto.

"Would you like to see the menu?" Trixie asked. "You'll be the first of my lunch crowd."

The stranger took his bright red coat and hung it up by the door. Then returned to his seat near John and glanced at the menu. He looked at John.

"Had you heard that story? I love it ... local history."

"Yep," John allowed. "Good story."

"I wonder when it happened? Gang stuff makes it sound like the eighties, or when drug gangs were on all the news, back when pot was illegal."

"More recent," John said. "Just this last fall."

"No way." The stranger was amazed. "Just last fall?"

"Just before the first real snow."

Trixie stood across the counter from the stranger, and leaned forward and whispered, "They planned the book club meetings in that booth, right over there," pointing toward the window area.

"Man oh man." He took a sip of his coffee. "You know these women?"

"Serve 'em all the time."

"Is it true, they tied them all up with string?"

"It was hay string," said John, "Regular string ain't strong enough for vicious gangsters."

"Man, these girls must be awfully tough."

"They're not girls, they're women, and you oughtta see 'em,

< 217 >

Trixie said, "They're really fearsome."

"Like movie stars," added John.

"I would really love to meet one of these women," the stranger said looking at Trixie. "Will you let me know if one comes in?"

"Oh, you'll know, they have quite a presence."

"They look like modern day Vikings, you can't miss 'em," said John.

"Superheroes is what they look like," said Trixie.

John realized he'd better get to work, so he stood and buttoned his coat.

"Duty calls." As he started to go, he paused. "Nice to talk to you, young man; I hope I'll meet you again."

When John was gone, Trixie paused in front of the stranger.

"You'd never guess that old cowboy was once the chess champion of Seattle, seven years in a row, and was never defeated." She gave him her sincere smile.

About ten minutes later Flicka came in and took the seat John had vacated. She was sporting a new haircut, short on the sides, standing straight up on top, adding four inches to her substantial height. It was dyed a bright green. She took off her Day-Glo yellow coat, glistening with snow that sparkled like diamonds, revealing an orange tank top and offered a quick look at the flower tattooed arm. She positioned the coat over her shoulders like a cape, unsure if she would be warm enough without it. So many bright colors all at once made it look like she'd just stepped out of a Marvel Comic Book.

She arched her back and stretched her long neck up like a cat and stuck her chin toward the ceiling for a moment. Then she seemed to relax down into herself, half closed her eyes and looked around at her surroundings.

Trixie came up on the other side of the counter, caught the stranger's eye, and winked, then glancing at Flicka.

"Coffee?" she asked.

< 218 >

Flicka smiled, nodded and sniffed the air.

The stranger, fascinated, was watching Flicka. Finally he spoke to her.

"This is a sweet town," he said.

She smiled inwardly, tipped her head slightly toward the voice, and let her eyeballs roll his way.

"It's a beautiful valley. Nice mountains, and a quaint village. Skiing only five minutes away," he said.

"Five minutes?" she said, looking at his face as though he were a baboon in a flower shop.

"Dude, you need a faster car!" she declared.

< 219 >

Branding

Direct sunlight poured through the window glass, making a distorted parallelogram on the warm wood floor. Centered in the light lay a black and brown striped cat, with four white toes and a white patch under his throat. He had notably long white whiskers, and the unusual habit of looking deep into your eyes, holding your gaze. His communication was telepathic. Neutered, his dreams probably focused more on crunchy cat food than lady cats or hunting. He might catch a mouse now and then, if it was slow, and didn't require too much planning. He was called Mickey, as in Mickey the Mouser, but that name was misleading.

Simon was seated at the kitchen table, with a cup of coffee, looking at the cat. He was not a tall man, but strong, and of substantial girth, more muscle than fat. His well-used, once black hat was upside down on the table.

"Sleeping cat looks like he owns da place." Simon said.

"That's a solar powered cat," Jake said. "He's getting charged up on the sun's energy right now. Someday all cats will be like that."

Jake looked closely at his old friend, to see if he understood. Simon spoke Spanish at home but was getting good at English. Television news had told him about global warming and alternative energy, and he sensed that Jake was being humorous.

"Solar powered, maybe, but you still gotta feed it, jes?"

"Yes." They both grinned and sipped coffee.

"Simon, you know that bay mare in the pasture?"

"Jes."

"Some criminals used her to smuggle drugs from Mexico. She's probably a racing Quarter Horse. No papers, but that's what she appears to be," Jake said.

"Jes. I heard this. They go very fast, race a quarter mile or less on a straight track."

< 220 >

"Well, there is no owner, and no brand inspector has called, so we have her, and I'd like to give her to you if you would like to have her."

"Oh My, Howdy Doody. Jake. I never had a horse of my own. Are you sure?"

"Yes. Sure."

"Gracias, thank you. Sure?"

Simon's dark face and black moustache released a large display of white teeth.

"I never had my own horse before," he repeated. "Muchas gracias, mi amigo."

"You can board her here, free, if you have no place to keep her."

"Okey-dokey, thank you Jake. How great is this?"

"Great," Jake said.

"I wanna name 'er Dorothy. Thank you very much."

"You're welcome," Jake smiled. "Dorothy it is."

They relaxed after that, looking thoughtfully at the cat, waiting for visitors.

"Good snow dis winter, maybe cows gonna be in good shape?" Simon wondered aloud.

"We'll soon know," said Jake. "We'll ride out and see. You can bring Dorothy. Would next week work?"

"Sure, I can go any day, but I hope it is not Friday, cause Jill has soccer game then."

"So, let's plan to go Wednesday then."

"OK Jake, sounds good."

"Meet at 4:30, jump the horses in and go. Get breakfast on the way, eat as we drive. Be horseback west of Delle before sunrise. Get home in time for you to have a late supper with Maria," Jake proposed, and Simon grinned.

"Jes," he said. "Das a very good plan."

"See if you have the radios, or maybe they're in the barn, and grab anything else you can think of, just put 'em in my Chevy.

Please make sure the radios are charged. I'll talk to Jimmy about doing chores. I'll have the trailer hooked up, and truck gassed."

"Okey-dokey." Simon said.

"We'll find out how the calving is going, or maybe, how it went."

It wasn't long before they were joined by John Farnsworth and Sam Skidster. Then they all went into Jake's office. Buster came in, too, tail wagging. The chairs were soft and comfortable, and Jake sat behind his desk.

"Well boys," Jake announced, "I got the call yesterday from Cindy Bollings. Byron wants to brand the third week in May."

"John?" Jake asked looking at the weathered face.

"Wouldn't miss a branding, Bud."

"Very good. Do you still have the camper back, for your pickup, John?"

"Same as last year. It'll sleep three of us easy. More, and I'll have to crawl over you with my spurs on, when I gotta pee, and at my age that's about three times per night. I'll bring it all set up, you guys just bring yer bags."

"So, Skid, we'll talk about what goes on, you just let me know what parts sound interesting. For sure the actual draggin' calves to the fire, right?"

"Yes, for sure."

"I talked to Byron, and he'd be glad to have you ropin' with us. It might be rope a pen, then wrestle calves. Or give shots or knives to testes, or somethin' not so fun. Then, next pen, back to ropin'. More than once, we had high school gorillas from the wrestling team, to flank and hold the calves. The point is, bring your back brace and leather gloves, 'cause it isn't all riden' an' ropin'. There could be some actual work involved."

"I'm in," Skid said.

"We leave Byron in charge, 'cause he owns the most cattle, and he's out there a lot. He is a serious cattleman, and his wife puts it all together. Byron's an excellent horseman and doesn't tolerate

< 222 >

yay-hoos. The cowboys will be mostly day workers, and they're the best around."

"Sure hope I don't embarrass myself too bad," said Skid, sounding concerned.

"You'll be fine. He'll have a little meeting with everyone, to remind us all how he wants it done. The cowboys work for many different ranchers, each with his own ideas," said Jake.

"At Delle we do it his way, no suggestions allowed," said John. "Won't be like Oklahoma or Texas, that's for sure. Nobody here is tied hard and fast, these guys all dally, and you'll see a few flat hats. Those guys are polite and all business in the pen. You can head or heel, be ready to do both. Just remember, it's not a timed event, it's efficiency, not speed, and be kind to the calves. Treat 'em like you own 'em!"

John paused, and added, "Those little white cotton team roper gloves might get you some comments and stares. If you need 'em, I'd get 'em real dirty first. And another thing, better get the rubber off your horn, we don't want jerkin'. Slip and slide is easier on the calves."

Jake smiled, but hoped John wasn't scaring Skid too badly.

"You'll sleep well," he promised.

"My first time with this particular bunch," said John, "a feller asked me if I was too hot, 'cause I was in a felt hat, and he was under straw. A snide remark, I thought. What a dipshit, but I think it was his idea of hazing the newcomer. Turned out, he was a fucking car dealer from Evanston, who liked to play cowboy, but, that dipshit could sure rope."

"You won't be the only first-timer," Jake said. "Cindy and Byron have an Aussie using them as home base, as he travels the West with his PRCA card, riding saddle broncs and making friends. Cindy thinks he'll be with us at the branding."

Jake looked at Simon, who was sinking low in the big chair. The solar cat had snuck in and was on his chest.

"Aussie means from Australia. Jes? Rodeo rider, huh?" Simon

< 223 >

was interested in rodeo.

"Yep. Byron said he's hot and cold, but when he's hot, he's hot."

"Hot now?" Simon asked.

"Apparently he started this year pretty hot," Jake said. "Cooling now."

"And we may have other visitors, too. There's always the friend of a friend. Some are good help, but riding among the calves, throwing loops into the dirt won't get you invited back."

"Anyway Skid, here's a quick overview," said Jake.

"We'll check on cows and calves next week, see how they wintered, Simon and I. Then scout them again in April, again about May first. See where they are and anticipate any problems. These are usually one long day, starting early, home for a late supper. You can join us if you like.

"Cindy said if all goes according to plan, we'd gather the third week of May, probably allow that whole week. Start Monday and probably be able to have our rodear, brand, and ship, starting on Thursday. Maybe get finished late Saturday if all goes well.

"The rodear is where we let the cows and calves mother up and we never rush that process. Getting it right can make or break a cowman's year.

"When we've gathered a truckload of pairs, we'll drive 'em to the pens. They will stay together through the branding, and they'll all get on the same truck together headed for their summer vacation in the mountains. That is the plan."

Jake stopped and sipped his cold coffee. "You guys want a fresh cup?"

There were no takers, so he continued.

"As we go scouting, we'll nudge them down the valleys, gullies, and washes, toward the flatlands, so when the big day comes, it'll go a little smoother. The big gather will have all the hired cowboys, and there're usually some volunteers; friends, children, and wives.

"On the desert we leave the dogs home. But I digress." Jake

< 224 >

looked at Buster, and said gently, "Good Dog."

Jake's lecture had raised some questions, mostly from Skid, and they spent an hour talking about Delle. Once they started, they'd sleep in John's pickup and meals would be catered until the last truck left. Simon would come and go as needed, but only during the day.

Skid asked if he could invite a horsemanship student or two to come help for a day.

"They could push groups of pairs from the rodear to the pens," Jake said, "other than that, they'd just be in the way. They could stay and watch, of course."

"If you wanna blend in, Bud, leave 'em home. They'll be about as welcome as a stray dog," advised John.

"Give those cowboys somethin' to talk about, for years," Jake said.

"Gosh," said John, with exaggerated humor. "Remember that year when that new guy, what was his name? Skip, Skid, maybe Slid? Somethin' like that, anyway, he wore white gloves and brought that cluster of rich trophy wives to the desert brandin' ... never seen so much lipstick or broken fingernails. Couldn't find a place to spit, shit, or pee. Couldn't even swear properly ..." John, having fun now, at Skid's expense.

"I guess the hazing has already started," said Skid. "Don't suppose I'll mention branding to the ladies."

"Jus' a moment, amigos, those ladies, Skid, ¿Tus amigas, son guapas?" Simon asked.

"Uh huh," Skid said. He was sorry he'd even considered the subject.

"I could bring them with me. I do not mind. They could come," Simon offered.

"No thanks, that's OK, Simon. Best we leave 'em home with the dogs," Skid said quickly, in the voice of a man on the edge of a cliff, invited to jump.

"No, no, Skid, I be glad to take 'em. It's no trouble, I gonna

< 225 >

go anyway. They can meet me here at seven, ready to go, we just load their horses and go, we'll be there, about, nine-thirty, ten, help move cattle from rodear to Delle; they'll be like cowboys in the West. Branding start, maybe one or two, after lunch, they watch through fence, no trouble, you know. I'll take the ladies home about five o'clock, get here, before eight."

Simon's enthusiasm worried the solar cat. When his zeal grew to excitement, it scared the feline into a high-powered exit.

"Okey dokey," Simon said. "I can bring Dorothy and some girls."

< 226 >

A Dream Horse

A cutting horse futurity is a contest for three-year-old horses. Most western states have them, a ritual of fall.

The National Cutting Horse Association Futurity is the big one. In Fort Worth in early December, it's for three-year-olds that have never competed before anywhere. It lasts two weeks and is a very big deal. One class, the Open, will have about five hundred horses competing for about a quarter million dollars.

Canadian rancher, Ian Tyson, wrote several songs about his addiction to cutting horses, and one was playing as Jake started his day.

> This colt that I ride is my joy and my pride
> So watch him now - you better watch him now
> This little stud's got the heart and the blood
> So watch him now - you better watch him now
> Cause I've had this dream forever it seems
> And it's time now to make it come true
> If everything gets right on this clear Fort Worth night
> You can see what this pony can do.
> The Futurity - the Futurity - the Futurity

Jake could type a letter on his computer, do a little basic bookkeeping, and check horses' or riders' earnings on the NCHA website, but that was about the extent of his ability with technology. So he felt a surge of pride when Skid was able to talk him through the process of calling up the Western Bloodstock site, and coaching him through it, to an early preview of a sale for two-year-old cutting prospects.

"Scroll down to number 149," Skid said, and waited a moment.

"Got it," Jake said. "Raging Metallic Cat."

"Watch the video and call me back."

It showed a young roan horse working in a pen of black cattle.

< 227 >

Jake watched that video, and many others. Most of the sale horses had the popular bloodlines, many from prestigious ranches. Well-known trainers were represented. Because they were just two years old started on cattle, the riders were shown helping them when they needed it. You could see these young horses were strong in the basics, watching the cows, reacting quickly, stopping and turning on their hind quarters. Bending. Expressive ears, pricked to the cow, or pinned back if challenged. Several wore hackamores, but most were in snaffle bits. Some looked more advanced than others. Many looked leggy and coltish, but a few appeared filled out and acted more mature.

Jake agreed with Skid about Raging Metallic Cat.

"Yep, he is ahead of the others. You seldom see one so mature and athletic at that age. He is amazing. But keep in mind, there is a big difference between a horse born in January and one foaled in July, even though both are two-year-olds on their papers."

"He's like a finished show horse, a great one," Skid effused. "That guy was picking him the toughest cows he could find. I never saw him help that horse once. Hand down, reins with two feet of slack."

Jake cautiously agreed, but warned, "He looked like a finished horse at two, but look again, I think the rider's using his legs quite a bit. And Skid, that video was one of the most professionally shot. No shaky camera here, so remember any bad stuff has most likely been edited out. A really nice horse, but I'm just sayin' ... a really professional video."

"Damn, I wish I had a rich client, looking for a futurity horse. That horse would be my choice. Work him justa little, keep him happy with his job, keep him sound. He'd be the one to beat. He's paid into Fort Worth, and that's where he should go," said Skid. "The National Cutting Horse Futurity in Fort Worth."

"Did Stef and Bill find their horses yet?" Jake asked.

"They have Craig Wilson's old gelding as the practice horse they both use, and Stef is trying out a nice horse from Wyoming.

But we'll see."

"Any chance Bill wants a futurity horse? You haven't plumbed the depth of their pockets yet, I don't think," Jake said.

Skid paused for a moment and said, "You may have given me a good idea. I wonder what that horse will sell for?"

"If two or more guys are looking at him closely, it could go into the six figures. Be sure to mention it's a huge gamble. He can bow a tendon or colic, quick as any other horse."

Skid is hooked into the dream, Jake thought. A horse like that could make a person's career, but besides a lot of money, he'll need a lot of luck. He knew Skid's optimism was fueled by hope while his own caution resulted from experience. Jake believed in dreams. Good luck Skid, he thought.

Over a week Skid talked to the owner of Raging Metallic Cat, and he talked to the rider in the video, a trainer specializing in starting youngsters on cattle, and Bill and Stef Jones. It sounded like a quarter million would buy the horse right away, and Skid sensed wiggle room in that price. Otherwise, the horse would go through the sale in Fort Worth, and might sell for a lot less, or maybe even more.

But Bill's answer was no, the gamble was too big. He wanted to get into cutting slowly, he said. Baby steps. Start in the shallow end.

"I want to learn the sport, one step at a time. Not interested in making a big splash," is the way he put it.

A smart answer, Skid knew, but not the one he wanted. He talked to his other clients and approached various amateur cutters he knew, just in case one of them had won the lottery. One of those he talked to was Wally Archer.

Wally saw the video and talked to Skid for over an hour. The dream found fertile soil in Wally and took root.

Wally had been riding, showing, and training his cutting horses for over thirty years. Like many others, his early passion had mellowed gradually, tempered by reality. The incredible highs, and the inevitable lows, fostered careful planning, and the managing of expectations. But Skid's excitement started to stir up the old fever. He had more time to ride nowadays, the time, the skill, the desire, but not the money. And, not yet the horse.

> *Cause I've had this dream forever it seems*
> *And it's time now to make it come true*
> *The Futurity · the Futurity · the Futurity*

... All I need, Wally thought, is a financial partner who could afford to gamble on a big finish. He knew the person he had in mind cared nothing for horses, but he had money he could risk, and was not afraid of a challenge.

And, Wally decided, he owes me a very big favor ...

< 230 >

Eloise

Hi Wally. It's me, Eloise." It was her chirpy voice on the phone.

"Hey, hello."

"So Wally, I talked to Prince today."

"Yes? You told him about my idea?"

"Well, he thought your proposal was very interesting."

"Did he go for it?"

"Well, I told him, you figured he could be your financial partner in an expensive horse. He'd buy the horse, and you would pay all the expenses to get the horse ready for the futurity. And if the horse made it to the semi-finals, the horse's value would soar, and if he made the finals, it would skyrocket even more, and if it ended in the top five, it would enjoy enormous stud fees the rest of its life, and the prize money would probably return the investment, and of course, if he won, you would be a legend in the history books."

"So, does he want to talk?"

"He said, 'What's a Futurity?'"

"So you explained a Futurity?" Wally asked.

"I did. I said three-year-olds. Cutting horses. Never before competed."

"So, what did he say?"

"He said, how fast is it? Can it qualify for the Kentucky Derby? Can it run in the mud? Is it a pretty color? I said I thought it was a cutting horse, probably just a sorrel, or a bay, could be a roan, probably too small for the Kentucky Derby."

Wally showed disappointment. "So what did he say?"

"Wally," she said quietly, "Prince said no."

She let him process that a few moments. Then she spoke in her sympathetic voice, "Honey, he said he wants to keep a low profile. I'm sorry. Maybe you can be partners in some other way."

< 231 >

"Oh ... Shit," he paused, accepting rejection. Slowly. "I guess I was getting too excited, too fast. It was a long shot, anyway."

"Prince does want to see you again, though," Eloise said.

"Oh, yeah? When and where?"

"He'll meet you sometime, when you know for certain where you'll be, and when."

"Well, I'm going to Kamas tomorrow, to do a job for him, at three in the afternoon. I could meet him just before, or sometime after. I'm not sure how long it'll take, so maybe before is best."

"I'd bet he'd love to meet you in Kamas. Where do you suggest?"

"In the Kamas Kafe, or maybe the empty lot next to Dick's Drive-In. Or the parking lot in front of Ace Hardware," Wally said, thinking out loud.

"Dick's might be filling with high schoolers; the Ace lot is big and might be good. That's probably best."

"Ace it is," said Eloise, "what kinda car will you be in?"

"I'll be in a dark blue Dodge pickup, short bed and four door cab."

"Plan on it, sweetie, unless I call you."

"Maybe he'll change his mind about the horse?"

"I doubt it, sweetie." And they hung up.

The Serious Sheriff

The sheriff was in the back booth of the Kamas Kafe when Jake came in. He took off his coat and sat across from Marvin. There was old gray snow outside the window, but it was warm, friendly and busy inside.

"Howdy."

"Howdy."

"If you wanna talk horses, Skid found a fantastic futurity prospect," Jake said with a huge, fake grin. "It's on your computer screen in the Western Bloodstock two-year-old sale preview, but it looks like a finished horse. Skid talked to the owner, and he's willing to give it away for only a quarter million."

Jake's smile expanded sarcastically until his entire face was involved. Proud of the smile, he held it as Marvin said, "Man, I'm so glad I'm outta that shit."

"Member how expensive it can get when you fall in love?"

"Yup. I remember."

"Skid's in love with a horse, sight unseen."

"Oh yeah?" said Marvin. "Love can make you stupid."

"Yes it can," said Jake, as an image of Darcy flickered in his mind.

"Sometimes it's hard to remember, they're just horses."

"Skid was gonna present the idea to Stef and Bill."

"Bill's too smart for that," Marvin said, "but I want to talk about your little crime wave."

"Me, too," said Jake. "I was at the big country store in Salt Lake City the other day getting some T-posts. While I was so close, I dropped in on Wally 'cause he has a buckskin gelding he was thinking of selling. It might work for the Joneses, maybe. Anyhow, in the process of looking at that horse, we were in the tack room a few minutes, talking, and I noticed he had an unusual knife on a small table, and it looked kinda like the one you are obsessed

< 233 >

about. I tried not to pay too much attention, but on the way home, I'm thinking, Wally was there at Buck's murder.

"And that got me going about a lot of strange stuff, wandering, sort of, and remembering that hunting accident, or murder, in the Wind Rivers, long ago. You had said there was a knife like that involved. As I recall, you and I were at his big party shortly before his hunting accident, and Wally was at that party, too. And I'm not sure, but I think I remember Peter talking to Wally about that up-coming Wind River trip.

"So, I'm probably imagining things. Certainly Wally is not a murderer, hell, we've known him for thirty years or more. I figure if he murders people we'd know by now."

Jake looked at Marvin.

Mildred, with the big hair and in her white outfit, slipped over, and poured them coffee.

"Sorry to be a little late gettin' to you two; we lost one in the kitchen, and Trixie came in late."

"Don't worry," Jake said. "She may have been dreamin' of Oklahoma."

"You guys eatin' today, or just drinkin'?"

"Just drinkin," they answered in unison.

Mildred vanished, and Marvin spoke quietly.

"There are only ten of those knives in existence, according to TJ, reporting from the hospital. TJ's is in an evidence locker, one is somewhere in Idaho, and one, we presume, is in Wally's tack room. I think one or two belong to the famous criminals: Prince and Frederico. Any way things are strange, and although Pedro, TJ, and Armando, have temporarily stopped trying to kill you, I'm still worried."

"Uh huh."

"I am now worried about Wally. Sure, we've known him at cuttings, but not socially. Ever been to his house?"

"No," Jake said.

"You have a deer rifle, a small pistol, and a cellphone."

< 234 >

Marvin said. "Anything else?"

"No," Jake said. "A vicious dog. Does he count?"

"If somebody wanted to kill you, how would they do it?" Marvin asked.

"I suppose they'd lie in a bush and shoot me with a deer rifle. Then call it a hunting accident," Jake responded.

"We know it's not Wally, but the knife makes me suspicious. If he ever calls you and makes a date, certain place and time, well, let me know," Marvin said.

"Marv, he's coming to my place tomorrow at three."

"How come? Has he ever come by before?"

"He's dropped in a couple times, over the last thirty years, just driving by and stopped to say 'hi'. Not recently. Probably twenty years ago, I must say this is very unusual. Drive all the way up here just to see my Derby horse. It's not for sale, and not even that special. We may not even be able to work a cow, the footing might be too sloppy," Jake said. "Now you're getting me suspicious."

"I think I'll come look at the Derby horse myself, tomorrow just before three," Marvin said, "I'll bring a loaded pistol."

Jake thought about that. Probably Wally had another reason to come up, and just thought he'd be friendly. Or maybe he wants to buy a Derby prospect or lower the price on his buckskin gelding. It could easily be anything, but it did seem strange.

"We could play it like they do in the movies," Marvin began. "I come out about two thirty, and park in your barn. Or you pick me up somewhere, so my car's not there. Then I hide in the hayloft or behind your round pen or somewhere, and you're wearing a bullet proof vest, and a wire. Wally points his gun at you, and you chat him up, and he confesses to all his murders, and when we have the evidence, I jump out of the bushes, and say 'Stick 'em up.' He turns into a puddle of piss, and we handcuff him."

"Sounds like fun," Jake said.

"Just kidding," said the sheriff.

< 235 >

"Let's really do it," Jake said. "I like it. Wally'll probably look at the horse, make me some lowball offer, I'll decline, and we'll all have a good laugh.

Marvin was serious. Thinking out loud.

"So, you pick us up, in town about two fifteen. Molly and me. We put your Derby horse in the round pen, with the solid fence, and put your Futurity horse in a stall in your barn. The stall next to the ladder so there's a good view looking down from the hayloft. Molly is up there, and I'm behind the round pen. I can move where I need to, without being seen. You'll wear a wire, and the Kevlar vest. Molly will have a long gun and her side arm, and watch the barn yard from the upstairs, hay door, left slightly open. In the barn she can look down from the hay loft. She'll have a pistol, in case the action is inside, below."

I'll be on the other side of the round pen watching through the cracks between boards. I can get pretty close if he pulls a gun. If he's innocent, he won't even know we'd been there."

"Yep, we'll do it. I'll have my pistol in case something goes wrong," Jake said.

"And," Marvin said, "you've got to keep in mind where we are, and steer things so the action is where we can see you, either the walled pen, the barnyard, or in the barn. Don't let him steer you into the house, or anywhere else."

"OK, sheriff," Jake said.

< 236 >

Shots Fired

Old snow, mud, and dirty gravel, entwined together in a drab example of abstract expressionism. Even the sky couldn't decide between dark low passing clouds, and a high ceiling of pewter gray. In the horse runs, where the ground was thawing, there was the pungent odor of manure.

At three in the afternoon as Jake strolled from his barn toward his pens, a dark blue Dodge pickup led a gray Mercedes down the driveway into Jake's barnyard and parked near the round pen. Wally jumped down from the pickup, followed by two men from the large sedan. Buster was watching, wagging his tail tentatively.

"Hi Jake."

"Wally."

"A couple of friends," Wally said. "Jesus Minundo and Frederico Juarez."

"This is Jake Oar," he told them.

"Good afternoon," Jake said warmly, as he put his hand deep into his jacket pocket and felt the fierce little pistol. They had stopped far enough apart that there was no handshaking, but there were smiles. The two strangers said nothing.

Jake led them to the gate, opened it, entered and moved left along the curving wall. The others all followed in, spacing themselves out a bit.

"This is my Derby prospect, Wally," said Jake.

The horse, a blue roan, had been acting edgy and distracted by something outside the back of the pen, but was now more interested in the people arriving. He snorted and looked at them.

Frederico closed the gate behind him and stood there, relaxed, with a hand still on the latch. No one was looking at the horse.

Quiet and smoothly, Wally's Smith and Wesson came out. Prince also was holding a pistol in his hand loosely hanging at his side. No one said anything for a long moment. Jake's hand was in

< 237 >

his jacket pocket, finger in the trigger guard, safety off.

Wally, who was facing him, suddenly turned, and shot Prince in the chest with a loud pop.

For the next three seconds moving targets and rushed shots rattled the air. Frederico jerked a gun out of his pocket, and shot Wally in the right shoulder, with a much louder bang. Jake yanked his weapon out, and shot Frederico, scratching his leg, with another pop. Frederico was opening the gate and ducking out. Another pop, this one from the far side of the pen. It nicked Frederico's left arm. He was out of the pen moving to his right, putting the wooden wall between himself and the guns.

Jake sprang after him, yelling, "Stop!"

He didn't, so Jake shot him in the thigh. Pop. As Frederico turned back with his gun toward Jake, Marvin burst around the pen. Distracted, Frederico glanced back just as the sheriff knocked him to the ground. They skidded about five feet through the mud, Marvin on top, the gangster's face leading the way like the cow catcher on an old iron locomotive. By the time they slid to a stop, one hand was cuffed, the gun twisted out of the other, and the hook-up was complete.

Marvin got to his feet, breathing hard.

Jake looked at him.

"Not quite ... the way ... we planned it ..." Marvin said.

"Pretty fun, though," Jake said trying his best to sound calm.

They looked in the round pen, assessing the damage. Prince, on his back, looked quite dead, the result of a professional hit. Bullet in the heart. Lifeless eyes rolled back.

Wally was quiet, sitting in the damp sand, back against the wall, holding a shoulder that must have been hurting. Buster was watching closely, keeping a little distance, smelling the blood. Two guns lay in the sand nearby.

The horse had been excited but started to calm down. He watched with great interest, then gave a snort and ran a few steps, then stopped and just stood looking, head held high with his ears

< 238 >

up and nostrils wide, eyes bright.

"Want to lie down, Wally?" Jake asked.

"No, I'm OK ..." he said. He obviously was not feeling good and didn't seem to want to talk or move.

Outside, with his face in the mud, Frederico didn't look very happy either. His gun was about ten feet away, near the wall.

"Holy cow," said Molly. "We're all OK here?"

"Fast and furious, there, for a minute," Marvin said. "Calm now, though."

She looked in the pen.

"Good afternoon," she greeted Wally.

"Howdy," he said, acknowledging her greeting, and started a reflexive gesture meant to tip his hat, only ended in a grimace.

"Stay comfortable, you don't have 'ta get up on my account," Molly said.

"It is nice to meet a gentleman, however. May I ask, who are you, anyway?"

"I'm Wally Archer," he said.

"Who's your friend here?" Molly wondered, looking at Prince, blood dribbling on the sand.

Wally looked over his shoulder.

"That use'ta be Prince."

"I think I'll call 911," she said.

"I just did," said Marvin.

Molly turned to Jake.

"Stand in here, out of the mud," she gestured to Jake. "I'm gonna undress you."

She worked deftly ... first the jacket, then the shirt, and then the Kevlar vest, and hung them over the wall. She carefully unstrung the little wire and recording device.

"Did 'ja get a good confession on this little thing?" she asked.

"Gunshots only," Jake replied.

"You are shivering. Here, put your shirt and jacket back on." She gave Jake a hug. "I'm sure glad you're still here with us. Lotta

< 239 >

times the cheese doesn't survive the trap."

"I got a little worried myself, when the fireworks started poppin'," Jake admitted.

Molly turned her attention to Marvin. "I'm glad I still got my sheriff. Although you look awfully dirty."

Marvin crouched next to his prisoner.

"Freddy, I'm gonna read you your rights," he said, and he did. Then he bent closer and said, "Mind if I ask you some questions?"

"No questions and no answers," Frederico said into the wet dirt.

"Suit yourself." Marvin left him, and carefully collected the guns.

A muttering came from the man on the ground.

"Freddy, is that you talkin?"

"I'm uncomfortable here."

"Ambulance on the way," the sheriff said. "Want me to hook you up differently."

"Fuck yes."

Marvin released one wrist. "Now you can lie on your back if you like," Frederico rolled over painfully. Now muddy on both sides, with his hands cuffed together in front, he lay quietly.

A little later Simon arrived. He'd heard the pop of gunshots and came to make sure everything was all right. After he listened to the tale, he drove Molly to town, so she could come back in the official sheriff car, with evidence bags and first aid supplies.

Next came an ambulance, and then two state patrol cars.

By five pm officers, participants, and the victims were gone, and Jake noticed the gate had been left open. He gathered a halter and went looking.

The horse was eating the old yellow grass sticking through a tiny patch of melting snow. Back in the barn, Jake and Buster fed the large animals and sat on the porch a short while. With the temperature dropping, he went inside and dug out his cell phone.

"Hi Darcy," he said. "Supper tonight?"

< 240 >

Park City Hospital

Well, well, well, Wally, you look better this morning."
"Mornin', Jake."

A tired looking woman in a dark red wool coat seated at the bedside, got up to leave. Jake took off his hat and smiled at her.

"Please don't leave on my account," he said.

"Oh no, I have to go anyway," and then to Wally: "Goodbye honey, I'll visit tonight." She bundled herself out of the door and into the hall. Jake watched her go. He was reminded of a Rhode Island Red hen leaving the chicken coop.

"Are you feeling all right?"

"I've been better," Wally said. He glanced at his bandaged shoulder.

"Unusual day, Tuesday."

"Yes."

"Wanna talk about it?" Jake asked.

"Don't know what to say."

"I could ask you some questions," Jake said, "How about that?"

"I've got a date with an attorney, in about two hours, and he's gonna tell me, don't answer any questions, unless your attorney is present."

"Yeah. But I'm not cops, or any kind of legal person. We're just two old friends in a bar having a beer, except we're not in a bar, and there's no beer. I could get two coffees, though. How about that?"

"All right. Get some coffee. Cream please, no sugar."

When Jake returned, he noticed the bed had been adjusted so the patient's head and shoulders were now several inches higher. In the chrome and white environment, Wally's pink cheeks were a much-needed touch of color.

They sipped coffee and looked at each other a while.

< 241 >

"Well, Wally, my first question is ..." and here Jake leaned forward, paused, looking into Wally's little blue eyes.

"WHAT THE FUCK?" Jake spat those words out.

"Man, I don't blame you for being pissed, but let's start with an easier question," said Wally.

"Here's one. Do you know a huge guy named TJ, that runs with a little group, Armando, Pedro and Cookie?"

"I've heard of 'em."

"Any idea why they want to kill me?" Jake asked.

"You met Prince Tuesday? Well, those guys usta' bat cleanup for Prince, I think that was what they were doin'."

"Reminds me," Jake asked, "whatever happened to Cookie?"

"Heard he was fighting infection for a long time. I think I heard he was OK, but he's not a pal of mine, or anything. Poor guy accidently got his hand cut off."

"How'd he lose his hand?" Jake asked.

"Farm accident, I heard. Do you know Cookie?"

"So, here's an easy one. That unusual knife in your tack room. What's its story?"

"No story, just a knife. It's normally in my bedroom, forgot it was in the barn."

"I heard there were only ten like that in existence. Means you're in a special cult or something."

"No Jake, it's just a knife."

"TJ had one like it. And you remember Peter Ernst. He died in a hunting accident a while back. He had one."

"Just a knife," Wally answered.

"I had heard that your pals, Prince and Frederico, had knives like that; what do you think?"

"How did you get obsessed with knives, anyway?" Wally asked.

"We're just two pals talking over our drinks. Can I ask, did you kill Peter, and did you kill Buck?"

"Course not. You better ask my attorney, if you wanna go there."

< 242 >

Jake looked hard at Wally.

"People been trying to kill me, so I guess you could understand my curiosity. And I understand your reluctance to talk about various murders, but if my questions offend you, you can shove that offense right up your ass."

"No offense taken," said Wally quietly.

Jake sat still, looking at Wally, and trying to cool himself down. After a few minutes he said:

"I do appreciate that you didn't decide to shoot me Tuesday."

They looked at each other some more.

"Thanks," Jake said calmly.

"You're welcome," Wally said, "you won't need that Kevlar vest anymore."

< 243 >

One Step at a Time

The Great Saltair was an abandoned pavilion and resort built in 1893, on the edge of the Great Salt Lake. Visitors could bob like corks in water far saltier than the ocean, and dance to exhaustion in the evenings. The western contemporary to Coney Island, it was important to many a youthful romance. Burned to the ground in 1925, it was soon rebuilt. Over the following years fire and recovery have been its legacy.

It sits west of the city, past the airport. There is evidence of bonfires to warm the homeless, remains of picnics and drug deals. Posters for underground bands, punk bands, and subterranean rock bands were disintegrating on the smoke-blackened walls. Its distinctive eastern European-influenced architecture is visible from the freeway.

Say goodbye to this historic building and travel west on Interstate 80, to another landmark, Delle, about an hour away. An abandoned gas station that had long ago dried up and was waiting patiently to blow away. And that is all there is, except about a mile west on a dirt frontage road are pens and loading chutes, made of railroad ties and heavy lumber. Both the station and the pens were usually covered with tumbleweeds, so freeway travelers seldom even notice them at all.

Simon arrived at the pens with Stef and Darcy, on a cool May morning that would lead slowly to a white-hot afternoon. This permanent sculpture dedicated to the livestock industry stood solid and strong. Cleared of their tumbleweed cloak, the pens were ready for work.

It was surrounded by pickups, horse trailers, campers, and motor homes. A temporary village. At the entry to the grid of posts and boards, stood a new green plastic rented Porta Potty. There was a brown canvas wall tent, and some cooking equipment,

< 244 >

collapsible tables and folding chairs. Except for nine horses, the place was deserted.

They unloaded their three horses, saddled them, mounted and rode west. Darcy was on Jake's gray gelding, Stef had her own horse, and Simon rode his large bay mare, Dorothy.

After about a mile, they spotted a dust cloud and heard the sounds of the first bunch of bovines coming from the rodear. Under Simon's direction, they moved well out of the way and were quiet as the group passed. These were not wild cattle, but they had been living on their own in the desert's rough terrain all winter, calving in the land of coyotes and vultures.

There were plenty of cowboys for the little herd, and several waved or called greetings to Simon.

After a few more miles they encountered a large group of cattle, the sound first far away, then loud as the animals came into view. With the cows calling for their lost babies and the calves bawling for their mamas, it was a quite a din of mooing and bleating. Separated during the roundup, hundreds of animals were spread loosely over about sixty acres of desert.

Sitting quietly on a low rise, Simon explained the action, as six riders slowly moved among the cattle. When a cow found her calf, it would start nursing. A successful reunion was called a pair, and when a rider was absolutely sure, he would drive them to a smaller herd held a quarter mile away.

Once the women understood the work, Simon took them to the little group being formed. They met a couple of the cowboys who gave them the job of sitting, watching, and allowing no pairs to escape.

"Don't scare 'em, don't crowd 'em, don't lose 'em. Just hold 'em, but not too tight," a friendly fellow suggested.

When the little group of pairs would fill a two-level truck, Darcy and Stef helped the cowboys push them to Delle, and into a pen. Then they rode back for more. That's how the morning went, just as planned.

< 245 >

Everyone gathered for lunch when five groups had been penned. Byron and Jake ate quickly, and with John's help, sorted mothers from calves in the alley between pens, and had the job done by the time the last cowboy was full of burrito and chips, and wishing he could catch a nap.

The actual branding, inoculating, ear marking, tagging, and castrating, happened in the one huge pen, one group at a time. The tools, medicine, propane heater, plus the forms for bookkeeping, were all organized on one side. This would be the center of activity.

Watching their first branding, Stef and Darcy were impressed at the way the action seemed choreographed. A calf would be caught, have unpleasant things done to it, and be released as fast as possible. Often it took less than a minute.

There were many people helping, trading jobs now and then, and trying to stay out of each other's way.

When Simon wasn't needed, he joined the ladies peering over the boards, and gave them a colorful play by play.

When those calves were replaced with a fresh group, John tied his horse up, lit a cigarette, then sauntered over to answer any questions. But after a short break he went back to work roping.

After an hour, Darcy and Stef took a little tour through the trailers, and saw where Skid had parked, near Jake's pickup and trailer. They got a bottled water from the scruffy cook washing dishes in a large pan of soapy water. They saw John's outfit on the western edge of the encampment. Then they wandered back, past the pens, to resume their position at the fence.

But there was a stranger there. He was tallish, just over six feet, with a canvas hat that suggested gardener or fisherman. He wore a bright yellow T-shirt and baggy neon blue nylon pants. Leaning on the fence he was focused on the activities. His neck and arms were deeply tanned. Stef stared at his elbows. They were pink and wrinkled as prunes. Wrinkles that had stories to tell.

< 246 >

"Hello," Darcy said.

He turned around, startled. His face was terribly old, and quite furrowed, but his eyes twinkled the color of robin's eggs. Those baby blues examined the two ladies carefully. Then he presented a huge smile that seemed to turn his face upside down. There was a tooth missing.

"Ladies," he said. "Good day."

"Yes, and getting warm," Darcy said.

They all watched the dusty work in silence for a long while.

"Real cowboys doing real work," he said finally.

"Yes."

"You don't see that every day."

"True."

"Very clever with their ropes."

"Yes."

He stood with a lady on each side of him, all of them focused on the branding. But since Darcy was the one saying yes, he looked at her.

"I thought they just played the guitar and rode over the prairie," he said.

"Or played football in silver and blue," smiled Darcy.

"What are we smelling?" the old man asked.

"That's the smell of burning hair," Darcy said, "Hot iron on cowhide."

"I never thought about that before; it must hurt."

"Probably does, but it's over quick," she said, "like a flu shot."

They watched for a couple minutes, as a calf was dropped on his side, the rope on his neck was removed and placed around his front feet, and the two ropers backed their horses stretching the calf, front legs south, back legs north. Two men held it down, and three more moved in quickly, and knelt, performing various duties. A cowboy carefully applied the hot iron to the calf's left side, high enough that it could be seen later, by a man on horseback. There was a sudden cloud of blue smoke, the unique strong

< 247 >

smell, and the squeal of the animal. About five seconds later the sound ended, the smoke cloud floated skyward, and the calf was free. That iconic tradition has been repeated in the West millions of times, marking a man's cattle. In some states it was required by law, other places it satisfies tradition.

"Western tradition, I guess," the old fellow said. "What are two nice girls like you doing out here?"

He gestured grandly to the vast desert, flat for a long way, rising to hills and low mountains in the distance. Everything looked dry, gray, and empty.

"Live nearby?" he asked.

Darcy gave him a sweet smile.

"I'm Darcy, this is Stef, and it's nice to meet you mister ...?"

"Nice to meet you girls. Name is Bradford Barnes. Now you might have noticed, we're a long way from anywhere. My question, watcha doin' out here?" he asked again, and showed them most of his teeth.

"We were playin' cowgirl this morning, but now we're spectatin'," said Stef.

"We have pals in there," said Darcy, gesturing into the pen.

"When they finish with these cattle, they'll take 'em to the mountains for the summer. That's where our homes are, up in the mountains."

"These hills don't look very inviting to me," said Barnes. "I'd expect you'll have a hot dry summer in front of you."

"Not these desert hills. East of Salt Lake City, there are real mountains with trees and creeks," Darcy declared. "That's where we live. In real mountains."

"How about you? Stopped out to check your mailbox and saw the dust and smoke. Came over to see what's goin' on?" she asked.

The man stepped back from the fence, so he could see both girls at once. He took the hat off and scratched his pale white forehead. His eyes sparkled but the rest of him looked ancient.

"I came from Ohio."

< 248 >

"You came to Delle, Utah, from Ohio?" Darcy was confused.

"Yes, I did."

"May I ask why?" Stef said.

The girls had turned around, facing him, their backs to the fence.

"It's a long story," he said. "I'm just passing through. I saw something going on here, noticed the smoke and dust way back. I knew when I'd get here, I'd stop and investigate. So here I am."

"Where are you headed?" asked Darcy.

"Headed to the ocean ... guess that tells you nothin', since there's an ocean on both sides. Don't mean to be coy, so, here it is. I'm headed west. All the way."

"All right," Darcy said. "To the ocean?"

"Girls, now that we're friends, I'll tell you. I am walking across America."

They stared at him.

"No way, get out ..." Stef said.

"You're not serious? Darcy asked.

"I'm flabbergasted," said Stef.

Darcy looked intently at the elderly wanderer.

"OK." she said, "I give up ... why?"

"Well girls, about ten years ago, I thought it would be a good idea, try for the world's record, maybe I could become the oldest man to walk all the way, from coast to coast. So I mapped out my route, laid my plans, so to speak, and started. First parts I did were near home, slept in my own bed for a while. Walk a few days, then rest a day or two. I was walkin' east for a while, then west from Columbus. Covered a lotta miles walkin' from home. I was plannin' on the record, but I wasn't in a hurry. When you're old, it doesn't pay to rush."

The women were paying close attention.

"Well, the first disaster occurred," and he paused for effect.

"Some old man I hadn't even heard of, Ernie Andrus, broke the record in the year 2016, at age 93. That kinda treatment will

< 249 >

break yer old heart. Took the wind outta my sails, for sure. I was too young, and too slow."

"But why are you still walkin' then?" Stef asked.

"Started and can't stop. Goin' for my personal best. Just doin' it for me."

He was thoughtful, and these girls were good listeners. "I'm learning life's lessons out here on the road."

"How old are you anyway, Mister Bradford Barnes, if you don't mind my asking?" Darcy said politely.

"I'm past caring. I'm only 89 but feel older."

Darcy excused herself, went and got him a chair from the dining area and a plastic bottle of water.

"Have a seat," she said.

The act of sitting seemed to exaggerate his age. When he was tall and straight, the wrinkles told the story. Adjusting the chair, moving around, any gracefulness was gone. The chair became his home and he settled in like a tired hound in front of the fireplace.

"How? How does a person walk across the country?" asked Stef.

"I have a support system," he explained, "A good friend named Daryl, with a van. He's retired and helps me when he can. He's about three miles further west, probably parked just off the road, somewhere, reading his book or something. When I get there, we'll decide to sleep in the van, or go to Wendover for the night. That'll get my vote. Have a buffet supper at some casino, might even lie around a pool tomorrow, then drive back here the next day, and continue walking west."

Stef did a couple of deep knee bends, then leaned back on the fence.

"You might be interested to learn, I've completed walking Ohio, Pennsylvania, Indiana, Missouri, California, and parts of Kansas, Wyoming, and Utah. And that's a lot of walkin'. I don't mean to brag, but there you are. Haven't touched Colorado yet."

"Your most memorable adventure?"

He squinted at Stef's question; possibly he was hard of hearing.

< 250 >

"What's your most amazing adventure?" she repeated.

"Well," he said slowly, "I fell in love with a younger lady in Kansas, and we shacked up together. I had to send Daryl and his van home for a week. It was like a beautiful interlude in my long walk. I think about her and those memories often. When I finish this, she said we'll get married, if I'm still alive."

He had tears in his eyes, and Darcy bent down and hugged his shoulders. They held on to each other a few seconds, and he caught the faint odor of lavender. She felt the thin frailness of his torso.

They all watched the fellows working in the dust for a while. There was no showboating there, just cowboys doing work they loved, using skills unique to their profession. Skid stopped at the fence, smelling of smoke, and said "Hi," and so did Jake and John, usually when their activities brought them to the neighborhood.

Simon appeared, coming up the fence outside of the pen, followed by another short cowboy packing a big grin.

"Dis is Phillip, ladies. He's here riding saddle broncos, takin' American money back to Australia. Dis is Darcy and Stef ..."

Darcy introduced Bradford, and they all had a short conversation that none of them understood. The Australian accent was indecipherable, but there was a lot of smiling and good feelings communicated.

Jake rode over and stayed long enough to meet Bradford Barnes, and chat a moment, before the hiss of the propane fire announced that they were back at work. Simon and Phillip returned down the fence and were gone.

Stef looked into Bradford's blue eyes and asked, "What do you listen to, walking down the road alone. Books or music? What's in your ears?"

He seemed to welcome the question, glad to get talking again.

"Can't have headphones on the road. Too dangerous. I have to listen for cars and trucks. 'Course, often there's things to see, and think about. But out here, where there's nothing, I'm in my mind.

< 251 >

I'm in there with myself.

"Really, I'm searching for the meaning of life. Not talking science here, nor religion. Important, sure, very important, but those aren't big enough. Platitudes that can start wars, but don't answer the question."

"Me, I'm after the big questions. The meaning of life. The real meaning. The why. And the how.

"What's really important is a personal quest. That's mine. You've gotta find it yourself. A belief system only takes you part way. There's more to it than that."

He liked these girls. He was playing the ancient sage, with curious students at his feet. He used the teeth he had to smile at them again.

"So, what is important?" asked Darcy.

"Good luck and health. Most important. You can't control where or when you are born, and you can't control your genetics. Those are simply luck, no way around it. It's only after that, after your birth, when you get to start to influence your own life."

The old gentleman scratched his forehead again. His hair was thin and white, the lonely fibers separated by visible skin, but he still had some, and he covered it again with the floppy hat.

"I'm gonna walk away, headed west, pretty soon, but I'll miss you girls, I surely will. Let me ask you, if this was fifty years ago, and we weren't fifty years apart, would you join me in forming a cult? Maybe save the world, or at least save some whales. Maybe stop a war? Live in the woods, grow veggies and make love in our spare time?"

Stef said "Yes," and Darcy said "Yes, for sure."

"Two girls teasing a helpless old man," said Bradford Barnes.

"Tell us where your roots were," Stef asked. "Like what were you doing fifty years ago?"

"Well, this is probably off a little, one way or another, but I worked many years as an air traffic controller, at the airport in Columbus, until Ronald Reagan fired us. Worked in a car plant

< 252 >

after that. Not a very interesting life, I'm afraid, not until
I decided to chuck it all, and take a walk. But ancient history
doesn't interest me. What I want is to pass some things I learned
on to you two. And this is it:

"When you get old, make sure you have something important
to do. Important to you, that is, because no one else will care.
Accolades, prizes, glory, do not mean shit. Pardon my French.
When the applause dies down, it's all forgotten, and you wonder
why it seemed so important at the time.

Find something meaningful to you, and you alone, that's what
will keep you getting up in the morning. That is what really
counts."

By now both ladies were seated on the ground with their backs
against the fence. Stef was hugging her knees and Darcy's legs
were straight out.

Bradford Barnes leaned forward and scratched a bright pink
elbow.

"I believe in you two girls, and that's the truth. You're special,
I see that. You're goin' places."

He examined the ladies again, this time with tired eyes behind
sagging lids. He blinked the periwinkle blues. They were moist.

"When we were teenagers," said Bradford Barnes, "we knew
everything. Then we spent a lifetime actually learning. You two
will someday find out that in old age we become reflective. And
just now you were witnessing my pontificating. Reflection leads
to pontification, apparently."

He struggled to his feet then, hands on the chair for support.
Hunched over, he pushed up, passing gas as he went.

Gas.

Although it came as a little surprise, the sound was like the
ripping of heavy cloth. A healthy sound, natural and unfettered,
just part of the getting-up process for the 89-year-old. The fart
rolled, unacknowledged, off into the desert.

< 253 >

In the silence that followed, he held the chair a while, before straightening on up. Then he stood quietly, establishing his balance, and the ladies got to their feet.

"You girls have made my day," he said. "Bradford Barnes. Look me up in the history books when you get home."

Darcy gave him her business card.

"Call us," she said. "We'll throw a party when you finish walking."

The two ladies walked with him a few yards. The first truck-load of cattle was just pulling out and turning east.

"Would you like a ride to your friend and his van?" Darcy asked.

"Nope, I'm not sharing you treasures with Daryl, that flirtatious rascal."

They all smiled their goodbyes.

"Here's the secret to life," he said. "One step at a time ... take it, one step at a time."

They watched his slow measured stride, as he headed west.

One step at a time.

Bonjour

A picture postcard in Jake's mail was a rarity. If there was one it was usually from a car dealer or new real estate agent in the valley.

When a card sporting a colorful scene appeared among some bills, he guessed correctly who it might be from. The picture side showed people walking along a river. A cityscape with garish peach clouds in an evening sky that was reflected in the water. Centered under the photo it said: "Paris au coucher du soleil."

Jake turned it over and saw Tina's signature.

"Hi Jake. Henry says Hello. His lazy brother is house sitting for us. He sold Henry's pet, the mini arab, on eBay.
We love Paris, it's terribly exciting. And we might not be home for a couple of months.
And Jake, here's news. I'm pregnant. A boy, I hope.
Love, Tina."
There was a postscript: *"Thanks, Jake, you saved my life."*

Jake felt like smiling. And so he did.

The Whorton Report

Irrigation ditches crisscrossed the Kamas Valley cutting it into pieces, like a giant puzzle. The bushes lining the waterways presented some of the early evidence of spring, with bright buds, on the end of each naked branch. It was an announcement that mud season would soon end, and green leaves were on the way.

In the round pen, the frozen sand thawed, became heavy and wet, then dry and soft, where a horse could be confident in deep stops and turns, his mind on his business, and not on the footing.

Jake's favorite horse held a determined, long-eared spotted heifer for nearly twenty seconds, mostly nose to nose. So when the young cow tried a quick stop and ducked away, Jake pushed his heels down and pinched the horse's neck. Then they sat quietly catching breaths, cow, horse, and rider. And then Jake noticed the sheriff's official car coming down the driveway.

He sat horseback at the gate waiting, as two men walked up.

With his leg, he pushed the horse close to the gate, and reached over it, to shake hands.

"This is Ray Whorton," said Marvin.

"Nice to meet you, Jake," said Ray. He was wearing slacks and a dark blue nylon jacket with lettering that read Fremont County Sheriff. He wore a silver belly western hat, with a narrow two-inch brim. He exuded a rather official presence.

"Likewise," Jake smiled.

Marvin had been looking at the sorrel horse, the finely chiseled head, expressive ears and intelligent eyes.

"I bet, old Ray here, has never seen a horse cut a cow," said Marvin.

"You're right," said Ray.

"Looks like your horse is warmed up," said Marvin, "and we're in no hurry."

Jake gave them both a smile and picked up his reins. Like all cutters, he was glad for any excuse to show off a nice horse. Jake thought about how to bump the herd, to get it against the far wall, without scattering cattle.

It was a good-looking herd, too. Mostly Black Angus heifers, raised right here, enjoying their last summer at home before a lifetime of winters on the desert calving, and summers up high. With them were ten long-eared cattle, partly Corriente, crossed with who knows what. Colorful and quick. Jake moved carefully.

He picked one of the fresh crossbreeds, eased her out, and slipped into position, and put his hand down, reins sagging, totally loose.

Suddenly the cow darted left, and the horse moved even quicker. After some dancing back and forth, equine and bovine faces only a few feet apart, the cow stopped, befuddled, frozen for a few seconds. Jake picked up the reins, and pinched the neck with his other hand, backed a step and let the heifer scoot to the herd.

Jake had been demonstrating his horse for Ray, but he was showing off for Marvin, his friend and earliest mentor. Ray saw the quick flashy horse; Marvin watched the accuracy and intensity.

It was sport when there was money to win, but like this, it was an art form.

Jake turned the horse all the way around, rode to the side gate, and opened it. Buster appeared, tail wagging, and by the time Jake came to the gate where the visitors stood, the dog had moved all the cattle out.

"I've seen it in video, but never in the flesh before. It's amazing," said Ray.

Jake stepped off and loosened the cinch. He knelt and took the white splint boots off and moved them to the rear cinch. Then he took a knot out of the tail and shook it loose.

"Is it as fun as it looks?" Ray asked.

"Yes, it is," Marvin said.

Then: "Jake, did you meet Ray in Island Park?"

< 257 >

"I'm not sure, I talked to a lot of folks that day; maybe, but I don't think so."

"I was late to the party," Ray said, "you'd gone, but I've read your report a few times."

They put the equipment in the tack room, gave the horse ten sips of water and returned him to the round pen to relax. Then they gathered on the porch.

"Ray's been in a motel in Salt Lake and I'm givin' him a vacation from the city, for a day or two," Marvin began. "Thought he'd like to see where the Shootout in the O. K. Coral took place. Show him the blood on the sand. And meet you, since you were there at the beginning, and maybe he could bring you up to date. You know, maybe answer any questions."

"Your little murder uncovered quite a mess of illegal drug business, and murder for hire," Ray said. "Prince and Frederico had a lot going on, and in many directions. The investigations are expanding, even as we speak."

"They were smuggling drugs in horses." That was Jake's statement but also a first question.

"They were starting to experiment with it. Using aged mares. It turned out to be too complicated. They shod the drug-carrying horses with aluminum so they could tell 'em apart, but it got more confusing than it was worth. For one thing you have to pick up a foot to see the aluminum.

"Take the drugs out, take the shoes off. They'd put the drugs in the vagina and keep 'em in with a little stitch they called a Caslick, named for the inventor. Then gotta get 'em shod, usually at a racetrack in Mexico. With shoes coming off and on all the time, pretty soon the hoof wall gets weak, or foot gets sore. And drugs going in and out, each time the little stitch goes in or gets snipped out, That's a lot of activity under a tail. First time a gangster doing this business got kicked in the nuts by a sore-footed drug horse, that came to a stop."

"Well, that's bizarre," said Jake.

< 258 >

"Aluminum shoes are rare, generally, but pretty common at a racetrack, so that added to the confusion.

"We think the drugs from your horse were inserted at a track in Mexico and were supposed to get replanted into a horse going to Canada, in a Texas trailer, but were never able to prove it. Also, possibly, they were just gonna be taken out of the mare and moved more traditionally, in somebody's glove compartment, or whatever. We had a room full of notes about who was going where and passing through Island Park at that time. How many horses came, and from where? Those kinds of questions. Everything was organized on yellow sticky notes.

Then one day a door was left open, and all our research blew into the hall. The computer jockeys said 'I told you so' but some of us trust the old ways. If the wind didn't do it, it would have been a computer glitch."

Ray paused. "But why should I burden you boys with our little internal affairs?" He scratched his elbow. "I sure do wish I knew who brought that mare up, though."

"So my big question is, who shot Buck?" asked Jake.

"We're pretty sure it was Wally," Ray said, "And while we're on the subject of Wally, we think he is responsible for at least six murders over the last thirty years. And it could be more, as many as nineteen. We have substantial evidence he was in the Wind River mountains when a friend of yours, Peter Ernst, was killed while hunting. It's documented that he flew into Jackson, Wyoming, and rented a car a couple days before, but no guide service is willing to admit any contact with him. Evidence suggests he was across the valley from Peter, but it is all circumstantial. And there was an old guide that claimed to know the details, but it turned out he was making it all up. It muddied the waters for a while.

"Wally has a very good lawyer, by the way. If I were to bet, I think he won't pay for either of these murders. However, there are some other ones under investigation, and I think some of

< 259 >

them will be successful."

"How come he killed Peter? Do you know?" Jake asked.

"Frederico gave us some early history on that. About twenty-five years ago a little group of wanna-be gangsters got inspired by those Godfather movies and formed a little family with big ideas. Except for Peter they were all just kids, seventeen to twenty. Peter Ernst was older, about fifty, as I recall, and kept telling them what to do and how to do it.

"He had some successful legitimate businesses, and crime was just another hobby for him. These young guys were high school dropouts and already knew everything. They surely didn't need another teacher telling them stuff. So they got fed up and decided to have him whacked. That's what Brando would do in the movie. We think they hired Wally ... started his new career."

"What's the latest with TJ and his crew?" Jake wondered.

"What you see is what you get. Totally vicious little killers. They are all put away now, 'cept Cookie. He's the worst of all for cruelty. He's in a rehabilitation program somewhere, far from bad influences, so I'm told," said Ray. "And while we're on the subject of TJ, I have a question for you two."

"OK, shoot."

Ray took off his hat and looked at Jake.

"I'm curious about the women that spent a night on the mountain after their ordeal. How are they coping?"

"Well," Jake said, "Darcy, the one that shot TJ, is fine, I know shooting another human, no matter what the circumstances, was huge for her and she re-lived that moment over and over for a while. She didn't question her decision, but it haunted her."

"You'll get to meet her at supper tonight, I hope," said Marvin.

"They all were offered counseling, but none followed through. Karen said she was too old for it. She likes to talk about that evening whenever she can get a listener. Tells a very good story too, I'm told. There's a local rumor that a famous writer is

< 260 >

talking to her.

"Darcy sees those women, sometimes," Jake said. "There were a couple three hours when they wondered if they were gonna get out alive. You don't forget that very quickly. And it built strong bonds among them."

"And that brings us to Carol DeClaire," Jake continued. "I get the feeling that the situation made her mad more than scarred. She's pretty much the same as before. Same humor, same opinions. I've gotten to know her much better lately since she bought a nice reined cow horse and loves to work cattle."

Jake looked at Marvin. "I think they were heroic and they're all just fine.

"When Marv told me the details, I was flabbergasted," said Ray.

"When we found the truck and the ladies, we were flabbergasted," Marvin said.

Flabbergasted or not, Jake wanted to know about Prince and Federico.

"The more we dug into those two, the wider it got. They were at the top, or connected near the top, of a lot of illegal drug business, murder, and many other rather clever, crooked adventures. Their fingers were in everything. Federico is probably going to prison for multiple crimes, in many jurisdictions. Wait and see. And everything involving Federico, involved Prince."

"What about the famous knives that Marv is always excited about?"

"Apparently in the beginning, way back, when the world was young, those five bad boys that I told you about got together, swore to be loyal, and took a blood oath. One of them, a nineteen-year-old, made the knives. Metal craft was his hobby. But soon they started killing each other. Peter, Prince, and Federico were part of the original bunch of five. TJ and Wally, and others we don't know, got awarded knives later in little ceremonies, for special extraordinary valor, or something. Go figure.

< 261 >

"Originally the knives meant a lot to them, but by now, they are just knives, I guess."

When Jake had no more questions, the conversation wandered to other subjects. No one seemed in a hurry to do anything but talk.

"Well," Marvin finally said, "let's see if that horse is cool, and I'll call Kay and Darcy, and see if they want to meet us at the Snake Creek Grill."

All three, four if you count Buster, went to the round pen. The horse was waiting at the gate. Jake put the halter on and opened the gate, but something caught his eye. Something small and shiny, mostly buried. Probably a hoof-pick. He paused, squatted and dug it out of the dirt.

It was an unusual knife. Part brass knuckles, part silver and steel switchblade.

"Wow," Jake said, "a knife. Here Marv, for your collection."

"Where you found it, I'd say it's Frederico's," said Marvin.

"I don't think they'll let him have a knife, where he's goin'."

All three men were looking at the knife, and although he was a step behind, the horse was looking at it too.

"So, you can keep it," Marvin said. His thumb was rubbing the mud off of it, exposing the silver design, and the finger holes in the brass part.

"No. For sure, it should be yours," Jake said.

"Not mine," said Marvin as he tested the switchblade mechanism.

"Marv, I'd say you earned it." Jake was serious.

"Not so special anymore," Marvin said looking closely at it.

"Nice craftsmanship, see here, how it fits together?" said Jake.

"That settles it then. Like the craftsmanship, keep the knife. It's yours, Jake."

"I've absolutely no use for something like that. It is obviously yours, Marv."

Ray was examining it closely now. "As much as I've heard

< 262 >

about it, this is the first one I've seen, in the flesh," he said.

"Keep it Ray, it's yours," said Marvin.

Ray looked at the other two, smiled his first big smile, and threw the fabulous knife forty feet, into the irrigation ditch.

Listening carefully, they all heard the tiny splash.

The End. Almost.

Epilogue

One day a letter came to the Summit County Land Conservancy office. It was addressed to Darcy and Stef. The penmanship was shaky, but readable. The return address and postmark suggested it had come from Kansas.

Darcy proposed lunch to Stef, and they met at the Kamas Kafe. Trixie brought coffee and the two women opened the letter together. It included a stick-on decorative heart, a dried pressed rose and a small photograph of a familiar old man and a short plump friendly faced lady with a grin.

> *Dear Darcy and Stef,*
> *You girls were like two beautiful flowers in the desert*
> *that was my long walk.*
> *I tried to tell you what I'd learned about life.*
> *I said you need a personal quest*
> *to keep you getting up in the morning.*
> *Something important to you and you alone.*
> *But thinking back, as I walked from*
> *Winnemucca to Elko, I realized that*
> *while I was speaking to you, I was listening to myself.*
> *My quest dissolved. And I realized my mistake.*
> *I had it all wrong. My real life is in Kansas with Myrtle.*
> *In trying to teach you, I taught myself.*
> *B.B.*

Millie and Trixie glanced at the booth.

"I think Stef and Darcy are getting rather emotional over a Valentine," Trixie observed.

"Maybe it's from Elvis," Millie said.

The End.

< 264 >

Author's Note

This novel is fiction. Many of the places are real, many of the little stories happened. I know how it feels to ride a cutting horse. And I met a man trying to walk across America, sea to shining sea. I met him at a branding in Delle. But everything else is fiction.

I had decided to write a story with sex, violence, murder, bad language and nudity, just to see if I could. If you think you recognize yourself or your friends in this book, you can forget the lawsuit. The characters and their adventures are all fiction.

And Wally (not his real name), if you're listening, I apologize. Somebody had to do the murders.

At one point in this novel Marvin's policing style is described as taking more from his cowboy life than time spent in the police academy. A lot of people wear big hats, but not many of them are cowboys. I like Buster Welch's description of a cowboy. Here is how I remember it.

"Suppose a man is riding home after a long hard day. He is tired and hungry. He sees a cow stuck in a mudhole. She is really stuck and to get her out is going to take a strong rope, a tough horse, and a lot of work. He knows that there is nobody to do it but him. And she's not even his cow. He also knows if he keeps going, nobody will ever know that he even saw her. But if he's a cowboy, he stops and takes his rope down and gets to work. No question."

That's Marvin.

Some people use the word 'cowboy' to explain a rogue cop in New York City. But that's not how it's used here.

< 266 >

Talking to Darcy, a woman of the future, Jake claims to be celebrating tradition with the sport of cutting and told her the story of the first cutting for prize money. Here is the full story ...

Boley Brown started as a cowboy but became a wealthy cattleman by the late 1890's. His ranch dominated Kent County in Texas. He built a beautiful house for his wife and held lavish parties. He gathered huge herds of cattle and assembled crews to take them north. He was a respected horse trainer with a real working need for good cutting horses.

In 1898 in Haskell, Texas, the first cutting contest for prize money was held. After the entries were closed, a cowboy came up, late, and wanted to enter. The gateman explained that rules were rules, and the entries were closed, sorry, no dice. When Boley Brown rode up to see what the commotion was about, the cowboy, Sam Graves, said he'd traveled many miles to enter the contest, and that he had the world's best cutting horse. The gateman repeated his no, but Brown persuaded them to let the stranger enter.

"If his horse is that good," he said, "I want to see it."

When Sam Graves had heard of the contest, he'd gone to the pasture for Old Hub, his favorite cutting horse, 22-years-old, retired and thin. He brought Old Hub to Haskell behind a buggy.

The contest resulted in a tie between Boley Brown on his big sorrel and Sam Graves on Old Hub. For a work-off Sam drew to go first. He cut on Old Hub without a bridle and the crowd went wild. Boley Brown didn't cut again, but went over and shook hands with Sam Graves, conceding the contest.

< 267 >

And describing Jake's ugly farm truck reminds me of a quick story.

Two Texans were talking.

"So, you say your place is large. Exactly how big is it?"

"Well, hell, I dunno. Lemme put it this way ... if I got in my truck some morning and headed east all day, at sunset I'd still be on my own land. Or if I'd headed west and drove all day I'd still be on my property."

"Yeah," the other guy says, "I usta have a truck like that.

Thanks to Ian Tyson for the use of words from a couple of his songs. The two of us shared a table in a bar in Fort Worth on a memorable night, when Russ Miller rode a horse named Dox Miss N Reno in through the front door.

"When we were teenagers, we knew everything, then spent a lifetime learning what we didn't know. In old age we become reflective, and sometimes reflection leads to pontification. You have been a witness to this phenomenon." Bradford Barnes said it, but I put the words in his mouth.

I'm glad you came along on this adventure. Thanks.

DW

< 268 >

Thanks

Thanks to some people whose tales have been stolen
and retold here. They include **H.** Linford, **M**et Johnson,
Buster Welch, **T**om Smart, **L**ee Patton, and **S**kip Slusher.
Thanks to people who have offered encouragement
and advice. **S**hel Weinstein, a long-time writing friend.
I listened to him read drafts of his stories as we explored
ski resorts all over the West. I drove, he read, we skied.
Tom Smart (who meets Buster's definition of a cowboy)
and his wife **H**eidi who introduced us to **M**ary Dillon, a
generous and amazing editor who cleaned the manuscript
and hoped the word "ladies" was not demeaning to women.
Kristen Case, a magazine editor we worked with for many
years and **D**ee Dee Richardson, struggled through an early
version. **T**he final edits were done by **M**ary Dillon, **T**om
Smart, **K**risten Case, and **E**lizabeth Hampshire. **L**ee Benson
gave his approval, and **R**oy Laycock wrote the first review.
Two books were very helpful: **W**alter Mosley's *This Year
You Write Your Novel*, and **A**nne Lamott's *Bird By Bird*.
Biggest thanks always goes to my wife **C**ha Cha who for
fifty years has placed her tracks beside mine. Here is a
direct quote from her: "Oh no. Not again."

Made in the USA
Monee, IL
30 March 2022

93349683R00163